Flashman and the Seawolf

Robert Brightwell

This book is dedicated to my father in law
Geoffrey Timberlake who has shown great
courage and dignity in fighting illness while
it was being written.

Published in 2012 by FeedARead.com Publishing –
Arts Council funded
Copyright © Robert Brightwell

Introduction

After George MacDonald Fraser did a superb job of editing the immensely readable memoirs of General Sir Harry Flashman after they were found in a Midlands sale room, I have always kept a lookout for further items relating to the Flashman family. I did once bid for a sabre that was said to have been owned by the general, but the price soon went out of my range as there are now so many enthusiastic readers of his published works.

So you can imagine my surprise when, back in 2010, I spotted offered for sale on eBay a bundle of unpublished manuscripts relating to the life of a Major Thomas Flashman and his exploits in the early 1800s. Fortunately for me, there was very little interest in the writings of this hitherto un-renowned soldier, and I was able to buy them with my opening bid.

Given the unusual name, I had hoped that the two Flashmans were related, and it seems that indeed they were. Thomas appears to have been the uncle of Sir Harry. There are even references to Thomas having lent money to Sir Harry's father (and complaining that it was never repaid) and so Thomas may have even funded Sir Harry's infamous education at Rugby school, which features in the book *Tom Brown's School Days*.

Beyond the name there are similarities in temperament too. While outwardly a brave and celebrated solider, in his personal memoirs Sir Harry admitted to being an amoral scoundrel and coward but with a gift for languages, horsemanship and for getting himself embroiled in just about every major conflict of the Victorian age.

In comparison, Thomas also has the uncanny knack of finding himself reluctantly involved with many amazing characters from his era – from forgotten but remarkable men like Thomas Cochrane to historical icons like Wellington, Napoleon and the noble North American Indian chief Tecumseh. He has if not fought then at least felt his guts churn in terror alongside them all.

Thomas, like Sir Harry, was also good with languages but seems to have had appalling luck with horses – resulting in the unexpected routing of an entire Spanish regiment in one incident, but that may be for another book. As for being immoral, Georgian England had a rather murky moral compass compared to the outwardly straight-laced Victorians of Sir Harry's era. The Georgians strayed from wild licentiousness to stifling honour codes depending on the occasion, and Thomas took every advantage of the former while invariably finding a way around the latter.

My role as editor has been restricted to checking the historical accuracy of the information and adding notes from subsequent research. Where it can be checked, a wide range of authorities confirm the detail Thomas provides, while his own personal perspective on the incidents and personalities in his career offer insightful context.

I trust that you will find the work informative and enjoyable. Thomas has broken his memoirs down into packets – much as his nephew did later on. Indeed, you might wonder whether his nephew, Sir Harry, ever saw Thomas's memoirs and whether they sparked him to write his own, refreshingly honest account. Certainly if you have not read them already, the memoirs of General Sir Harry Flashman VC, reluctant hero of Afghanistan and countless other places, are strongly recommended.

Robert Brightwell

~~~~~~~

Chapter 1

I am near seventy now and have met many incredible people
and witnessed some astonishing sights in my time. From
ambushes and treachery, the feel of cold steel against your
throat in the dark to pitched battles on land and sea, I've
witnessed heroism, incompetence and slaughter, often while
desperately trying to find somewhere to hide. I have been
white with fear disguised amongst Napoleon's Imperial
Guard, terrified more times than I can remember fighting
with Wellington's redcoats and more than a bit alarmed with
the tomahawk-wielding warriors of Tecumseh. But when it
comes to all those that have led me into danger, one stands
clear above them all, partly because he had two prolonged
attempts at getting me killed. But also because, as well as
being the bravest lunatic ever to wave a blade, he was the
most cunning in battle, if a naive fool when the trumpets had
stopped.

At my time of life if you think of a brave comrade then
usually you are also thinking of a man with whom the grim
reaper eventually caught up. There are only so many times
that you can charge shot and shell before your luck runs out,
which is why I was rarely to be seen when charging shot and
shell was required. But Cochrane is still with us; indeed, I
had supper with him tonight and our jawing over old times
has spurred me to put pen to paper. His name struck fear into
French and Spanish alike and Napoleon himself called
Cochrane the 'Loup der Mer' which translates as sea wolf.
He has written his own memoirs, of course – full of
bitterness over those who wronged him – and doubtless
others will write about him too. But they don't get across
what it was like to fight alongside him, how he inspired you
to believe that even the most suicidal action was no more
dangerous than lighting a cheroot.

But I can't start my tale with Cochrane. No, this story
properly starts a few months earlier, in the summer of 1800.
I was eighteen and had just finished at Rugby School, with

the headmaster Henry Ingles giving my old man a less than glowing report of my prospects. As the third son I wasn't the 'heir' or even the 'spare' to my father's fortune, and for that first summer he left me to amuse myself on the family estate, which was probably a mistake.

"Why do you want to know how our brother George is doing in the dragoons?" asked Sarah Berkeley coyly before sharing a conspiratorial glance with her older sister, Louisa, sitting on the other side of the drawing room. "Are you thinking of joining the Army too?"

Louisa joined in: "Now why would you want to do that? I can't think why you would want to leave the area after all the fun you have been having this summer." Louisa said this with a look of wide-eyed innocence. "There is no reason – perhaps living near a windmill – that is causing you to look to your career, is there, dear Thomas?"

"Not at all, and I trust that you have not been listening to idle gossip," I blustered.

The girls laughed happily, not believing me for a moment and enjoying my discomfort. I was surprised that they had heard of my troubles with the miller's daughter, for he lived a village away, but the Berkeley sisters were notorious hubs for local gossip. They were the prettiest girls amongst the local quality for miles around and so were invited to all the balls and dances, which was why they always seemed to know what was going on. Sarah was just sixteen, the prettier of the two and an artless flirt. Louisa, the same age as me at eighteen, was more of a wicked tease. We had grown up on neighbouring estates and seen a lot of each other. I enjoyed their company, although now they liked nothing better than trying to embarrass me.

"So the miller is not after your blood for getting his Sally pregnant then?" asked Sarah.

"Certainly not," I lied. "But a chap cannot work diligently around his father's estate for ever. I need to find a suitable career, somewhere else. As George joined the dragoons a few months ago, I thought I would tool over and enquire what he has said of the life."

6

They both laughed at this and Louisa said, "What he says of the life depends very much on to whom he is writing. Papa visited the garrison last month and collected some letters from him. Sarah, why don't you read Thomas the letter he sent to us."

Sarah found the letter in the bureau and recounted, "He asks about our health and tells us that life in the dragoons is very dull: marching, riding, drills. The only entertainment he mentions is playing whist with his brother officers and hearing a singing recital by a Miss Marchbanks. Is that the kind of life you were hoping for, Thomas?"

Well, it did sound a bit of a frost, but I was not sure that George would be completely honest about all aspects of Army life with his sisters. Maybe I would have to take the day's ride to the garrison and see for myself.

As if reading my mind Louisa said, "I bet you would love to read the account of Army life that he sent Edward Carstairs." I would indeed. I knew both George and Teddy Carstairs from school. They had been in the year above me and had both been wild then. George would be far more honest with Teddy, although I could not see Teddy sharing his mail with George's sisters.

Louisa reached into her blouse and pulled out a second letter with three large blobs of wax on it. "This is his letter to Edward, which fell open before we could send it on."

"But it has three seals on it – how could it fall open?"

"It fell onto a hot iron that melted the wax through the paper," said Sarah smugly. "Do you want to know what is in it or do you want to discuss its provenance?" They were both looking excited now and I was sure that more embarrassment was about to come my way, but I also really wanted to know what was in that letter.

"Perhaps I could read it myself?"

"Oh no, where would the fun be in that," smirked Louisa. She opened the letter and read aloud: *"Teddy, you must speak to your father about a commission. Army life is everything we had hoped. There is no chance of being sent overseas for the foreseeable future and so we are left to*

7

*enjoy life in the garrison. There are hunts at least twice a
week, horse racing, gaming and gambling of every
description and parties in the mess every weekend. The
prettiest local girls attend and fling themselves at all the
eligible bachelors. I partied last weekend with a Tallulah
Marchbanks and ended up having her in my rooms, taking
her horse artillery style until she sang like a steam whistle.
There is a cornetcy coming vacant next month, make sure
your father knows. Yours, George."*

I was stunned, partly from hearing the sisters talk of such
things and partly because Army life sounded just the thing
for me. My first clear thought was to wonder if I could get
that cornetcy before Teddy Carstairs heard about it. That the
sisters had stolen his mail could work in my favour.

My musing was interrupted by Sarah asking, "What is
horse artillery style?"

Well, at that point in time I had no idea, never having
heard of it before. I could guess it was a way of performing
the capital act, but quite how this involved horse artillery
was beyond me. Of course I was not going to admit my
ignorance to the sisters and so I simply replied with as much
dignity as I could muster, "A gentleman would never discuss
such things with a lady."

"Really," said Louisa. "So you didn't go horse artillery
style with Sally Miller or with Ruby at the Fox and Duck or
the Parson's new dairymaid or with that girl you were seen
with in Jarrod's hayloft?"

My God, they were well informed, and I thought I had
been quite discrete. The only thing that they did not know
was that it had been the dairymaid in the hayloft.

"Again, a gentleman never discusses such things."

"I don't think he knows what horse artillery style is," said
Sarah. "Shall we show him?"

Louisa smiled wickedly and moved her hand up to her
blouse again. My imagination was working overtime. What
was she going to do or pull out of there now? If I had taken
the rest of that summer to guess, I would not have predicted
that a respectable young lady would have kept the three

8

cards in there that she now threw onto the table in front of me. They were pornographic drawings.

"These were enclosed with George's letter to Teddy," she said.

The top one with the caption 'Horse Artillery Style' showed exactly what was involved. This is not the place to go into such details, so I will just say that all that hauling of guns must give a man a strong back. The second one, called 'The Wheelbarrow', required finding a lady with arms as strong as a canal digger's, and as for the 'Viennese Oyster' position, well, it just doesn't bear thinking about.

I must have gone red with embarrassment and the girls were laughing loudly, almost muffling the sound of carriage wheels pulling up outside. I looked around at the door, worried that Lady Berkeley may come in to see what the jollyment was all about, and pushed the cards back to Louisa.

As the laughter subsided Sarah went to the window. "Why, the miller has come calling. Oh, and he has just seen your horse, Thomas."

"Jesus, no!" I charged up to the window and took a peek around the edge of the drapes. "You witches, that is the bloody coal dray."

They were off into peals of laughter again.

"So you *have* got Sally in the family way," cried Louisa. "Everyone's been talking about it. You had better speak to your father before the miller does."

I rode home thinking about what to do next. The girls were right: I did need to speak to Father. Sally was claiming she was pregnant and her father was starting to kick up a fuss over it. Of course they knew that marriage was out of the question. What they really wanted was to be paid off from the Flashman fortune to give her a new start. Looking back, the Flashman family had for generations been running an unofficial benevolent scheme for such fallen women in the locality. It would seem quite generous if you overlooked the fact that they had also been responsible for the women 'falling' in the first place.

9

With several people in the village bearing a striking family resemblance, I was pretty sure that my old man had used the Flashman benevolent fund on several occasions himself and so would not be as offended as people are now under the prudish influence of Vicky and Albert. Why, back then the Prince of Wales had probably married bigamously and would mount just about anything apart from his wife, most politicians saw a mistress as being an essential source of gossip and the Devonshires were living openly in a *ménage à trios*. In fact, the only politician who seemed to live a life beyond reproach was Spencer Percival, and when he finally got to be prime minister he was assassinated by a lunatic, which shows what demonstrating restraint gets you.

No, the problem with the Sally incident was not that I had been bulling my way round the village but that I had not yet decided what I wanted to do with my life. School had proved that I was not academic smart. I also clearly was not Church material. Back then all the talk was of the Navy, as they were beating the French and Spanish everywhere they found 'em. But at eighteen I was already much older than many midshipmen, who normally started at around twelve. There were also exams, such as in navigation, to pass before you could progress. I had hated mathematics at school, with all the angles and calculations, and did not want to be the oldest midshipmen the Navy had ever had.

Apart from some fashionable cavalry regiments, the Army at that time was considered second rate. It had been beaten by the colonists in North America and had not covered itself with glory in various other expeditions such as in the Low Countries. But on the plus side, you could buy your rank, so you did not have to languish as an ensign or cornet all your days, and for the most part regiments spent their time in barracks.

I pictured myself tooling around town in my sharp red uniform coat and officer's trappings with a pretty girl on each arm and parties in the officers' mess each night. If I thought of actual fighting at all, it was shouting orders and seeing neatly ordered files of troops marching off to obey my command. Yes, my ignorance was appalling, and if I knew then what I know now I would have jumped straight on a horse, ridden to Canterbury and begged the archbishop to let me become a parson!

My father generally kept to himself; my mother, who had been a Spanish contessa, had died some years ago, and so it was not often that we had a father and son talk. I remember clearly walking into my Father's study that evening and meeting that piercing glare from under his bushy eyebrows. He was around sixty then, still pretty lean and energetic and with a mind as fast and sharp as a trap. He had eaten alone as usual and the supper dishes were pushed to one end of the table. He had been reading some papers but put them down with a resigned sigh as I approached.

"Hello, Papa. I was wondering if I might have a word?" I said, sounding brighter than I felt.

"Yes, I thought you would be dropping by. I had the miller calling for me this afternoon in a fine old state. Apparently you have 'defiled' his pure daughter. Although from what I hear from the gamekeeper, she has also been defiled by half the county. The child could be yours, I suppose?"

"Ah yes, well... err... it could be, yes." We were getting to the point rather more quickly than I had expected. I had rehearsed a bit of a speech about how the girl had led me astray, only a saint could have resisted and so on, but realised at once that this was not going to wash. If he had spoken to the gamekeeper about Sally's reputation, he was bound to have found out what I had been up to all over the estate during the summer months, if he had not known already.

"Well, I have agreed to give her a dowry and the miller is lining up some local lad to marry her, but it would be best for you to be out of the way for a bit."

"Yes, Father," I said, looking suitably crestfallen. "I have been thinking about that. I was wondering if a career in the..."

"I have written to Castlereagh," my father interrupted brusquely. "He owes me a favour and will be able to find a place for you. It won't be glamorous or well paid – you will need an allowance on top of the salary – but it will get you on the ladder. You need to start thinking of a career."

"Oh, but I have, Father," I said, all eager now we seemed to be talking along the same lines. "In fact, I was thinking of joining the Army."

My father sat back in his chair and fixed me with a firm stare. I sensed that he was looking at me for the first time in ages, sizing up my build; I was tall but still had some filling out to do. He looked into my eyes as though trying to assess my character. I held his gaze for as long as I could but then looked away. Growing up I had been closer to several of the servants than my father, whom normally I saw rarely, but I sensed that instead of just dealing with me as an irritation, this discussion was going to be different.

"Sit down, Thomas." My father reached for a cigar in a box on his desk and then, after a moment's hesitation, he did something he had not done before: he offered me one too. I had experimented with cigars at school and smoked a few times at inns during my recent summer of debauchery, and so I reached forward and took one. After we had both gone through the ritual of snipping the end off the cigars and lighting them from the candles on the table we sat back and stared at each other through a smoky fog. I was determined to appear like a man before my father and so was trying hard not to cough and hoping that he could not see my eyes watering through the smoke.

"Thomas, you cannot imagine the horror of a battlefield. I was at Marburg and swore that I would never see one again."

I knew he had done some army service when a young man and had fought at Marburg in '60, but this was the first time I had heard him talk about it.

"We fought on a riverbank early on a hot summer's day. There was a thick river mist. I was in charge of an outpost platoon that was supposed to warn of the enemy approach, but in the fog we lost our bearings. We heard marching and crept forward, unsure if we would find the French or our own British and Hanoverian troops. The French came out of the mist, like ghosts in their white coats."

He paused to take a sip of port and then continued, his eyes looking at one of the candlesticks as though lost in his memory.

"They were only fifty yards off and saw us easily in our dark red tunics. I heard some shouted commands and within a few seconds they had stopped and fired a volley in our direction. We were hugely outnumbered with half a dozen of their muskets aimed at each one of us. The crash of their fire was deafening. I felt a tug at my coat where a ball passed through and I am sure I felt the air move as a ball passed close to my cheek.

"For a second I was frozen and then I looked to my right. The man next to me had been hit in the chest and head. The back of his head had exploded out and he was already dead before he started to fall. Further down the line nearly everyone seemed to be hit, several already falling, a couple still standing and staring with shock at the growing crimson stains on their shirts. I looked round and the man to my left was on his knees holding in his guts and rocking back and forth and starting to whimper.

"I must have stood there several seconds before I looked again at the French. The smoke from their volley had hidden them but now they started to appear, marching out of the smoke with their bayonets iron-grey in the mist."

Now he looked at me and spoke more briskly to ensure that I got the point of this story.

"I turned and ran. No thoughts of military glory, just survival. I ran. I did not know in which direction, only that each step was taking me away from those bayonets. Only five of our section survived that encounter." He paused to take a puff on the cigar. "As it turned out we had done our job well from the Army's point of view. The French started to move in the direction we had run, thinking we were running back to our lines. The volley gave away the French

13

position and the British infantry attacked their flank, again coming out of the mist and finding the French facing the wrong direction.

"The mist melted rapidly as the sun came up and revealed a sight I will never forget: the regiment that had attacked us was now mostly dead and dying in the field where they had found us. They had been attacked by our infantry and our cavalry had ridden 'em down when they broke.

"I wandered the field of dead and dying until I found the bodies of the men I had been with. One was still alive and I held his hand while he died. He made me promise that I would do more with my life than rot in some foreign field and I kept that promise."

I stared with shock; I had never heard my father talk so openly and honestly about his past. For a moment he seemed embarrassed himself and then he pressed on.

"Now, I don't doubt that when you think of the Army you think of all the attractions of the officers' mess and the effect the uniform will have on the ladies." Well, he had me there. That was exactly what I was thinking about.

"But we don't have an army on the continent now, Father. I will have plenty of time to learn soldiering."

"You don't survive by learning soldiering, at least not unless you are a general." He was talking with passion now and he banged his hand on the table to make his point. "It is luck, boy! When the balls start flying, it is sheer bloody luck if you survive unscathed. Look at Marburg. We killed six times the number we lost – why? Because some silly fool got himself lost and blundered into their lines. You are only here because some very long odds came off that all those Frenchie balls went wide. I know it and I don't want to see a son of mine gamble like that."

He took another sip of port and puffed again on his cigar before continuing calmly. "This world is corrupt, you must know that. Soldiers and even generals are pawns in the games that politicians play to gather influence and destroy their enemies. They move the pieces and grow fat from patronage and sleep comfortably in their beds while they send others to die in the blood and the shit. Look at James; he knows how things work."

My father had helped my brother James find a position with the Navy Board overseeing ship repairs.

"Why, he tells me that private dockyards are ten times more efficient than those run by the Navy Board where every dockyard manager and clerk grows fat on the wages of nonexistent workers."

As it turns out both my father and brother were wrong there: the situation was even worse. In 1803 a parliamentary commission found that three hundred men could build seven ships a year in private dockyards, but in naval yards with three thousand men officially paid on the books they could barely manage to repair seven ships per year.

"No, I'll not buy you a commission in the Army. You will go to work for Castlereagh. He is at the centre of things at the moment, so there is plenty of opportunity to make an impression. Give it until you are twenty-one and then we will talk again. Remember, while I am alive I can pay you an allowance, but when I am gone, James will inherit the estate and he will have his own children to support then. You need to secure an income and you won't manage that on half-pay in a regiment."

~~~~~~~

Chapter 2

So that was it, the die was cast. Whether Sally really was with child I never discovered. I saw her again four years later and she gave me a very surly look. She had a child on her hip then but it was hard to judge the age. Anyway it could not have been mine for it was an ugly little squirt.

I left for London the day after talking to my father. I did not sleep well that night as my father had given me a lot to think about. Up until then I had taken it for granted that I was part of a wealthy family. I had not thought too much about the future and had tried to ignore the fact that in time the bulk of the wealth would go to my brother. My father would leave me some funds so I would not be penniless, but the estate, the London house and most of the investments that supported the house and estate would go to James. It was the way it had always been with families: the eldest son inherits; and I did not begrudge my brother his wealth. But now I had to start on my own way in the world and it seemed the sooner, the better.

It was nearly noon when I left on horseback with a pack pony for my luggage and Jasper the groom as bodyguard. The old man had given me ten guineas for the journey, far more than I needed, and a note for another fifty drawn on his bank to tide me over until I got established. While the roads were safer than they had been, a wealthy young man travelling alone with a lot of luggage was asking for trouble. So I was glad to have Jasper alongside; his presence would help deter any thieves. We each held horse pistols in our saddle bags but any sensible man would only use these if he was desperate. It was virtually impossible to hit someone from a moving horse and so these blunderbuss-type pistols scattered the shot over a wide area. The result was that you were likely to only wound and enrage an attacker while the recoil could easily break your wrist, leaving you defenceless.

At a leisurely thirty-miles-a-day pace it would take around two and half days to reach London and Jasper was good company. He had been a soldier too, although he seemed strangely reluctant to talk about it – perhaps my father did not want him to give me ideas. Instead he talked about his days as a drover driving animals to London, joking about the noise the geese made when, to protect their legs for the journey, they herded them over trays of hot tar to coat their feet before walking them in sand. Protecting the animal's feet was essential for the drover, for if they would not make the distance, he would not be paid. Jasper told me how once his father had made him give up his socks and one boot to make some shoes to protect the feet of a prime sow. We passed some pigs on the journey and they all wore little woollen socks with leather soles and we checked the drover's boy had his boots on.

Now you may be wondering why I am wasting your time with these bucolic memories. Well, I didn't realise it then, but country life in England was about to undergo the biggest changes it had seen since the Black Death plague in medieval times.

When I took that journey most country people we passed were self-sufficient through the use of common land. Each village would have some fields that everyone from the squire to the poorest peasant could use to graze sheep, cows or raise pigs. Other fields were for crops, with many laid out on a strip system dating back to before the Norman Conquest.

This was about to change as landowners were realising the value of this common land and getting Acts of Parliament passed so that they could enclose them, throwing off the common folk and leaving them to starve or move on. An Act of Parliament was passed the following year which made the process much more straightforward and ultimately saw over a fifth of the land of England enclosed.

Many of the peasantry I saw on that journey were soon to be forced from their land and most would wind up in cities or the growing industrial towns in the north. There jobs were being created through new technologies such as steam in cotton mills or foundries or mining for coal.

There are many nowadays who say these workers have a bad lot and compare their lives to some rural idyll that they enjoyed before. But let me tell you that there was plenty of bare-arsed poverty in those villages when we passed through them. In a factory your income is not dependent on the weather or your pig dying unexpectedly. There was no poorhouse then; if you could not feed yourself, you had to beg, and in many villages we had to push our way through scabrous children and some adults in rags begging for coins.

On horseback we were not tied to the coaching inns which did their best to fleece travellers of any money they had. Instead we stopped at inns that Jasper knew from his droving days. They turned out to be very comfortable and with hearty meals made from animals that had got 'lost' from the flocks. Over the two nights we dined with some farmers, a lawyer heading north and a parson. All were red-cheeked, cheery fellows until the conversation turned to tax – which it invariably did. To pay for the war with France and Spain the government had just introduced a tax on income. The government was already taxing all manner of things, from tea and tobacco to sugar and even windows, and this catch-all tax was seen as the last straw. Of course we all conveniently ignored the fact that the brandy we drank after the meal while we joined in the cries against government corruption and greed was probably smuggled tax-free from France.

On the afternoon of the third day we approached London. Even after travelling roads well covered with animal dung, we could almost smell London before we saw it. London was growing fast but it was a city of big contrasts between rich and poor. The new buildings springing up on the outskirts were not keeping pace with the growth in the population. Poor people were crammed into every available space with tenements and slums down every alley. At the same time areas were being cleared for the wealthy in the centre of town and new, spacious villas and terraces were being constructed. This compacted the poorer areas even more. The streets were filthy from the human waste thrown into the road and people were everywhere. Several times Jasper had to use a cudgel to keep prying hands from the pack horse and sometimes we had to spur the horses through crowds to avoid being waylaid.

My brother had bought one of the new townhouses in a smart terrace in one of the better parts of town. Before I rang the bell I stood with my back to the door and surveyed what I could see of the city. Another identical terrace was being built on the opposite side of the street but over the scaffolding you could see churches, warehouses and a sea of buildings of every description down to the distant river. This city was where I had to make a name for myself. It was where things happened, a growing empire was controlled and lives won or lost. It was my new home. With mounting excitement I turned back and pulled on the bell chain.

My sister-in-law welcomed me to their new home. I liked Emily; she was far too good for that pompous brother of mine but they seemed happy together. She showed me around and pointed out the new furniture and decorations in the latest regency style. They were pleased to have me as a guest until I found work and could support myself.

That evening they took me out in a cab to see the sights in the town. As we passed the old St Stephen's Chapel in the Palace of Westminster that now served as the House of Commons, my brother James brought me up to date with what was happening in Parliament.

William Pitt had been prime minister of Britain since I was an infant and so complete had been his control of Parliament it was hard for me to imagine anyone else in the role. But it seemed that we were heading towards a constitutional crisis as Pitt and the King were directly opposed over the issue of Ireland.

A French invasion of Ireland four years earlier had failed only due to bad weather and there had been a major uprising by the Irish themselves just two years ago. If the French were to get a foothold in Ireland, it would give them a new invasion launching point and there would be many disaffected Irish who would join them. It would be a disaster for the rest of Britain. Pitt and Castlereagh, the secretary for Ireland, were determined to bring Ireland fully into the union of England, Scotland and Wales to make it less likely they would break away or support an invader. But this involved giving Catholics the same rights as Protestants to sit in Parliament. There was huge opposition to this from the establishment, led by the King himself.

Pitt had just got the Act of Union passed in Parliament which added Ireland fully to the Union of England, Scotland and Wales, with a new Union Jack flag created as a result. There were rumours, though, that the King would block the proposals to give the same rights to Catholics. This would leave Castlereagh humiliated as he had given assurances to Catholics that this equality would be part of the bill. Relations between the King and the prime minister were at an all-time low.

"Castlereagh will see you," James said, "but you need to be careful. Both Pitt and Castlereagh seem to think that they can talk the King round, but I have heard that the King is completely entrenched. Even if he can find you a position if Pitt resigns, so will Castlereagh, and your post may go with it. If you get into an office, try to quickly make some friends amongst the Whigs too, as they could soon be in power."

This did not fill me with confidence that I was about to start a long and prosperous government career. In fact it looked like after seventeen years of stable government I had chosen exactly the wrong moment to try to look for work.

If I was depressed at my prospects before then, I certainly was not encouraged by my meeting with the man himself. In the end I finally introduced myself to Castlereagh, not at the Irish office, but at his home at Cleveland Square. I was there exactly on time but had to wait half an hour as he was running late from the House of Commons. His wife, Emily, was very apologetic and organised tea while I waited, and when Castlereagh finally appeared he also apologised but seemed now in a rush for another appointment. We met in his study and he read my father's letter and said that he would try to find me a position. He was tall and I dare say handsome, with a soft Irish brogue to his voice.

"What skills do you have, Mr Flashman? You speak French and Latin, I suppose?"

"From school, sir, yes. And Spanish, as my mother was from Spain and she taught us."

"Interesting, that is more unusual, although not a lot of use in Ireland. But leave it with me, Mr Flashman. As you will know, it is a difficult time at the moment, but I do mind your father well. He has helped me in the past and I would like to return the favour. So let me look out for the right opportunity and I will be in touch."

As I was about to take my leave the door opened and a much younger man strolled in.

"Dammit, Robert, that blasted bitch has done it again."

At that moment he noticed me in the room and came to a sudden stop. Castlereagh, with a weary smile, introduced us.

"Thomas Flashman, I would like to introduce the impetuous young fool that is my brother, Charles Stewart." We shook hands as Castlereagh added, "Thomas has only recently arrived in London and is from a fine, respectable family and so I don't want you leading him into any of your haunts of depravity."

"As if I would, dear brother," said Stewart in the same soft Irish accent while giving me a wink. "New in London, you say. Well, you'll be looking for places that sell hot buns and fine French pastries, I'll be bound, and I know all the best ones, as anyone will tell you. Now don't worry, brother, I can think of a spotlessly clean place to which I can take our Mr Flashman that will wash off that country dirt and leave him in fine fettle for whatever you have planned for him."

Castlereagh gave a resigned smile. "Mr Flashman, you had better leave us while you still can, as I must detain my brother for a word in private."

I left the room but instead of leaving the house I waited in the hall. After a few minutes Stewart came out and grinned broadly when he saw me. He was around twenty-two then, tall, broad with sandy, curly hair, and normally he had a

21

devil-may-care attitude. But as I discovered later, he was a troubled man, and occasionally, when drunk and with company he trusted, he revealed his tortured inner self. But then I knew nothing of this; I just saw someone who could save me from stumbling blindly around by myself and introduce to me the best places to have fun in London. Both my father and my brother had stressed the need to make the right connections and the brother, well, half-brother as it turned out, of my new patron seemed a good place to start.

Stewart, for his part, was delighted to take up the challenge of introducing me to the best parts of London. Making sure we both had fun took his mind off his own troubles and right then I think he wanted to forget a lot of his recent past, and so my induction began immediately and with relish.

~~~~~~

Chapter 3

For a young, vigorous man with newly awakened sexual appetites, London back then was in some ways just one huge house of entertainment. Some chap called Colquhoun had estimated in 1797 that there were fifty thousand prostitutes in London, which was approximately ten per cent of the total female population. If you went to places like The Strand and Covent Garden, you would find that figure hard to believe, and put it much higher. It was impossible to walk more than a few paces down the street without being accosted.

Those with coin in their pocket could have every vice and depravity satisfied. Alternatively, like me, they could learn of a whole load more vices whose existence they had not previously known. Courtesans ran from the exquisite specialist at fifty guineas a night in a top-class brothel to the hundreds of streetwalkers who would take you up an alley for a pint of wine and a shilling, and doubtless throw in the pox for free. Indeed often they would not bother with the alley; it was not uncommon in the rougher parts of town to see a tart with her skirts up leaning against a wall while the punter bulled away at her, often with other whores standing nearby yelling encouragement or criticising his stamina.

For a better night and six guineas you could visit a quality bagnio house and have a good dinner, a bath and a keen young woman. The women there were literally cleaner, especially if they joined you in the bath, which many did, and the madams assured clients that they were free from disease. There were houses that specialised in black girls, Indian girls or men if that was your taste. There was even a barge moored on the Thames which ran a restaurant on the first floor and a brothel on the second. The dinners were poor and the wine rough, but later the rocking of the boat with a girl astride you was very pleasant.

I never went, but there was even a house of correction where the poor women prisoners were given the choice of starving to death or whoring themselves to the warders.

Their keepers would act like pimps and male visitors could have a female prisoner, willing or unwilling, for the whole night if they tipped the warder a shilling.

Alongside all of this went the elite of polite society, known as the 'ton', ruled by the likes of the duchess of Devonshire and her set, who talked in an affected babyish accent which others in their crowd sought to ape. They ruled the social scene through the institutions like Almack's Assembly Rooms, which was like a high-society casino and dance hall. Entry was decided by a committee of society harridans that met every Monday night and decided who was 'in' while snubbing those whom they thought were nouveau riche. They gave those who were approved an annual voucher for ten guineas allowing access to the club, and to demonstrate what appalling judges of character they were, they gave one to me after an introduction from Stewart. The origins of the Flashman fortune, while possibly tainted by slave trading and piracy, were sufficiently old to pass muster.

Stewart had first taken me to a bagnio that specialised in Turkish delicacies called Mustafa's, or 'must have her' as he pronounced it. The authenticity of the establishment was dubious; I was in Turkey a while back and did not see any of the 'authentic meat pies' on offer that Mustafa assured us were staple fare in Constantinople, but he did also do a good venison and lamb kebab. The huge guard at the door who called himself Achmed was no more Turkish than I was, with a rather obviously false drooping moustache. However, once inside the facilities were excellent, with a huge, marble-lined Turkish bath and some very enthusiastic girls. In most establishments you chose your girl and then went to a room for privacy, but here it was a more social arrangement. While there was a male masseuse available if you wanted a proper Turkish bath first, most people chose a girl to help them with the bathing process and things progressed naturally from there in one of the large plunge pools, on or against the marble slabs or leather couches.

While Mustafa insisted his girls were clean, Stewart was sure that liberal dosing of soapy water before, after and often during a bout would keep him free of the pox, and as we both stayed clear of disease, who is to argue that he was wrong? My own personal favourite was a girl called Jasmine, with raven hair, almond eyes and a glorious olive complexion. She had a slim waist and the most perfect breasts that you could cup in each hand. Given the sociable setting you could not help noticing the activities of other couples nearby, which was also arousing.

On my first visit, after some very intimate soaping, Jasmine and I had just settled sitting on a marble massage slab, slippery with soap and with her astride me while I nuzzled those perfect breasts. Distracted by a squeal, I looked across at Stewart some yards away, who had hauled himself to his feet with his girl still wrapped around him with her ankles crossed in the small of his back. He caught my eye and shouted, "Ten guineas I can beat you round the main pool."

Well, I am a gambling man and the way I saw it I had a good six-yard head start and a lighter jockey. So, reaching down to cup Jasmine's soapy rear, I was up in a moment and charging for the edge of the pool while Jasmine clamped on and yelled encouragement. With Stewart roaring behind me we ran on the towels at the edge of the pool for grip and cleared the first hurdle of a pair coupling at the edge of the water. Down the far side of the pool we were still in the lead, although I could hear my new friend was gaining ground. Other patrons and girls were now yelling encouragement. Around the final corner we went with a portly gentleman and his girl holding a towel across the path as a finishing line. Then as Stewart came alongside he nudged me hard to fall into the water.

I surfaced laughing and crying "Foul!" and "Steward's enquiry, surely!" with Jasmine still in place. Stewart and his jockey jumped in afterwards and the old boy with a towel shouted it was a void race – and he should know, as it turned out he was a High Court judge. Stewart introduced to me to a couple of other junior government types who happened to be sharing the pool with other girls at the same time. One was a senior official at the Foreign Office and the other worked at the Treasury. I realised that Stewart's friendship would make getting known in the right social circles easier – and a lot more pleasurable – than falling off a log.

Over the next few weeks I spent a fair bit of time with Stewart and some of his crowd, and it was certainly an eye-opening experience. I started taking fencing lessons with him, not because I expected to fight but because that was a fashionable way to take exercise just then. There was also a surplus of fencing masters in London, many having fled from the French revolution. Our teacher was a Monsieur Giscard and we would spend many an afternoon with foils and rapiers learning the formal positions and ripostes that are allowed in a sporting fencing match. With the padding and blunting of points we battled away for many an hour without suffering a scratch. There was also cock fighting, bear baiting and horse racing. I recall we saw some chap called Belcher become boxing champion, mercifully after just seventeen rounds as his last bout had taken fifty-one. We watched cricket and saw a chap called Robinson experimenting with cricket pads to protect his legs, but they kept falling off and impeding his runs.

In short I had fallen in with a fast crowd at a time when being an effete dandy was all the rage. This was the age of Beau Brummel, who had heightened the concept of fashion for men, which was closely followed by the Prince Regent, or 'Prinny' as he was known, and all the smart set about town. Tailors quickly caught on to the opportunity of fleecing the rich for the most fashionable cuts and colours, and these clothes became extortionately expensive. I was never in with Prinny's crowd but I did overhear someone once ask Beau Brummel how much he thought it should cost to keep a single man in clothes. He replied that, "With tolerable economy I think it might be done with eight hundred pounds a year." This was at a time when the average wage for a craftsman was just a pound a week.

It was a crazy time. I recall seeing one man positively weep because he could not get a cravat in the right shade of plum. I remember having a silk black-and-yellow-checked waistcoat that I was inordinately pleased with and wore as often as I could. I thought it made me look quite the dandy at the time. Strangely enough, I saw it again a few years ago when the housekeeper showed it to me as she was sorting clothes for charity. I was happy to see it go as it would never fit me now and I thought it would help some local yokel stand out stylishly from the crowd. A few weeks later I was out riding and damn me if I did not see it adorning a scarecrow in one of the fields. Yokels around here have no sense of style!

Yes, London in the late summer and autumn of 1800 was probably the most carefree time of my life. For a young man without care and commitments and with gold in his pocket it was a playground of delights. Yet the fashionable crowd I fell in with were hard drinking, hard playing and so obsessed with being seen wearing the right things and in the right places that they almost made having pleasure hard work. Even at my young age it seemed frivolous, false and meaningless and I struggled to understand how anyone could really get that upset over the right shade of plum. Oh, I enjoyed all the parties, the flirting and the days watching horse racing and other sports, but in a world where men were fighting courageously on land and sea and where we were surrounded by the poor's very real struggle for survival, obsessions with such trivia as clothes seemed ridiculous.

Looking back after a long and eventful life, I realise now that they were just trying to give their lives purpose. The playboy set were not involved in government, were horrified by the thought of discipline in the forces and, led by Prinny, the wastrel in chief, they just wanted to show that their life had some meaning. Prinny's personal example certainly did not encourage the fashionable set to lead more meaningful lives. He was thirty-eight then and already weighed eighteen stone due to his greed and gluttony. The duke of Wellington described him as "the worst man I ever fell in with my whole life, the most selfish, the most false, the most ill-natured, the most entirely without one redeeming quality".

Prinny had also run up debts of over six hundred thousand pounds by the time he was thirty-three, which meant that the fast set struggled to keep up with the fashion. A few had great personal wealth, but others gradually got deeper into debt and faced disgrace and ignominy. Some ended up in debtors' prison; others shot themselves; one or two ended up in the new United States. Even Beau Brummel ended up fleeing to France to avoid bankruptcy and died a pauper.

As I did not have an income I was certainly living beyond my means and was getting through what little money I had faster than a duchess in a hat shop. I did not hear more from Castlereagh and the bank draft my father gave me was quickly used up. I had borrowed another twenty guineas from my brother, who was appalled at the speed I had got through the first fifty and did not approve of my friendship with Stewart. What my brother did not know was that I had also borrowed another hundred in my own name from my father's bank.

Things came to a head when I came home one evening and was handed a letter from my father who had evidently been given a very one-sided account of my activities from James. I was furious – peached on by my own brother. Mind you, he always had been a pompous telltale, so I should not have been surprised. My father had sent more money, but now James was to pay me an allowance like some bloody schoolboy. Well, I was not going to put up with that, and my brother and I had a blazing row before I stormed out again. I was livid, and what made me most angry was that I knew that until Castlereagh came up with a job I would probably have very little choice but to go along with this allowance plan.

I skulked home the next morning still feeling bitter and found my brother busy thrashing one of the maids who had broken some favourite ornament. The girl was wailing piteously as he kept lashing her with a cane and I used the diversion to slip past unseen.

I laid low until I heard him call for a cab and leave with his wife, Emily. I slipped back downstairs to order a late breakfast but found the maid still sniffling in the hall. At the sight of me a cunning, crafty look came into her reddened eyes. "Master Thomas, I knows 'ow you can get your own back on Master James if you want."

Well, that was a damned cheek if ever I heard it and I told her not to interfere in the affairs of her betters and sent her away to get me some breakfast. But my curiosity was piqued and I was still brooding when she brought in the tray. The cunning minx must have known I would be hooked, which is why she brought the tray herself rather than send one of the other maids.

"All right, how could I get my own back on James?"

"Beg pardin, sir, but Master James and Miss Emily are strugglin' to have children, sir. They have gone off to try Dr Graham's electric bed."

Well, I had heard of Graham – who hadn't? He is the only man I have known to make any money out of that completely useless invention, electricity. While scientists keep publishing papers on it, not a single practical use has been found. But Graham, half medical man and half quack, had used it to create his Temple of Health, with its centrepiece, the Celestial Bed.

The bed was designed to help couples conceive and had a gentle electric current pass through it that was supposed to improve fertility. It also had crystals and bells on it that would make music as the bed moved. In the past, scantily clad girls were employed to cavort about to help the more feeble men get in the mood for conception. In fact there were rumours that Emma Hamilton, Nelson's mistress, had started her career acting as the goddess Vestina at Dr Graham's. The bed had been used by the cream of society including Prinny, dukes and duchesses and various politicians, and was seen as quite respectable. Dr Graham had made a fortune, but unfortunately had spent even more and eventually sold up.

The bed was now owned by another quack, claiming to be a 'sexologist'.

Well, it was interesting news, but I did not see how it would help me get my own back on my brother and said so.

"But I knows the 'tendant and 'e will let us in for a shillin'."

"Good God, girl, I don't want to watch my own brother mounting his wife. Get out!"

"No, sir, you don't unnerstand. We don't watch, we turn the 'andle that makes the 'tricity. The 'tendant says that if you turn it fast, you can make them hop and jump, sir."

I considered this as I munched on some toast. I had heard that electric shocks could be quite painful. It was a shame Emily would have to suffer as well, but she had chosen to marry the stuffed shirt and so now she had to suffer the consequences. I could get in there, give them the shock and slip away; they would never know it was me. I was also curious to know what electricity looked like when it was being made.

"All right, tell me where it is and get me a cab," I said, having made my mind up.

"I 'as to go too, sir, or they won't let you in."

"What? I am not travelling around London with a maid. Tell me where it is and I will get in all right."

"I am not telling you, so you 'ave to take me too. I want to turn the 'andle as well." She stood there with her jaw stubbornly set and I was beginning to understand why my brother had thrashed her.

"All right, get your coat and call for a cab."

We arrived at a discrete-looking establishment off Pall Mall a short while later, and after the maid had spoken briefly to someone inside, we were taken down to a room in the basement. In the centre of the room was a machine with metal cogs, wheels and levers. There were some metal cables leading from the apparatus through the ceiling and I could hear people moving about on the floorboards above me. A couple were whispering and then a voice asked if they were ready and my brother's voice replied that they were.

The attendant who had shown us down took hold of a big handle attached to a wide wheel on the machine and started to turn it slowly. There was a mechanical whirring noise that gradually built up and the attendant said that it was important that we kept the wheel at this steady speed. The maid – I had discovered that her name was Sarah on the journey over – promised we would and I took hold and started turning at the same rate. The attendant stood there watching us for a few minutes but finally he was satisfied and left us to go back upstairs.

My arm was starting to ache already but as soon as he was gone I started to quicken the pace of the wheel. It must have been attached to some gears and the sound increased to a continual hum. Within a few moments I heard Emily say that the bed was tingling and it was hurting. Then my brother, the gallant fool, suggested that she go on top so she was in less contact with the bed. Knowing my brother was now getting the full charge, I turned the wheel even harder and soon heard him gasp, but Emily was making entirely different noises and evidently greatly enjoying the new experience

"Oh yes, James, don't stop."

"I can't stop. The bloody electricity is convulsing my muscles."

"Oh God, yes, that is good."

I was starting to feel that I was getting more detail of my brother's love life than I wanted, and as my arm was now truly aching, I stepped back to give Sarah a go. They may call females the weaker sex, but the years that maid had spent scrubbing at steps had not been wasted. She had clearly built up strong arm muscles and, doubtless powered on by memories of her recent thrashing, she went at the wheel like a demon, far faster than me. Her arm was powering that wheel like one of the new-fangled steam engines while above us the couple were shouting even louder.

"Oh James, this is fantastic, oh, oh God, oooh God, oh don't stop."

"Dammit, it bloody hurts, it really bloody hurts, and it is getting worse. I cannot take much more."

As another minute passed Emily could be heard reaching new heights of ecstasy and my brother could be heard yelling. His shouts ended with "Oh Jesus, this is too much, ouch, that was a spark, Jesus, there are bloody sparks now, oh Christ, my balls, I can feel my balls sparking, arrrgh."

This last groan coincided with a final climaxing shriek of ecstasy from Emily. As the sounds of pleasure subsided above us the maid stopped turning the wheel and we could hear the attendant's footsteps rushing down the back stairs. It was time to go.

We were out of the front of the house in a moment and back into the cab, which I had kept waiting for us. We laughed all the way back to the house, recounting our favourite moments until the tears streamed down our faces.

James and Emily arrived back at the house half an hour later and you can be sure that I had left the drawing room door open and sat in a chair that gave me a clear view while I hid my smile behind a paper. Sarah was scrubbing the hall fireplace as she had been for the last twenty minutes. How we did not give the game away I will never know, as I ended up shaking in silent laughter with a handkerchief shoved in my mouth. Emily came in first, looking radiant with a face flushed red and very dishevelled hair. My brother positively limped into view a few seconds later. He was not wearing a wig and most of his hair was sticking straight up. He winced every time he took a step and had a cut under his eye, which I later discovered was due to one of the crystals falling off and hitting him in the face. He looked furious and they were arguing as they crossed the hall.

"I tell you, we should have got a refund."

"We can't do that, James, or they will not let us come back."

"Come back? Are you mad? We are never going back there! It was the worst experience of my life."

"Well, it was one of the best of mine. So if you want a son and heir, you had better be willing to go back."

They disappeared out of earshot after that and the maid winked at me through the door as she went back down to the servants' quarters. If there is a moral to this tale, it is this: if you must thrash your servants, be careful not to beat the ones who know your secrets.

~~~~~~

Chapter 4

While electrocuting my brother had been fun, it did not change my financial situation, and so when Stewart called around that evening to collect me for a visit to a club, I explained that my clubbing days were, for the moment, over. Gentleman would typically go to enormous lengths to avoid admitting that they were financially stretched, but by then I knew Stewart well enough to be straight. He had on a couple of occasions been very open with me about atrocities in Ireland and the horrors that sometimes kept him awake at night and I felt I could be open with him in return. Telling him I was out of gelt would not be as bad as him thinking I had just tired of his company.

To my surprise, he did not seem that bothered that I was down to my last ten guineas, with only the prospect of a pitiful allowance.

"Do you play cards?" he asked.

"I played a bit at school," I replied. "But surely I could lose as much as I could win? I need a more secure source of income than that."

Stewart grinned. "Don't worry, Flash, I guarantee that you will not end this night with less than you started. I know just the chaps to get you flush again."

We went to a quiet club in Piccadilly where he sought out two other gentlemen. I won't name them, but they were both in their thirties and immaculately dressed in expensive clothes and in the latest fashions. They were clearly educated men and had the languid air of men with time and money to burn. We started to play cards, but to my surprise after a while Stewart said that he had to leave but that my new friends would see me right.

The game of fashion at the time was faro, which was more like roulette than cards. The thirteen cards from a single suit, normally spades, were laid on the table to form the board and then a whole new pack was shuffled and put into a card shoe to stop them being tampered with. Someone

34

was selected as banker and people placed bets on what card number or rank would come out of the shoe; it did not matter which suit. The cards were drawn in pairs: the first was the banker's card, and if you had money on that card, you lost it; and the second was the players' or winning card, and if you had money on that card, it was doubled.

If it sounds simple, it was. Purely a game of chance in theory, but while we were only playing for small stakes, I was soon down by three guineas.

"It is time we showed you the system," one of the new fellows said. "You bet on the low cards until you see an ace and then you bet on the high ones. When you see an ace again, you bet on the low."

"But surely the odds are the same?" I saw them exchanging pitying glances. "My God, are you saying the deck is rigged?" I whispered. "But I saw you shuffle it."

Another deck appeared almost magically in the dealer's hand. "You saw me shuffle *a* deck," he said, "but not the one we are playing with. Don't worry about your losses; this is just a practice session for richer pickings later this evening."

"But how will you get the cards into the shoe?"

"Don't you worry about that," the other one said. "You just play for small stakes until I give you the signal. Then gradually, and I mean gradually, you increase the stakes as you start winning. Put in a few small bets on the other end of the board so you lose a bit too."

"So you mean we are guaranteed to win?"

"Yes, provided you don't behave like a gannet in a fishmonger's. You need to keep natural and do what we tell you. If anyone suspects what is going on, you will be ruined. But here is the most important thing: when we give you the signal you cash up and leave. Oh, and we will be round later to collect ten per cent of your winnings as our fee."

We left for Almack's where there was a gathering of the wealthy set which included some aristocratic gambling addicts. Chief among these was Georgiana Duchess of Devonshire who when she died in 1806 left gambling debts of twenty thousand pounds. But this was just the tip of the iceberg, as during her lifetime her husband and various friends, including Prinny and Thomas Coutts, the banker, had paid off many times this amount in other gambling debts. There were others too who lost similar sums, all playing a game where officially the odds were even, which gives you a good idea of how widespread rigged decks were in those days.

I changed my ten guineas into counters and we slowly toured the tables. Then one of my new friends indicated a table in the corner of the room that had a spare seat. Sitting around the table were a matronly old lady, whom we will call Lady S, and her daughter, whom we will call Lady D. Both were dripping in jewels, with the mother wearing diamonds and rubies around her neck while the daughter had a stunning sapphire tiara. I had seen them both before and knew them to be closely related to one of the wealthiest families in the country. I will not name them, as if this fell into the wrong hands, their family still has great influence.

Two other gentlemen I did not know were also at the table, one of whom was the current banker. I politely asked to occupy a vacant seat and sat down next to Lady S. The two men seemed to be coming to the end of a long night and had clearly a lot of drink on board. In contrast the ladies were excited and fixated on the cards while drinking sweet wine and largely chattering amongst themselves. They seemed to have made a small profit for once and were feeling very pleased with themselves. In such an intimate gathering I could not see how the deck could be switched. As it turned out I did not see it happen, for I had just looked away to a disturbance as Lady Bessborough's hair had caught light – they wore it in a big style then and she must have walked too close to a wall sconce candle. They got it out quickly and she was being ushered from the room when I felt a hand on my shoulder, which was the signal that the job had been done.

Well, now I knew that the winning card would be in the bottom seven, but I did not want to cover them all as that would have been too obvious. So I put two guineas on all of the odd numbers up to seven and the last guineas I had on the jack, just to even things out a bit. The first pair of cards out was a double, threes, which meant that the shoe moved on to the next player, Lady S. She re-organised the large pile of counters in front of her to make room for the shoe and could not resist looking greedily at the small piles in front of me and the other players.

On average, as you might expect, I won on every other hand and let the money ride where it was won. I was soon up to twenty guineas, I had lost my stake on the jack and then the first ace appeared and I slowly started migrating my stakes to the other end of the board. As I won the size of my stakes gradually increased from two to five and then to ten and twenty guineas a card. It was normal to keep all your money on the table, as you only lost it on the losing card. Sometimes I won several hands on the trot; other times there would be several even cards in succession and I would not win at all. But apart from when I was slowly moving my bets after an ace, I rarely lost a bet.

The gamblers had reminded me in our practice session that it was important to show excitement as I won, as though I was surprised by my winning streak. But even though I knew I was going to win, it was still genuinely exciting and it was not difficult to look pleased. Lady S's daughter, Lady D, claimed that I must be carrying luck with me that night and decided to shadow some of my bets, taking money off her mother in the process. One of the other men at the table decided to bet on the even numbers as I was betting on the odds, but as he covered them all he won and lost in equal measure.

Three aces came and went and my stakes gradually migrated up and down the board accordingly, growing all the time but keeping to odd numbers plus jacks and kings as though that was my system. The other players congratulated me on my good fortune, even Lady S, who had been obliged to send for more counters.

Eventually a footman brought me a message on a tray. I already knew it would say that my father was asking that I return home urgently. It was my signal to make my excuses and leave.

Wishing the other players good fortune, I gathered up my counters and walked to the cashiers.

From a ten guinea stake I made three hundred and fifty guineas that night, which was provided as an impressively heavy velvet bag full of gold coins. I felt very vulnerable taking that amount home through the streets of London in a cab, but the next day I was able to pay off my brother, the bank and the gamblers with their ten per cent fee and still have over two hundred to live on.

I saw the gamblers several times at clubs in subsequent years. They were professional villains who planned carefully to enjoy retirement rather than go to the gallows. They had made it clear to me that their help was a one-night-only event, as if one player won too regularly, it would raise suspicion. Everyone they helped owed them a favour, and I suspect that there were various lawyers and perhaps even judges who had a vested interest in keeping them out of the courts. Certainly whenever I saw them I would look around and try to spot whom they were helping this time. Invariably if you looked carefully enough you would find a gambler having a surprisingly consistent winning streak. If you waited, you would see they would make a point of quitting while they were ahead rather than losing their winnings later in the night as most genuine gamblers normally manage to do.

The amounts lost at clubs such as Almack's were truly staggering and clearly my friends were not the only ones cheating. Whole estates would change hands in a single night. There was even a rumour that the affections of Lady Melbourne were sold by one of her many lovers to another aristocrat for thirteen thousand pounds to clear a gambling debt. James Fox, the Whig leader, managed to run up gambling debts of a hundred and twenty thousand, which were cleared off by his wealthy father. All this on a game where officially the odds were even.

I would have been ruined and disgraced if I had been caught, but evidently many fortunes were made in this manner and if you were careful like the gamblers, people were rarely caught. The gamblers took the risk of swapping the deck and they were careful not to be seen with me afterwards.

That night's work solved all my money problems and gave me a healthy profit, but I never gambled seriously on faro again. It is far too crooked for me.

~~~~~~

Chapter 5

Two days after my card success I received a message inviting me to dine with Castlereagh. I hoped that this meant that my employment prospects were picking up. I had immediately used some of my gambling money to rent some rooms of my own in a respectable looking area near the centre of town. My new landlady, a shrill woman called Mrs Partridge, had let me a well-furnished apartment in a large old house with a sitting room and bedroom with laundry and cleaning provided. This meant that I was able to escape from my brother's prying eye, which was just as well as I was still struggling to stifle a laugh every time I saw him limp around.

It was the first time I'd had a place of my own and now there was a chance of a job too. To celebrate I spent the afternoon with Jasmine at Mustafa's. I went there for two reasons. Firstly because I had been getting increasingly fond of Jasmine and spending more and more time there. Secondly because Mustafa had broken the cardinal rule of a brothel owner and given me credit over recent visits and I needed to pay him back.

I was now a well-known regular. Achmed, the doorman, recognised that anybody who saw him in daylight more than once would not be fooled by his Turkish disguise. So for me he dropped the salaam greeting and "May a thousand angels bless the pleasure of your eminence" or similar claptrap and replaced it with "Evnin, guvnor, good to see you agin" and usually some comment on the latest sporting news. Mustafa would often invite me into his office for a chat over a glass of strong, sweet coffee. As a break from the usual pleasures, Jasmine and I would walk in the park. It turned out she was not Turkish either; her father had been from North Africa and her mother was Spanish.

"Welcome, welcome!" cried Castlereagh as I arrived at his London home later that evening. Then, in a lower voice, he added, "Charles has been drinking all afternoon. He is in one of his depressions. I am relying on you to stop him getting embarrassingly drunk tonight as half the Cabinet will be here. One of them wants to meet you too; there might be a job in it for you."

Before he could say any more Charles Stewart wove through the small crowd in the drawing room to thrust a drink in my hand and say, "My God I am glad to see you here. This night is set to be a dull affair. God, what a crowd." He was looking at the six other men, including his brother, who were going to dine with us. "That is George Canning over there," he said, pointing to a balding man with an energetic manner who was jabbing another guest vigorously in the chest to make a point. "He is just too clever by half; can't follow him when I am sober never mind when I am drunk."

"Isn't that Pitt?" I asked, pointing to a pale, grey-haired man on the far side of the room. Most of the names of the leading politicians were familiar to me from the papers, but they did not carry illustrations so matching faces to names was difficult if you were not familiar with this type of gathering.

"Yes, that is him, talking to Wilberforce. Robert is worried about his health. Look at him, he looks much older than his forty-one years. That is what seventeen years as prime minister does to you." Pitt did indeed look drained, but he was still talking animatedly to Wilberforce, who I knew was the anti-slavery campaigner and a long-time friend of Pitt.

"Who is that?" I asked, pointing to another younger man who had just joined Pitt and Wilberforce.

"No idea," said Stewart brusquely, "and if I don't know 'em, he can't be that important. Now come on, are you going to nurse that drink all night? I need another."

A short while later we moved into the dining room and I sat near the bottom of the table with Stewart, already realising that restraining him from being obnoxious was going to be a forlorn task. Pitt and the senior Cabinet members sat at the other end of the table but the stranger

Stewart did not know came around the table and sat next to me.

"William Wickham," he said, introducing himself. It was not a name I had come across in the papers but he clearly knew me. "You are Thomas Flashman, aren't you? Castlereagh said we should have a chat."

"Err, yes. Do you work with Castlereagh in the Irish Office?"

"Course he doesn't," interrupted Stewart loudly. "I would bloody know him if he worked there. Who or what are you, sir?"

"Well, I am sort of linked to the Foreign Office, at least the work I do is for their benefit." Wickham spoke calmly with a smile, ignoring Stewart's aggressive tone.

I noticed that Canning had looked up at the mention of the Foreign Office – until recently he had been foreign secretary – and he had given a wry smile at Wickham's words.

Clearly Wickham was well known to Canning, but Stewart, gazing glassy eyed across the table at Wickham, had missed all of this and continued, "Foreign Office are the last to know anything. Bloody foreign governments run rings around us. Half of these French *émigrés* seem to be spying for the French to keep family members safe on the other side of the channel. This Napoleon chap the French have got now seems to know what he is doing. He will give the Foreign Office a run for their... for their..." He look puzzled as though he could not remember what he was going to say and then just finished loudly and abruptly, "The Foreign Office know nothing." To emphasise his point he banged his fist down on the table, knocking his wine glass over to spill red claret all over the white tablecloth.

Castlereagh looked in mute appeal at me and tried to start another conversation at his end of the table, but before I could do anything Wickham was standing and reaching across the table for Stewart's glass. "Here, old fellow, let me refill that for you." More drink was the last thing that

Stewart needed and I suggested quietly that he might want to have a rest as he had taken a lot on board already.

"Nonsense," said Stewart. "And miss all this fun?" He pointed to the other end of the table. "Anyway I am hungry and want to eat." He gestured to a plate of soup that a footman had just put before him.

Wickham had poured just a half glass of wine for Stewart. I thought that if that was his idea to slow Stewart down, it would not work as Stewart was bound to complain. But then as Wickham picked up the glass with his right hand to pass it across, I saw a white powder fall into the drink from something hidden in the palm of his hand. He looked up and saw that I had noticed and just grinned and winked. Wickham swirled the wine around the glass to mix in the powder and then placed it before Stewart.

It took Stewart a moment to notice the wine was there, but then, as I expected, he was quick to complain. "What is this…? Mr Foreign Office, half measures? You are not paying for this wine, my brother is, so fill the glass up."

"I do apologise," said Wickham, still calm and smiling. "Why don't you drink that now and I will give you another full glass."

Stewart threw the wine back in one gulp and belligerently passed his glass back for a refill. I watched him closely. He took another swig of the fresh wine and put the glass down next to his soup. His eyes had been glassy before but now they seemed to lose what little focus they had and he started to sway in his chair with a slightly puzzled look on his face.

"You might want to move his soup," said Wickham quietly, "or he will be in it in a moment."

I got up quickly and moved around the table and had just got his soup dish and wine glass out of the way when Stewart's head hit the table with a loud thud.

"Good God," said Castlereagh, looking in astonishment down the table. "Did you hit him?"

"No, sir," I replied. "He just passed out."

"Oh, I don't mind if you hit him; it was quick thinking, the mood he was in. Well done, Flashman." Evidently

Castlereagh still thought I had brained his brother and was happy about it.

My host then whispered to his butler and a couple of moments later two of the footmen gathered Stewart's unconscious form and carried it away.

"Will he be all right?" I asked Wickham quietly.

"Oh, he will be fine, but he will have a sore head in the morning."

We were interrupted by Pitt trying to involve us in the conversation that they had been having at the other end of the table.

"Tell me, Mr Flashman, are you a Catholic?"

"No, sir, I am not. Church of England. But to be honest, I visit church as little as I can."

"But, sir," said Wilberforce, squinting at me with his weak eyes, "you need to have faith as a beacon to guide your life."

"Not now, William," smiled Pitt. "You can leave your evangelical Bible thumping for later. So, Flashman, do you have servants? Are they Catholic?"

"I have just rented some rooms and I have a housekeeper. I have no idea what religion she is."

"Would it concern you if she was a Catholic?"

"No, or I would have asked when I took the rooms."

"Exactly," cried Pitt triumphantly. "You see, things have moved on and Catholicism is less important to people. We have passed the Act of Union creating the British Isles and everyone within its borders must have the same rights, for it is a single nation. Catholics in England have the right to vote and so should Catholics in Ireland, and they should also be able to serve as members of Parliament."

"You are preaching to the choir," said Castlereagh grimly. "But that is not how the King sees it."

Pitt took a deep breath before he responded. "If the Irish do not feel included in the Union then with their Catholic majority they could break away and the King would lose that dominion as well as America. We have quelled a rebellion already and invested a fortune in time, money and titles to get this far; we cannot go back now."

"Yes, but the King is convinced that to allow Catholic emancipation he would be breaking his coronation oath to protect Protestantism."

"But that oath is over a hundred years old. Times have changed. Since then laws relaxing restrictions on Catholics have been passed and other restrictions are routinely ignored."

"The Gordon riots were only twenty years ago, tearing up London and attacking Catholics," interjected Canning.

"Popery was just the excuse; there were political, economic and plain criminal motivations behind those riots too."

The debate continued like this for much of the evening. Despite looking tired, Pitt dominated the conversation with passionate debate, surrounded by friends he trusted who argued their cases with equal vigour. The wine flowed and it turned into a long night. Pitt drank prodigiously of port that had been prescribed years ago to help with his health. He partook of his medicine enthusiastically, downing at least two bottles by himself before the rest of us moved on from claret to port. At one point he got up mid-debate and, unbuttoning himself, went behind the screen in the corner of the room where he was in full flow in every sense of the word. With his finger jabbing the air above the screen to make the point that he would resign if the King did not back down and his piss splashing in the chamber pot in front of him, he continued to make his case. I had been used to people leaving the room if they wanted to use the jakes, but everyone took this as normal.

Castlereagh's dinner finished around midnight. It had been an illuminating insight into government and had introduced me to some of the key men, but Wickham had not told me about the new job. When I asked, he told me that he would tell me later, and it was only as we stepped out of the house that he pulled me to one side, out of earshot of the others.

"I understand that you speak Spanish, is that right?"

"Yes, my mother was Spanish. She and her Spanish maid taught me."

"Have you ever been to Spain?" he asked.

"God, no. My mother's people have land there, but when she married my father they acted as though she had married a devil and cut her out of their lives entirely."

"Excellent. I need someone I can trust to deliver a message to an agent in Spain."

"What… but I don't understand. I thought you worked at the Foreign Office, and aren't we are war with Spain?"

"Technically I am under-secretary of state for the Home Department, but in practice I run a network of agents across Europe. I am Britain's spy master, which is why your friend Stewart did not know me. I spend much of my time in Switzerland."

"But surely you have couriers to do that kind of thing?"

"Oh we do, but rather a lot of them have been getting caught recently. Your friend Stewart was right about that: many of the French *émigrés* are persuaded to spy for France to protect relatives there and now they are getting close to the Spanish community in London too. If I was to ask one of my Spanish agents to visit Spain, there is a good chance word would get out. I need someone I can trust who has no links with the Spanish community here, and Castlereagh suggested you."

"But won't it be dangerous? I have never been to Spain. I don't know any of the customs. I would stand out like a sore thumb."

"Oh, don't worry, you will only be in Spain for an hour or two at the most. A ship down to Gibraltar, then another boat, Navy probably, to take you up the coast to a small town. You will just need to slip ashore at night and pass a message to an agent and possibly get a despatch in return, and then your work is done. You will be well paid for the trip too."

My mind was reeling. I had been expecting some post in a London ministry; it might have been dull work, but it was safe. Now I was being offered foreign travel and the chance to mix with spies, albeit briefly. Fool that I was, I believed the assurance that it would not be dangerous. It would be a grand adventure, and if Wickham or Castlereagh were to write to my father to say I was going abroad on government business, he would find it hard to object. If I were to refuse work that Castlereagh had pushed my way then he may not offer work again.

"Are you sure I will not need to be in Spain for more than a couple of hours?" I asked, just to be certain.

Wickham laughed. "Don't worry, it will be straight in and straight out. The agent you are passing the message to is an elderly Catholic priest who has not left the town in years. He will be there, waiting in the church. He is the courier at the Spanish end who will pass the message on."

"All right. My father wants me to stay in London, but if he does not object, I will do it."

"I will send a note to him tomorrow. We should have a reply by the end of the week, and in the meantime, I will arrange another meeting so that we can discuss this further."

Feeling suddenly excited and important that I was to play a part in government affairs, I wished him good night and then looked for some transport home.

Several of the ministers, such as Pitt, had carriages waiting. I did not, but two men with a sedan chair were hovering conveniently to hand and I climbed aboard and gave them the address. At night it was dangerous to go alone in any part of the city, and with my finest clothes and shoes I did not want to walk through the filth on the streets. I was also partly drunk after all the wine that night, but not enough to stop my mind buzzing about the chance to travel abroad and start a government career. They got me to my rooms quickly, but as I paid them I noticed a strange thing. One of the men, the boss of the outfit by his attitude, was wearing an exceptionally good pair of shoes, albeit covered in mud. Normally such fellows wore the roughest boots. When I commented on his footwear he looked surprised and then explained that he had won the shoes in a wager on a cockfight. This did not really explain why he was ruining them with his sedan chair work, but I did not dwell more on it and went to bed.

~~~~~~~

Chapter 6

Three days later I received a note from Wickham asking if
we could meet in a coffee shop in Jermyn Street. He was
sitting at a table in the corner with another figure hidden
behind a newspaper. As I got closer I saw that the other
person was a lady in riding clothes. Society women were
rarely seen in coffee shops, which were a male domain, and
with their hooped skirts they would normally struggle to get
through the throng. But this lady did not look English or part
of the society set. She wore a slim riding skirt and jacket in
brown over a quite low-cut white bodice and a jaunty hat
with a feather in it.

Wickham looked up at my approach and stood to shake
hands and introduce his companion as Consuela Martinez.

She turned to me and said in Spanish, "It is a pleasure to
meet you, Señor Flashman. I understand that you are new to
London. What would you say are the finer points of the
city?"

Well, looking at her in her rig – she was showing an
impressive amount of cleavage – two attractive points sprang
to mind immediately, but I gathered my memory of Spanish
to reply promptly, "While the cathedrals and mansions are
impressive, nothing can compare to the beauty of the ladies
you meet in coffee shops."

She laughed at the compliment but gave me a shrewd and
calculating look. Then she turned to Wickham and said in
English, "His Spanish is really very good, almost like a
Spaniard."

"Excellent," said Wickham. "Well, you have passed the
Spanish language test and I have heard this morning from
your father that he is happy for you to work for the
diplomatic service. I am glad to welcome you aboard."

"What is the mission about?" I asked.

"Well, we have had the Spanish fleet blockaded in Cadiz
for months now. But it is draining on the fleet to keep a
squadron there on blockade duty, and despite making some

feints to draw them out for battle, they have stayed in port. We want to destroy them before they can join up with the French. We have an agent in Cadiz and we think we can use him to get the fleet to sail."

"But how?"

Wickham glanced briefly at Consuela, who was paying close attention. "I will give you the full details when you are ready to sail." He pulled a sealed paper out of his pocket. "But in the meantime… what is it?"

I had just noticed a man sitting two tables away behind Consuela. Apparently engrossed in coffee and a newspaper, he looked exactly like the sedan chair driver of the other night. This time, of course, he was expensively dressed and he was not sporting a moustache as he had been before, but I was sure it was the same man. I had only given him a puzzled glance, but Wickham had noticed my momentary distraction.

"Oh nothing, just thought I recognised someone, but it can't be."

"Thomas, in my line of work we don't take coincidences lightly. Who is it and where have you seen him before?"

"He looks like the sedan chair driver who took me home from Castlereagh's after I had finished talking to you the other night. He does not have a moustache now as he did then. But now that I think about it, I recall that the driver was wearing much better shoes than the average sedan driver, which I thought was strange."

"So he could have been watching me that night and decided to follow you as we had been talking. But how the devil would he know we were meeting here?"

Wickham pretended to brush some dandruff from his shoulder to steal a glance at the stranger, who did not notice. Unfortunately Consuela was less subtle, scraping her chair when she looked round, and the stranger looked up. Leaving some coins on the table, he folded his paper and started to leave.

Wickham turned to Consuela. "My dear, would you do me a service and trail our friend to see where he goes."

"It will be a pleasure," she said with a grim smile. With a nod to me, she sprang lightly to her feet and set off after the man, who was now heading out into the street. I felt sorry for the stranger if he turned and challenged her. She exuded a sense of danger and I would have bet a guinea that amongst the folds of her dress was a razor-sharp stiletto knife that she could expertly wield to defend herself.

I asked, "Is Consuela one of your agents?"

"Oh yes, a recent recruit but a very capable one. She was in Spain recently and the information she brought back was very valuable. Now, here on this paper are details of the carriage to Southampton and the ship you will be taking to Gibraltar. I will meet you before you get on the carriage and give you some letters for our agent and details of where to find him."

He started to count off tasks on his fingers. "I will also give you a letter signed by Pitt confirming that you are a diplomatic courier and asking all British subjects to assist you in your efforts to deliver your message. That should help you get a Navy ship in Gibraltar. I know the governor there well and he will certainly assist you. We will also give you some gold to overcome any obstacles you might meet along the way.

"Don't worry about receipts; we are much more relaxed about that in our line of work than the Treasury, if you get my meaning. What you don't spend you can keep.

"Now, I must get going. I wish you good day."

With a cheery wave Wickham was out of the door and my career as a courier began.

When I returned to my rooms I found an invitation from Stewart. He had forgiven me for knocking him out, which is what his brother had told him had happened. He was embarrassed about how he had behaved at the dinner and grateful I had stopped things getting worse. Castlereagh had reserved a box at the Vauxhall Pleasure Gardens that evening for some of the new Irish peers to keep them onside during the continuing difficulties with the King, and I was also invited. Given that this was the Pleasure Gardens I was expected to bring female company, and it was the kind of place men brought their mistresses rather than their wives. I knew just who to invite.

Jasmine was delighted to come, although it cost me a new dress for her. We hired a carriage and crossed London Bridge and passed through the gates of the gardens into a magical world. With a two-shilling entrance fee, the rough sort were excluded and everything was designed to delight. An orchestra played in the centre of the gardens while couples promenaded around the beautifully kept flower beds or lingered among the many alcoves and deep recesses in the large hedgerow walks. These walks, particularly at the masked balls they held in the gardens, were notorious as places of wild debauchery.

We decided to leave that sort of thing for later and went up to the supper box hired by Castlereagh. There were nearly a hundred of these boxes spread across the park and Castlereagh had booked a large one holding a dozen people. It was like a room on stilts, with a balcony facing the orchestra and stage in the centre of the park. You could see over the crowds to watch the entertainment and the fireworks that followed and enjoy the lanterns that were lit as darkness fell, and in the meantime a supper would be served in the box. That night the food was good, the wine excellent and the orchestra played popular show tunes with various singers. I had a beautiful girl in my arms and as the lanterns started to shine through the darkness it seemed to be a magical night. The only thing ruining the romantic mood was the presence of ten very drunk Irishmen, and so we decided to take a stroll.

I had no doubt that we would end up in one of those dark, secluded hedgerows, but initially we walked along the better lit flower gardens and across the intricately laid lawns. Many other couples were doing the same, although I noticed a rough-looking sort with a scarred face on his own. He stuck in my memory because he looked so out of place. The entry fee normally put his type off, but if they came, they did so as a couple. This villainous-looking cove was the only man I saw walking about on his own. More worryingly, wherever we went in the gardens when I looked around I could see him loitering in the shadows. We went to the north end and then the south; he was there both times. Then we took a turn around the orchestra and weaved between the couples picnicking on the ground and he was there again, and this time I noticed that there was also a very large accomplice on his own behind him.

In hindsight, the sensible thing to do would have been to go back up to the supper box, but I thought the maze of thick hedges would be the ideal place to lose him. Then, when we were sure he had gone, I could get to grips with Jasmine. Of course she thought I was making up the scarred man just to get her into the hedges, but followed on willingly. We took several twists and turns, interrupting a few couples along the way, until we got to the end of a straight corridor of hedges and stood in the dark corner at the end to see if we were being followed.

Five minutes passed and then Scarface appeared at the end of the row, clearly looking for somebody. When he saw us he started off in our direction. We did not delay but moved quickly around the nearest corner and tried to shake him off again with more twists and turns. Once, we caught a glimpse of the fat accomplice too, but he did not see us.

Now Jasmine was getting worried as she had seen that the scarred man really was following us, but I was sure that after a dozen turns and dodging around various other couples he would not get us this time. Again I found another long corridor of hedges to watch from and checked that we had another gap in the hedge as an escape route.

Five minutes passed and then ten. The fireworks had started now and rockets were swooshing into the sky and exploding with loud bangs that caused ladies to scream and turned night briefly into day in their flash. There was the crackle of other fireworks burning on frames nearby and smoke smelling of rotten eggs began to drift through the hedges. We would be even harder to find in this smoke.

I began to relax, and was just having a quick fondle of Jasmine and thinking of disappearing into an alcove when I felt her stiffen as she looked over my shoulder. I turned around and sure enough Scarface had found us again. I grabbed Jasmine and ran down our escape route. The problem in planning an escape route in a maze is that it can sometimes finish in what could prophetically be called a dead end, and that is what happened in this case. I whirled around, looking for another way out, and found none. I looked for a gap between the hedge plants but they were too tightly planted and there were no gaps big enough under the foliage either.

Jasmine screamed as Scarface came round the final corner to find us again, but with the fireworks continuing no one would take any notice. He stopped and stared at us for a moment and then moved slowly forward. I saw something metal gleam in his right hand. I had no weapon and I was just about to suggest that we both try to make a run for it as he could only catch one of us when the huge accomplice also walked round the corner and started walking quickly towards us without making a sound.

We had backed into the corner. My heart and my mind were racing. I had some coins I could throw them and we could try to dart past, but something told me that these were not common muggers. Scarface stopped again just six yards off and watched us as though weighing up how to attack. As Jasmine took in another big breath to scream the big accomplice pulled out a cosh and with a swift blow… laid Scarface out cold on the ground.

"Evenin, guvnor, you looked like you needed some 'elp," said a grinning Achmed, taking off a broad-brimmed hat that had kept his face in shadow.

I could have wept with relief. It turned out that, knowing how rowdy the gardens could get, Mustafa had sent Achmed to keep an eye on Jasmine. He did not want any former clients seeing her and thinking they could take liberties when she was out with the quality, as he put it.

Achmed escorted us out of the gardens and into a carriage. What with the relief that the danger had passed and the fact that I had been with Jasmine all evening without anything more than a quick fondle, I was feeling monstrously horny. I decided we would return to my rooms together. It would be nice to enjoy each other and some privacy in my own new home, a bit like we were a proper couple. I asked Achmed to tell Mustafa to expect Jasmine back in the morning, and then we set off for a night of passion that had Mrs Partridge repeatedly banging her broom on the floorboards below us and telling us to keep the noise down.

~~~~~~

Chapter 7

I suppose that we have all woken up at some point in our lives in an unpleasant manner. With a massive hangover in a provost's cell, or remembering you have goosed the general's daughter and your career is ruined, or even in a strange bed with a hideous old trot and desperately hoping that you haven't mounted her, or at least that you will never remember it if you have. I've done 'em all and plenty more besides, but for sheer horror none compare with the way I was awoken next morning. Those memories have stayed fresh and raw in my memory all my life for reasons that will be clear later in my tale. Aye, and when I have woken up to all those other ghastly situations, well, at least I have been able to roll over and think, 'It could be worse.'

It was the suddenness of it that hit me the hardest. Normally consciousness comes on you in waves, one memory after another, and you have time to adjust, but I am still not sure what hit me first back then. One moment I was blissfully unconscious, sleeping with a beautiful, naked girl in my arms, and a second later I was gibbering in terror. Thinking back, it must have been the twitching of Jasmine that started to wake me; I have a vague recollection of her clutching at me and her leg drumming against the bed, but I might have imagined that. Then, before my eyes were open, I became aware of something warm and wet on my chest and shoulder and only then did I feel the prick of a sharp blade at my throat.

My eyes opened then all right, to find that evil, scarred face from the night before leaning over me.

"You just keep quiet, boy, or you will get the same treatment," he said.

It was dawn and the curtains were thin and so the room was filled with a dull, grey light that made him look even more sinister, but I still did not understand. Then, with the knife still against my neck, I twisted my head slightly to look at my beautiful Jasmine. Her eyes were closed as if still

56

asleep, but her body was still twitching and then, as I looked down further, I saw it. Beneath her sweet red lips and proud chin on her slender throat was a hideous, red, gaping gash. Her throat had been cut and between us we were covered in blood that was still pulsing from her body. From my neck down all I could see was blood on our bodies and soaked through the sheet which covered us.

"Ooh," was all I could say as I looked on that sight. I was struggling to comprehend in the second or so I had been conscious what was happening.

Scarface then spoke again although I only remembered the words later when thinking back. "Now you are going to give me the paper Wickham…"

The reason that I did not listen at the time and that the sentence was never completed was because Jasmine suddenly opened her eyes and looked at me. In this charnel house of horror she was still alive.

That hideous moment brought me to my senses, or perhaps took me further away from them, as I ignored the knife at my own throat and just erupted from the bed, shouting. One moment I was in the bed, the next there was a flurry of blood-soaked sheet and I was on the floor on the opposite side of the bed from Scarface, scrabbling under the pillow. It was instinct. I don't remember consciously thinking about the horse pistol until the great big thing was in my hands and both my thumbs were hauling back on the hammer.

By then Scarface had disentangled himself from the crimson bedding that had covered him as I leapt up. He had started to spring across the bed, knife in hand. When he caught sight of the pistol his face was only inches away from the big muzzle. I fired. The flash in the pan and the noise from the big gun was deafening in such a confined space and Scarface was snatched away as though someone had yanked him back by his collar to the other side of the bed.

I stood there, frozen in shock. For a second or two I was deaf from the discharge of the pistol, and with the room half full of acrid smoke from its firing, it seemed surreal. Maybe ten seconds ago I had been fast asleep in paradise and now my lover watched me through the haze with the fixed, glassy stare of the dead and that awful second mouth under her chin. Scarface had taken a faceful of scrap metal at point-blank range. Judging from the new blood spatter on the opposite wall I thought he must be dead, but as my hearing recovered I heard a sickening gurgling from the other side of the room.

Then I heard a noise in my sitting room and the door into the bedroom moved slightly to give the person a better view. He could see Scarface's side of the room but was hidden from me. I heard a low whistle as he saw the body of his accomplice.

"I have another pistol if you want more of the same," I squeaked as I swung the pistol to cover the door, noticing how ridiculously high my voice had got. I instantly realised as I looked down it that I could not fool them with this gun, as a tendril of smoke was still coming from the barrel, indicating that it had just been fired.

Frantically I looked around for something else to use as a weapon, but the newcomer showed no sign of wanting to call my bluff. Unlike Scarface's cockney rasp, his voice was more educated, with a foreign accent I could not place. "You are a dead man, Mr Flashman" was all he said, and then I heard him move across the other room and leave my apartment.

The second he had gone I started for the saddlebag in the corner to reload the pistol, but my hands had now started to shake so violently it was impossible. I moved across to look at what had been Scarface. He could more accurately be called Bubbling Raw Meat Face now, and as I watched his chest heaved a final sigh and then simply stopped, leaving the room in heavy silence. I looked across at the beautiful Jasmine and shuddered again at that dreadful gash across her throat. I could not bear to look at it and picked up one of her petticoats from the floor and draped it across her chest and neck so that only her face was visible.

I whirled round as I heard more movement in my sitting room and snatched up the poker from the fire grate; it was the only weapon I could see. After a second the head of my landlady, Mrs Partridge, appeared around the door. Now at this moment of deep personal crisis there were many things I would have welcomed from Mrs P: an offer to get help, a comforting embrace or even a strong cup of tea. What I did not need was her jaw sagging as she looked at my naked, blood-spattered body clutching a poker over two grisly corpses and then her taking a deep breath and screaming "Murder! Oh, terrible murder! Somebody get the town watch!" as she ran out of the door, doubtless waking up the entire street.

It brought me to my senses and no error. I had no witnesses for self-defence and no wish to risk the mercy of the court when a rope and the gallows were a possible outcome. That's if I got to court; it would be easy for my unknown enemy to arrange my murder in jail. I would be surrounded by villains with little to lose who would probably kill me for a bottle of gin.

I quickly threw on some clothes and packed my valuables into my saddlebag with the pistol; the rest I would have to leave behind for now. I could hear a commotion on the stairs as people entered the front of the house to the still-strident appeals of Mrs P, but luckily my rooms faced the back. I pulled up the sash window and squeezed out. With my saddlebag over my shoulder I jumped down onto the outhouse roof and then down to the ground. I was away into the grey dawn before anyone entered my rooms.

I ran a few hundred yards down the alley and then stopped in a doorway while I worked out where to go. They knew who I was, so would probably watch my brother's house. I could not go to Castlereagh or Stewart at this time of the morning and I needed to tell Mustafa what had happened. I did not want anyone else telling him it was me, and I instinctively knew that he would believe that I had not killed Jasmine. There was, after all, the body of the murderer still on my floor – although probably little chance he would be identified without a face. Yes, bizarre as it might seem, a Turkish-themed whore house was the safest place for Flashy that night.

Ten minutes later, after a run across town, I was hammering on the door of Mustafa's, which was eventually opened by a bleary-eyed Achmed. I was out of breath, my face was still blood-spattered and some of the blood on my chest had now soaked through my shirt: I must have looked a proper state. After looking up the street and seeing I was alone, he rushed me into Mustafa's office. The old man was got out of bed while I sat weeping in a chair as recent events caught up with me. When Mustafa came in I started to tell him what had happened. I knew Jasmine was one of his favourites. With Achmed adding in the detail from the night before, Mustafa was convinced of my innocence and soon all three of us were weeping and drinking brandy to get over the shock.

After a while Achmed was sent to get an undertaker to recover Jasmine's body and a message was sent to summon Wickham, telling him it was urgent as someone had tried to kill me. I was not going to go to Wickham myself with those killers looking for me.

Wickham arrived an hour later, looking slightly surprised at the oriental surroundings of the room in which we met. "Well, Flashman, I was not expecting this: a meeting in a Turkish brothel. What on earth is going on?"

Well, I told him and he sat down on one of the couches in amazement.

"Good God," he said when I had finished. "So you killed one of the villains but the other, the one you did not see, is still at large. And the poor girl dead too. I am so sorry, Flashman. I had no idea that you would be in this much danger. And you say that they knew about that paper I gave you too?"

He sat back to think for a moment and then said, "Well, it is clear that you will have to leave London for a while and not be seen in any of your usual haunts." Here he glanced curiously around the Turkish-themed boudoir in which we were currently sitting. "They know a mission is being planned but they don't know where or what it is, or they would not be trying to find that paper. They certainly want to stop you reaching Spain. The sooner that we get you away, the better."

"What, you still want me to go to Spain? After all this has happened?"

"Of course. It is the safest place for you now. You will be killed for certain if you stay in London, and I have just arranged passage for you on a ship to India. Only the captain and I know that it will be dropping you off at Gibraltar on the way. They may watch the ships bound for the Mediterranean but they will not watch the East India Company ships."

He put a bundle of documents on the table with a cloth sack that clinked. "Here are the letters I told you about. There is an extra letter to the governor of Gibraltar to let him know what is happening. In the sack are some silver Spanish dollars, some gold escudos and some large gold coins called onzas. Now, I am sure that I was not followed here, but they will be looking for you. They may track the girl's body back to here and watch this place, and so we should get you away as quickly as possible. The company ship sails tonight."

"Tonight! But I can't possibly get to Portsmouth by tonight."

"No, it sails from the docks here in London. Gather your things here and I suggest that you take my carriage – the driver can take you straight to where she is moored as we have just come from there. I will walk back. If you need any extra clothes then ask the captain to send a crewman for them, and on no account go on deck before she sails. You should be in Gibraltar before any agent here can send a message to Spain. We are fortunate the ship is sailing so quickly."

"But will it be safe to come back?" My mind was whirling at the speed of events and for a moment I thought I would be trapped abroad and murdered if I ever showed myself in England again.

"Of course. Once your mission has been completed you will be of no interest to the agents here as you will already have done what they are trying to stop you doing. I would not rush back, though. You have plenty of gold to live on; stay low in Gibraltar or some other friendly port until the outcome of your mission is known."

"But you haven't told me what the outcome of my mission is."

"Haven't I? Goodness, no, I haven't, have I? With all the rush I completely forgot. Your mission is to get these documents to the priest in a small coastal town called Estepona. The priest's brother works at the Admiralty in Cadiz. The Spanish admiral in Cadiz, called Moreno, is a very proud man and a capable sailor and he knows that the English fleet blockading Cadiz would destroy much of the Spanish fleet if it put to sea. He is therefore wisely staying in port, which ties up a whole squadron of our ships in the blockade."

Wickham patted the packet of papers between us. "These papers include copies of British Admiralty orders to Admiral Saumarez, who commands the Cadiz blockade, to send half of his fleet back to Gibraltar to guard a convoy in the Mediterranean. There are also copies of orders from the Spanish government to another Spanish admiral, ordering him to Cadiz to take command of the Spanish fleet and show more vigour against the enemy. Both copies are, of course, fake. The hope is that Moreno will be stung into sailing against what he thinks is a weakened English fleet before he is relieved of command. Once the Spanish fleet has sailed, and hopefully been destroyed, then you will know it is safe to return home."

A few minutes later I was bundled into Wickham's carriage. At my feet was the saddlebag with my few possessions in it and in my coat pockets were the letters and the heavy bag of coin. In one day I had changed from being a simple diplomatic courier to a man on the run with the destruction of a whole enemy fleet at stake.

~~~~~

Chapter 8

I will spare you the details of my journey to Gibraltar aboard the company ship. The weather was awful, particularly across the Bay of Biscay, and I spent most of it flat on my cot or heaving into a wooden pail. Eventually, as the ship turned east to sail along the bottom of the Spanish peninsular, the weather calmed a bit.

At the end of the third week we sighted Gibraltar. The ship was anchored in the harbour and a boat was launched to put me ashore and pick up some provisions before it continued on its journey. This was my first time abroad and I sat in a borrowed boat cloak at the stern while the launch was rowed to a jetty. I had lost a fair bit of weight on the journey as I had eaten little, and while the sun was noticeably warmer, I still shivered a bit under the cloak. The harbour was dominated by the great rock of Gibraltar and was full of shipping of all shapes, types and sizes. It had been a British possession for less than a hundred years, and as we drew close I saw the buildings were unlike those of home, with more white walls and balconies than a British port.

I was left on the quayside with my luggage in a canvas sack beside me. I explained to the harbour master that I had despatches for the governor and he organised a cart to take me to the residency, which turned out to be an old convent. It only took a few moments as the convent was at the southern end of the main street. There were a couple of sentries outside but I could not find anyone inside. I wandered through the hall and a couple of reception rooms and then I heard a strident woman's voice calling, "Charles, Charles, where are you?"

I moved to the door nearest to where the voice was coming from, but as I got close it opened and a grey-haired old man backed out of it and bumped into me. He whirled round and whispered, "Who the devil are you, sir?"

"Thomas Flashman, sir. I am here with despatches for the governor."

"Well, keep your voice down and follow me."

He led the way across the room and then through a small door hidden in the panelling and then up two flights of a narrow spiral staircase. Eventually we emerged in a small attic room and he quietly locked the door behind us.

"Dammit, in my lifetime I have had the ignominy of having to personally surrender to both George Washington and Napoleon Bonaparte, but neither were as persistent as Mrs bloody Harris. What is the point of having armed sentries when you can't have unwelcome guests shot, what?"

"Are you the governor, sir?" I asked hesitantly.

"General Charles O'Hara at your service, sir," he replied. "Governor of this fine bastion, ready to repel all invaders apart from that frightful harridan patrolling the floors below us."

His eyes twinkled in a well-worn face as he looked at me. He was sixty then, and he had indeed surrendered to George Washington at Yorktown as Cornwallis had been too ill, and he had also surrendered to Napoleon in Toulon when the young Captain Bonaparte had first gained fame commanding the artillery in the siege of the city. Following that encounter O'Hara had spent two years in a Paris gaol, threatened with the guillotine. He was there in the Luxembourg Prison in Paris during the height of the terror. While he was one of the few to leave with his head still on his shoulders, his health had suffered ever since.

He sat at the small desk in the room and gestured me to the chair opposite.

"So, young man, what despatches do you have for me?"

I reached into my jacket and passed across the letter addressed to him and sat quietly while he read it.

"So you are from Castlereagh, are you. Well, you are some distance from his Irish office domain now, but I see that Wickham is involved too. Sound man, Wickham. So you want to land in Spain, do you?"

"Just to land a despatch to an agent, sir. I am not planning on stopping."

"Be sure you don't, and be especially sure you do not fall into the hands of the French. Their hospitality is worse than a Brighton guesthouse and the haircuts they offer are a mite too close for my liking, if you get my drift."

"I will be steering well clear of France, sir, and I speak Spanish. I just need someone to row me ashore for a couple of hours."

"Aye well, the French have got agents in Spain too. They have to as the Spanish could not organise an orgy in a brothel. But you are in luck as the very man to take you is in port at the moment."

He picked up a telescope from the drawer of his desk and walked across to the window that gave a view of the bay. "Yes, the *Speedy* is still there, although Christ knows what he is doing to her now."

He walked across to the fireplace and yanked on a bell pull and then sat back down. "Lord Cochrane is the man for you, sir. In any matter requiring cunning and skulduggery, the chap is a virtual pirate. The previous commander of the *Speedy* captured nothing in three years; on Cochrane's first mission he came home with a flotilla of ships he had taken from the enemy."

The door opened and a young man walked in.

"Ah, Taylor," said O'Hara. "Would you go down to the harbour, find the *Speedy* and give Captain Cochrane my compliments and tell him I would be obliged if he would wait for a passenger that I will send along presently."

To me he added, "I will need to give you some written orders for Cochrane to cover this assignment, as he seems to have antagonised his naval superiors despite their share of the prize money he earns for 'em."

The young man turned to go but O'Hara called him back. "Taylor, has that bloody woman left yet?"

Taylor smiled and replied, "Yes, sir. I told her that you had gone to inspect food stores in the harbour and that you would be away for the rest of the afternoon."

"Well done, Taylor, well done indeed. Peace and tranquillity reigns once more in Government House."

"If you don't mind me asking, sir, what does the Harris woman want with you?"

"She wants what all women want, young Thomas," O'Hara said as he reached for a quill and pen and started writing. "Don't fool yourself into thinking that is something that they get between the sheets – bigod no, that is just a tool to get what they really want, which is power and influence. Mrs Harris has set up some society rooms in town and wants my patronage to drink and game there so that the rest of local society follows. Well, I won't do it.

"Let me give you a word of advice, Flashman: never play cards and drink at the same time. I did, and in eighty-four got so much into debt I had to leave England and hide on the continent. Cornwallis lent me the money to clear my debts and return. He offered me a job in India too when he became governor general, but the heat here is bad enough in summer."

He finished writing and sprinkled fine sand over the letter to soak up the surplus ink from a pot on his desk. "Is your Spanish good?"

"Reasonably good, sir, yes. My mother was Spanish; she taught me."

"Excellent. My mother was Portuguese; we are both mongrels then. Now, take this to Cochrane and be sure to visit on your return to let me know how you succeeded."

Editor's note: The following chapters will seem to many readers as scarcely credible, or similar to incidents from novels featuring Hornblower or Jack Aubrey. However, all incidents, with the exception of the landing in Spain and Flashman's personal conduct, have been confirmed as historical fact. Cochrane was the real Hornblower or Aubrey, and it is clear that both CS Forester and Patrick O'Brian, plus many other authors over the years, have taken considerable inspiration from Cochrane's exploits. While the landing in Spain has no historical record, many of the tactics used in that action, such as the 'bug pit', were used by Cochrane when defending Fort Trinidad in the town of Rosas in 1808, so perhaps Cochrane tested them here.

The cart was still waiting outside and it took me down to the naval dockyard where I was directed to a berth that should have held the *Speedy*. But there had been a mistake: instead of a sharp-looking naval brig there was a decrepit-looking Danish coaster called the *Clomer*. Having learnt a little about ships from my time on the company ship, I knew this boat was far too small to be a sloop. In fact, she looked barely capable of a trip across the bay. I was just about to climb back on the cart when on deck strolled a tall, ginger-haired officer in what looked like a well-worn Navy uniform. He was checking some supplies against a list in his hand. As I stood hesitantly at the end of the gangplank, he looked up and asked absently, "Can I help you, sir?"

"Err, yes. I am looking for the sloop *Speedy*. Could you direct me?"

"Aye, step forward down that gangplank and you are aboard her, sir."

"But it says *Clomer*," I said, pointing at the name painted on the side of the ship.

The stranger stopped what he was doing and turned with a smile to give me his full attention. "Tell me, sir, does this boat look in any way like a Royal Navy sloop?"

I looked across the quay to where a couple of naval ships lay moored. Both had broad cream stripes along their sides interspersed by black gun ports and the white ensign flew from their mast heads. On the closest one I could see that the decks were holystoned white and the rigging was all squared away, so that all the yards were tidy, and hanging exactly perpendicular to the masts with sails evenly furled along their length. In contrast the *Clomer*'s sides looked like black slabs, with no stripe or marked gun ports. There were uneven folds of sails along the yards with one of them hanging at a distinct angle to the mast. It was also much smaller than a naval sloop, or even the smaller class of naval brig. If it was a Royal Navy craft, it was the smallest in the harbour. The armament seemed in scale with the ship: instead of big naval cannons, the only guns mounted behind the hidden gun ports I could see were little bigger than the big duck hunting gun that my father's gamekeeper mounted on his skiff to use on the lake at home. The only shipshape thing visible on the *Clomer* was the deck. As I looked down on it I could see it was clean and all the coiled ropes were stowed away tidily for quick use.

The stranger watched with some amusement as I looked carefully at his ship and the neighbouring naval vessels.

"In truth, sir," I replied, "it looks very little like a naval vessel. Just the decks look tidy; the rest looks quite neglected."

Bearing in mind that some naval officers had fought duels over insults to their ship, the stranger seemed quite delighted by my criticism.

"Excellent, sir, excellent, for that is quite the intention. Step aboard His Majesty's ship *Speedy*, currently disguised as a rotten old trading scow from Denmark." He bowed theatrically. "Cochrane, her gallant commander, at your service, sir."

"It is a pleasure to meet your lordship," I replied.

"Oh, please drop the 'lordship'; call me Thomas. I take it you are the gentlemen whom O'Hara sent me the note about; Flashman, wasn't it?"

"Yes… Thomas, I'm Thomas Flashman."

"Ah, too many Thomases; it will cause confusion. Call me Cochrane and I will call you Flashman. Is that your dunnage?" asked Cochrane spotting the canvas sack that held my possessions. "Excellent, glad you did not bring too much; as you can see, space here is somewhat limited. I take it this is your first time on a Navy ship?" Without waiting for an answer he continued: "Well, you have done better than me. When I joined my first ship as a midshipman I had a sea chest almost as big as me, which was too large to fit down the hatch. So the first lieutenant had it sawn in half!"

Cochrane laughed at the memory. He exuded energy and enthusiasm: already he was bounding towards a small hatch in the deck calling, "Follow me, sir, and I will show you to your quarters."

He led the way down to the smallest cabins I had yet seen. The deck was no more than five feet high between the beams and as low as four feet under the beams so that constant crouching was required. Someone of Cochrane's height was almost bent double. I was shown to a cabin made of canvas screens that was already dominated by one large cot suspended from the ceiling, but Cochrane assured me that there was room for another. I was to share with his younger brother, Archibald, or Archie, who was my age and one of the midshipmen.

Already I was feeling claustrophobic and I asked if we could go back on deck. Cochrane just laughed and said "The space does take some getting used to" as he led the way back to the sunlight.

"I need to get to Estepona," I said as we got back onto the upper deck. "Will the *Speedy* be able to get me there?"

"That is only thirty miles up the coast. Don't worry, Flashman, the *Clomer* is much more seaworthy than she looks."

"Why have you disguised your ship?" I asked.

"Ah well, you always have to look for ways of turning disadvantages into advantages," said Cochrane, leaning back against the rail. "When I first saw the *Speedy*, well, let's say I was just as unimpressed as you. She is the smallest Royal Navy warship I had ever seen with a pathetic armament of four-pounder guns. Do you know I can comfortably walk around this deck with the output of both broadsides in my pockets? We tried bigger guns and they damn near shook the boat apart. Despite her name, she was slow and ungainly too. In short, there were a lot of disadvantages."

Cochrane smiled wryly. "But if I did not think she looked like a warship then there was every chance that enemies would dismiss her too. That was an advantage. We increased her speed by replacing her main yard with one we sort of borrowed from a captured ship of the line in the dockyard, so that in light winds we can make good speed. We can spot a nice, fat coaster at dusk and be between it and shore by dawn, giving it nowhere to go. The cannons might be small, but the gun crews are good and accurate. Since May we have captured nearly twenty ships, which has given us a tidy sum in prize money."

"So why the disguise?" I asked again.

"Because now whenever an enemy ship sees the big mainsail of the *Speedy* it heads straight for the nearest port. Our reputation precedes us."

He caught the eye of a big, blond seaman who had just come up on deck and winked at him. "So now we look at the disadvantage of having a big, thick Danish bosun whom no one can understand and we turn it to an advantage by disguising ourselves as a Danish coaster."

"Vitch ve name efter my dog," added the blond seaman, smiling.

"Meet Eriksson, our bosun – and Danish master should the wrong people come visiting," said Cochrane.

Now, these days if someone suggested I put to sea in a boat that looked as though it would find the Serpentine lake in the park a challenge and bunk down in a glorified rabbit hutch, well, I would damn their eyes and storm back to the governor for something looking more substantial and reliable. But then I was just eighteen and still reeling from the recent changes in my life. In the last few months I had left school, left home, tried to fend for myself in London, been nearly killed and killed someone myself, and now I was effectively on the run. Looking back, I was probably desperately in need of some stability and a sense of belonging. It is the only explanation I can think of for why I spent the next two nights before we sailed sleeping on board that ridiculously small craft rather than decamping to more comfortable lodgings ashore. But by doing so I discovered that the strength of the *Speedy* lay not in its guns or speed, but in its amazing crew.

While there is lots of talk of jolly Jack Tars and Nelson's love for his sailors, in reality the Royal Navy back then was a brutal institution. The Navy was ruled by fear. Several ships and even fleets had mutinied in previous years, and one of the recent changes had been to station the marines' quarters on ships between those of sailors and officers to help protect the officers from their own crews. Life was easier on the company ships, as I had witnessed during my short passage to Gibraltar, with a calmer, more professional approach by skilled sailors who had joined for the pay and not due to the press gang.

But on the *Speedy* the atmosphere must have been unlike that on any other naval vessel. There was an easygoing respect between all officers and the crew, whom the officers knew by name. Despite being the commander's brother, Archie was shown no favouritism and spent time learning a wide variety of skills from the sailors. I remember on the second afternoon he was learning how to patch a sail and managed to sew a stitch through his breeches as well. His brother was all for roving the sail to the yard breeches and all, but William Parker, the only lieutenant, pointed out that we were already in disgrace with the port commander for the disguised appearance of the ship. Leaving the harbour with a pair of breeches flapping from the middle of our topsail would guarantee we were never given a decent berth again.

Two fifteen-man prize crews had already been despatched with prizes back to their home base of Port Mahon in Minorca. The seventy men left as crew might have been packed in more tightly than in an African slaver, but they were proud of their ship. Even on the company ship the crew were wary of talking to the passengers, but here, as I had little to do, they would often stop and talk. Invariably they described how they had outwitted enemies and the prizes they had captured. Often the stories centred on Cochrane's cunning and ingenuity, and they had a genuine affection for him. This was not least because, due to prize money, he was slowly making them rich, but they also recognised that he was sparing with their lives. Indeed, not one crewman had been killed due to enemy action since Cochrane had taken command. On the *Speedy* there was never a flogging, and rarely did the officers have to reprimand any of the crew.

The air of confident professionalism that prevailed on the ship started me to thinking about my own skills and abilities. On my first night with the officers crouched round the wardroom table I had explained the events that had brought me to Gibraltar. Barrett, the wardroom steward and chief gossip to the crew, had ensured that everybody knew that 'the young gennelman' had already despatched an enemy agent.

On the second day while on deck Guthrie, the surgeon, asked if I would be handy in a fight if, as was likely, the boarding of a prize featured in the forthcoming trip. I foolishly mentioned that I had taken some fencing lessons in London, which caused Cochrane to look up with a smile. Cochrane ordered up a weapons chest and I was invited to demonstrate the positions I had learned. There were no delicate foils in the chest similar to those that I had been used to, just stouter cutlass-type weapons, and by now several of the crew were drawing near, sensing that entertainment was in the offing.

Cochrane introduced my performance to those watching by shouting, "Now, lads, this is how a French fencing master teaches gentleman to fight."

I picked up a cutlass, which seemed devilishly heavy compared to a foil, and adopted the first pose, shouting "Position one!" and then moved on to two. By the time I had got to three there were howls of laughter from the crew, and so I deliberately exaggerated the flouncing about for the remaining moves so that they laughed with me rather than at me.

"Well," said Cochrane, still smiling, "I am sure that will come in useful somewhere. Eriksson, perhaps you could demonstrate some of your own fighting positions."

Eriksson and another crew member picked up cutlasses and pistols and faced each other. Eriksson shouted "Position one!" and rushed at his opponent, sweeping his sword away with a strong diagonal cut and, still pressing in, pretended to knee his opponent in the testicles. His opponent imitated a cry of pain and folding in agony whereupon Eriksson feigned to bring the sword hilt down on the back of his head. Position two involved pulling out the pistol and shooting the opponent just beyond the sword's reach, and position three comprised throwing the empty pistol at an opponent's face and then pretending to skewer the opponent when he instinctively deflected it. In short, nothing Monsieur Giscard would have approved of, but tactics much more likely to keep me alive in a pitched battle on a crowded deck.

Afterwards Cochrane sent Eriksson and me off to a quiet area behind some warehouses, where we could practise some moves without mockery from the crew. Eriksson swapped the horsepistol I still had as my only weapon with a brace of pistols from the weapons chest and we spent some time shooting bottles so that I could get used to firing the guns. He advised that around twelve feet was the maximum effective range in the heat of battle. Having used pistols numerous times since, that is something I can confirm. In fact, that afternoon with the giant Dane gave me skills that saved my life on numerous occasions to come.

If all the talk of pistols, cutlasses and boarding pikes (long-handled axes with sharp hooks on the back of the blade) was a bit alarming, I comforted myself with the fact that Cochrane was yet to lose a man in action. If I had known what was to come, I would have taken evening classes in weaponry with Eriksson every night!

Despite having a tiny, scruffy-looking ship and guns more designed for a duck hunt than a man o' war, both officers and men were extremely confident about their prospects for more prize money. I remember wondering at the time what they would be like with a proper ship. As it turned out, when given a frigate years later Cochrane was even more successful. On his first cruise his share alone in prize money was seventy-five thousand pounds and he

73

returned with five-foot-tall, solid-gold candlesticks lashed to all three masts from a captured treasure ship.

With all preparations for the *Speedy* complete and the harbour master anxious to get what he saw as an embarrassing spectacle away from his wharves, I treated the officers and Guthrie, the surgeon, to a final meal ashore on our last night in Gibraltar. I used some of the funds given to me by Wickham for expenses, which seemed only fair as the *Speedy* was helping me complete my mission. We went to one of the best taverns and after Cochrane took some gentle ribbing over the state of the *Speedy* from some of the other naval officers there, we settled down to some good food. It was mostly fish and shellfish as fresh meat was hard to get with Spain blockading the border, but there was some fine wine that had been smuggled in. As we got to the port and cigars Cochrane started talking about how he had joined the Navy.

"My uncle was a naval captain and he signed me up as a midshipman on the books of four different ships when I was a young boy. I did not serve on any of them at the time; it was just so that I would have seniority on the lists if I did enter the Navy. I was eighteen when I joined my uncle's ship as a midshipman, but officially I had already been in the Navy for ten years.

"Initially the first lieutenant hated me; he was the one who sawed my sea chest in half as it was too big. But he was a superb seaman and I leant pretty much all I know from him. My first few voyages were patrolling along the Norwegian coast and then protecting the fishing and whaling fleets near Nova Scotia. No fighting at all, but plenty of time to learn the craft of sailing a ship, and in some rough seas too. They were good times, though."

Cochrane suddenly smiled at an amusing memory. "On most ships there is a pet animal or two, and my uncle had a parrot on his ship. The bird had learned to imitate the call of the boatswain's whistle, and sometimes piped a call so correctly that it threw the ship into confusion. We even blamed the parrot for some of our own mistakes if we could get away with it, and as it was the captain's pet, little could be done. I remember one time when the mayor and his daughter from some Norwegian town paid a visit to the ship. The girl was being hauled aboard in a bosun's chair when the bird whistled the call for 'let go'. The poor girl ended up in the sea with the mayor and my uncle shouting at the crew to haul her back up before she drowned. How the lieutenant hated that bird."

~~~~~~

Chapter 9

We set sail on the third morning I was with the *Speedy*. It was a bright, sunny morning and winds from the north-east helped push the little ship on at a decent clip. The crew all seemed to know what they were doing, with little need for anyone to shout. Which was just as well as a few looked more than a bit delicate from the last night on shore, but others were happy and joking about the new prizes they would capture.

For a while I too found it bracing to feel the deck moving under my feet in response to the wind, but when we got out into the main straights of the channel the currents were stronger and the movement seemed more violent. As a result, after a while my old seasickness returned; this time it seemed worse than before. I began to wonder if the seafood we had enjoyed the previous night was as fresh as the tavern keeper had said, although everyone else was fine.

With the high probability of enemy spies in Gibraltar watching ship movements from the harbour, Cochrane steered an easterly course when in sight of land as though heading out towards the main Mediterranean fleet. In late afternoon, with the land a very distant smudge on the horizon, we put about and started hauling on a more northerly tack. With the prevailing winds Cochrane estimated it would take just two days to reach Estepona. He would arrange our arrival at night, and I would slip ashore in a boat, deliver my messages to the old priest and then be away again before anyone noticed that I was there. It seemed straightforward and I began to feel the overwhelming confidence of the rest of the crew – ah, the *naiveté* of youth!

To add to my good humour Cochrane rated me as a midshipman in the ship's crew, which meant that I would get a share of any prize money, which could be a tidy sum if this trip was as successful as their previous voyages. I was repeatedly assured that Spanish coasters and merchants put up very little resistance. Their crews were supposed to be demoralised and I would only be required to join boarding parties and look like a fearsome pirate. The absurd folly of this advice became only too obvious just the next day!

Overnight the wind weakened and a thick mist developed over the ocean, but as we were so recently from land we were sure of our position and pressed on northwards as fast as the wind allowed. As dawn broke the ship looked eerie, sailing in this white cloud, and even on such a tiny ship I struggled from the tiny poop deck to see either the bowsprit or the top of the mast. While we could see little on deck Cochrane sent a lookout with a telescope aloft where he thought the mist would be thinner.

Sure enough two hours later, as the mist started to thin as the weak heat of the winter sun eventually burned through it, the lookout reported seeing the tops of some masts to the east. God knows how they tell these things from a few sticks poking out of the top of a cloud, but he was sure it was not a naval ship and from the spacing he felt it was a large merchant. Wolfish smiles spread across the faces of the crew: a single merchant taken alone and by surprise in the fog would make an excellent start to the voyage. A course was set to intercept this new craft, but the mist was thinning all the time and would not hide us for long.

The thing people forget about sea battles is the time they take. You read about them and about how this fleet intercepted that fleet and imagine that it all happened fairly quickly. In reality things happen very slowly, leaving those with a nervous disposition plenty of time to get windy about the likely outcome – and with my heaving guts, I was literally windy already!

However, as the morning pressed on the gossamer threads of mist were stripped from our goal like a teasing harlot, and by noon she was revealed. That masthead lookout deserved a bonus in my book, for she was exactly as he had predicted: a nice, big, fat merchant. She was over twice our size but seemed lightly manned, and there were no painted gun ports along the side. The crew were delighted as she was worth a pretty penny to all of them – and to me, I remembered.

77

Cochrane was already working out the size of the prize crew she would require when the situation took a very unpleasant turn.

There are times in your life when everything could change on the tiniest chance, a split-second making the difference between life and death. One of those moments happened then as we drew close alongside the merchant, about a hundred yards off her. I swear to God that Cochrane had inhaled the breath to shout the order to start the attack when the enemy revealed a surprise of their own. Along her plain sides two rows of a dozen gun ports appeared and seconds later a lot of very large bronze muzzles were pointing in our direction.

I gaped in horror. Along our decks the gun crews were crouched behind the bulwarks ready to reveal our own relatively puny surprise, and still blissfully unaware of the guns facing them. A ship's boy was prepared with the flag halyards to run up the naval white ensign. If we had revealed either the flag or any of our hidden cannon first, we would have been blown instantly to matchwood.

I looked across at Cochrane, who instead of being worried just looked annoyed and muttered something about having "caught a Tartar". The crew watching Cochrane from the guns began to sense something had gone wrong and one started to put his head above the parapet to see.

"Keep your heads down, boys. That merchant has just revealed itself to be a powerful Spanish frigate," said Cochrane calmly.

I looked across and sure enough, the Spanish ensign had just broken at their mast, and now one of their forward cannons boomed to send a shot across our bows in the international signal to heave to and stop.

"It looks like we will have to use our Danish tricks sooner than I thought," said Cochrane, and then he turned to the small, scared-looking ship's boy crouching at the flag locker behind him.

"Don't worry, lad, we have plenty of tricks to play yet. Take off the ensign and run up the Danish flag, quick as you

78

can. And get that other flag I talked to you about ready to run up the mainmast when I give you the signal."

He turned to face the crew and, conscious that sound travels well over water, asked quietly, "Eriksson, where are you? Time for you to go on stage. Come on, up to the poop and give the orders to heave to."

A grinning Eriksson stomped happily up to the stern, seemingly unconcerned by the gaping muzzles pointing in his direction. Cochrane, in his shabby blue coat, gave a smart salute as he descended the deck, leaving the big Dane apparently in charge. He had only gone a couple of steps when Eriksson's big voice started to boom: "Stand by to..."

"In Danish, you bloody idiot," Cochrane hissed at him.

"Ja," said the Dane and then louder "Stavved at hiventil", or something like that.

The crew just stared, puzzled, at Eriksson until, in an exasperated voice, Cochrane hissed, "Oh for God's sake, forenoon watch only stand by to heave to – but do it slowly and slovenly – remember, we are not Navy. The rest of you, stay hidden. A coaster this size would not have a big crew."

You can imagine how I felt as I watched the situation unfold. My early confidence had disappeared up the gun muzzles facing us. The haphazard Danish disguise did not seem likely to fool a child from this distance. Already I could see the Spanish decks alive with men who were starting to lower a boat. The frigate had probably been sent specifically to look for the *Speedy*, which had been pillaging local shipping, but clearly they did not yet realise that they had found their prey. As soon as they were aboard they would swiftly discover that only one of us could speak Danish and then that we were the actual ship they were looking for. We could expect no mercy after that. Despite the fact that we were a naval ship, the Spanish viewed the crew of the *Speedy* as little more than pirates after its activities along their coast over the previous year.

Wickham's message looked destined to be undelivered, and I thought of O'Hare's warning about being captured and French hospitality and remembered that the Spanish also used some of their prisoners as galley slaves. In these winds we could not run from the Spanish, and in any case they would open fire the minute they saw signs that we were not standing to as requested. Even the rest of the crew seemed tense. Some were watching Cochrane hopefully, as though he was a magician about to pull a rabbit from a hat, but I could see no trick serving here. I imagined the horror my father would feel when he discovered that I had ended up a galley slave chained into a fetid Spanish warship patrolling the Mediterranean until it was sunk, no doubt with me still chained to it. But then I realised that my father never would discover what had happened to his son, as I doubted the Spanish offered a mail service to galley slaves.

As we came to a stop the rocking of the boat seemed more pronounced and I began to feel queasy again. I moved to the middle of the ship where the movement seemed less pronounced, muttering that I was going to be sick.

Cochrane looked up sharply at this; he had been crouching, watching the enemy ship with his telescope. "Don't you dare disgrace yourself in front of the enemy, Mr Flashman," he said sternly.

I nodded an acknowledgement, thinking that I was not capable of speaking and obeying his order simultaneously at that particular moment. I shut my eyes and swallowed back the rising bile and was only vaguely aware of Cochrane ordering Barrett, the steward, to bring a cup of salty porridge on deck and another seaman to bring one of the dirty lamps from the foc'sle.

By now a boat with around thirty heavily armed sailors and a young officer had put out towards us. I slumped down out of sight with the rest of the hidden crew behind the bulwark. I could hear the officer in the Spanish boat shouting at us and Cochrane prompted Eriksson to reply.

"Tell them we are the *Clomer* from Copenhagen. We have been to Algiers and are bound for Marseille. Do it in English but with your nice, strong Danish accent as though you are struggling with the language."

I heard more shouting from Eriksson as he passed this message on and then someone again calling from the approaching boat. They were speaking English back to the Dane, asking why he had changed course to approach their ship. It was a good question and no error, as the only ships likely to approach what looked like a nice, fat Spanish merchant ship were other Spanish ships or someone looking to take her. It was clear that the Spanish strongly suspected we were the latter.

Cochrane hissed to the ship's boy, "Now, lad, run up that other flag."

I opened my eyes to see what nationality we were going to claim now. For a moment I thought it was the red and gold of Spain, but then I saw that the flag was all yellow, which meant nothing to me. A sailor nearby saw my confusion and whispered, "That there's the Yellow Jack. They fly that when the crew is sick."

Cochrane was whispering to Eriksson again and a few seconds later I heard Eriksson shouting to the Spanish boat that was halfway between the two ships now.

"Ve haf plague om bord," he yelled, gesturing at the flag. "Ve sailed to you to see if you had a doktor or medicine to help. Three crew are dead and six are still sick. They got sick after Algiers."

This last detail was key as most people in the region had heard that plague had indeed broken out at Algiers. In Gibraltar and countless other ports there were measures in place to stop the contagion spreading. I could hear the officer in the boat shouting back to his ship in Spanish; he was passing on the message to his captain and asking what he should do. I could not hear the reply but after a few moments the officer in the boat shouted that they still intended to board.

"Get your crew to stand well back – if they come close, we shoot!" shouted the officer.

"Blast," said Cochrane. "I thought that would work."

Then I heard a shuffling and when I opened my eyes again he was crouched next to me. "Don't worry, Flashman,

81

we will soon be out of this fix. Just close your eyes for me, will you."

I was too ill to argue and so shut my eyes and a moment later I felt his hands touching my eyes and cheeks; he seemed to be smearing something greasy on them. Well, I have never worn makeup in my life and this really did not seem to be the time and place to start.

"What the devil are you doing?" I asked, struggling to get away from him.

"Just trying to make you feel better. Now drink this, and if you must be sick, please do it over the side, there's a good chap."

He passed me a cup of what looked like milk. Judging that I could not feel any worse, I took a deep draught of it. I had swallowed one mouthful when the saltiness hit me and then I felt the bits in my mouth and knew I was going to sick. I stood and twisted round and felt my stomach heave just as I got my head over the rail. I sent an arc of vomit several yards into the sea and was then dimly aware of the Spanish launch just a few yards further on. In the stern sheets stood a young officer in a smart blue coat generously adorned with lace. But it was his face that took my attention as it was fixed on me. In a single second his expression turned from one of haughty disdain to disgust and then horror. I was beyond any acting myself; my stomach continued to wretch as I hung on to the bulwark muttering "Oh God" repeatedly.

Only later did I understand the full spectacle provided to the Spanish officer. Having been ordered to board a ship that could be potentially infected with plague, he was understandably apprehensive. As he approached its side he saw a wild creature with sunken eyes and cheeks, courtesy of some lamp black marking from Cochrane, appear and void the entire contents of his stomach over the side.

After a few seconds frozen in shock, the officer noticed some of the former contents of my stomach drifting towards his launch and that seemed to tip him into action. Shouted orders followed and the launch turned about and headed back to the ship as fast as it could go with the officer shouting to his captain that it was plague for certain.

Cochrane got Eriksson to shout again, asking if they had a surgeon and medicine to keep up the pretence, but the only word I picked up from the officer's reply was 'loco', meaning mad.

One of the men started a cheer as the boat rowed away, but Cochrane cut that off quickly. "Quiet, lads. We do not want to ruin the effect now. Not after Mr Flashman has valiantly given his guts to see them off."

And with that he came up beside me, where I was still slumped over the side, retching, and patted me on the shoulder. "Well done, Flashman, well done indeed. You see, your illness was a disadvantage and we turned it into an advantage."

With that he went off, whistling to himself, and leaving me still feeling like death warmed up but with a strong urge to punch him on his supremely confident nose. It was a feeling that would occur many times again during my association with Cochrane.

~~~~~~

Chapter 10

We stayed wallowing stationary in the sea while the Spanish frigate sailed north-west in the direction of Minorca, where the *Speedy* was officially stationed. The crew were jubilant at the success of our deception, with Cochrane soaking up the praise at his cunning and 'Flashman's broadside' being hailed as a masterstroke. I was also congratulated as though I had been in on the plan all along, and grudgingly had to admit that it had been a good idea. In fact, having expelled what had been making me ill, I was also slowly feeling a lot better. One of the seaman fetched me a scrap of mirror so that I could see my face and I began to fully understand the look of horror on the Spanish officer's face, for my appearance would give children nightmares. A combination of Cochrane's ministrations and my wriggling about to avoid them had created a hideous mask of shrunken eyes and cheeks, while another mark, presumably incurred while I was trying to escape, looked like the shadow from a growth on my chin.

Ignoring the calls that I looked better as I was, I washed the muck off in a bucket of seawater and felt more refreshed. Remembering my conviction less than an hour ago that I would end my days chained to a Spanish galley, I too felt the need to go and congratulate Cochrane for getting us out of the fix. He received my words with a grin.

"Ah, don't worry yourself, Flashman, and I am sorry for using you like that. I needed you to take a good gulp to get the effect. If I had told you what was in the cup, you would have sipped and we could have been lost. But truly, I am sorry I had to act so. I thought that the Algiers story and quarantine flag would work, but they were a damned suspicious bunch on that boat."

"Do you think they were looking for the *Speedy*?" I asked.

"Oh, undoubtedly," he replied. "We have taken twenty prizes along this coast and they had disguised themselves exactly like something we would have found hard to resist. Well, we did try and take it, didn't we? I am just damn glad they revealed their surprise before we did. We have obviously been hurting them if they have gone to all the trouble of preparing a disguised frigate. Now we will set sail in a while as I want to reach Estepona at nightfall. Will that serve you, Flashman?"

Well, that brought me up sharp. For a while I had forgotten about the landing and had just been recovering from the scare that the frigate had given me. But now, just a few hours later, I was to be on the enemy shore. I remembered Wickham's words – "straight in and then straight out" and that I should only be ashore for a couple of hours – and tried to take some comfort from them. After this recent fright I really hoped he was right.

Both Cochrane and Parker shot the noon-day sun with their sextants to confirm our latitude so that we could be sure of coming in on the right spot. Having cruised the coast before, they were already roughly familiar with its outline, although it was hard to see as we approached with a blinding sun setting behind it. As darkness fell the leadsman started taking soundings, and after the sun had set there was still light in the sky to confirm that we would be coming on to the small bay just to the south of town.

I went and got changed into some clothes that I had bought in Gibraltar after Cochrane pointed out that my London clothes would stand out a mile in a Spanish village. I was soon wearing some patched old breeches, a rough shirt and a long coat with some sturdy boots. I also had a wide-brimmed hat which would leave my face in shadow to complete the outfit. I pushed both of my new pistols into my belt but behind my back, so that they were not visible when the coat was open. The farmer I was pretending to be would not normally be armed. I then pushed the letters into one of the pockets of the coat. By the time I came back on deck you could make out the white line of the surf where waves broke on the shore and the crew were lowering one of the boats.

We planned to make the landing just after midnight. Cochrane came up to me as I got ready to go. "I will wait here until an hour before dawn, which should give you plenty of time. If anything goes wrong then I will come back tomorrow night as well."

He gave me a rough map showing where I would land in relation to the town. The church was by far the tallest building and so should be easy to find. Sensing my nervousness, he added quietly, "You will be fine, Thomas. Just go in carefully and slowly, and if there is any sign of trouble, come back."

Archie led the eight-man boat crew that rowed me ashore. All of the oars were wrapped in rags to reduce the sound of splashing and the crew pulled strongly through the low waves to beach the boat on the shore. I was about to jump out but Archie got two of the seamen to carry me so that my boots would not get wet and covered in sand, which could arouse suspicion.

"I will walk with you to the ridge and hide in the dunes," he said. "I can watch the town from there."

We crouched down as we approached the ridge and I got my first look at Estepona. It was dark but the silhouette of the buildings was clearly visible and there, in the middle of the dark huddle of buildings, was one that was unmistakeably a church, with the tall bell tower next to the main building sticking up like a finger pointing at the sky.

Archie seemed excited by the moment too. He patted me on the back with a whispered "Good luck, Thomas" and I slithered forward over the dunes so that I did not create a silhouette on the skyline. This was it. This was what I had come all this way for, and with the crew of the *Speedy* risking their lives to put me ashore, I had to see it through. As I moved, crouching, down the slope between the bushes and plants growing on the sand, I tried to convince myself that there was nothing to worry about. Wickham was the expert in this sort of thing and he had predicted a simple in-and-out job. I could be back up these dunes within the hour if things went well. But somehow I could not convince myself. The hairs prickled on the back of my neck and a feeling of foreboding grew as I approached the town.

Behind the dunes there was a road along the coast and this led into a street that seemed to go to the centre of town. As I got to the end of the street the town was still silent, not even a dog barked. I pulled my hat down low over my brow to hide my face and tried to walk as quietly as possible. There was sand in the street which muffled the sound of my boots.

As I reached a crossroads I found a grotto to the Virgin made of stone with a niche in front where people had left offerings, and in between the stones were some scraps of paper where people had left prayers. On impulse, I reached into my pocket and took out the letters. There was a gap between the grotto and the wall behind and I slid the letters into the gap. If the priest was there, I could retrieve them or tell him where to find them. If something was wrong, they would not be found on me, which might just save me from being hanged as a spy.

One street further on and the road opened out into a square which I would have to cross to the reach the church. I paused on the corner. Two lights were visible in the buildings surrounding the square, but still the town seemed eerily quiet. It was at this precise moment that the moon came out from under a cloud; while not full, it provided enough light to see the open ground I would have to cross, and for people to see me. There were some abandoned market stalls and a horse trough and some trees in the centre to provide some shade.

Taking a deep breath, I set off across the square. As soon as I started moving I had a strong feeling I was being watched, but I was committed now and to dart around would just raise suspicion. I kept walking, glancing left and right, but could see no movement. Now I was at the church door and there was a great ring handle. I twisted it slowly to avoid it banging, but it made a screeching noise that in the silence sounded loud enough to wake the dead. I pushed the creaking door open and slipped inside.

The church was lit by around a dozen candles, some on a stand near the confessional but most centred around the altar where a grey-haired figure dressed in a priest's robes knelt in prayer. I shut the door behind me and felt a surge of relief. An old priest alone, just as expected. I felt foolish now for leaving the papers at the grotto.

I walked slowly down the aisle as the old priest got up and, with the aid of a stick, turned to walk towards me. Something was not quite right. To this day I am not sure what triggered my sense of alarm. Perhaps he had got up a bit too quickly to see me, faster than his subsequent limping would have indicated possible, or perhaps his limp just wasn't right. Whatever it was, relief was replaced with suspicion. I glanced about the church. There were lots of dark corners and recesses, but we seemed to be alone. With a growing sense of unease, slowly I continued to walk down the aisle.

"Can I help you, my child?" the priest asked in an old, quavering voice.

We were just yards apart now and the candles from the stand by the confessional lit his face more clearly. I noticed that the skin under his grey beard seemed to shine more than the rest of his face and then it hit me like a blow, I recognised him. The skin shone because it was glue and the beard was false. Beneath the grey hair and false beard was the same man I had seen twice in London, once with a sedan chair and the second time in the coffee house with Wickham. I stopped and must have gaped in recognition for the agent realised that the disguise had not worked and straightened up, looking disappointed.

"Welcome to Spain, Mr Flashman," he said. "I am glad you did not keep me waiting long. Your presence was reported to us in Gibraltar, and as we knew where you were going, we had lookouts along the coast. You have some papers, I believe, for a British agent? Perhaps you would be kind enough to hand them over."

My mind was racing. "How did you know I was coming here?"

The agent smiled triumphantly. "Mr Wickham is a very trusting man. He leaves papers where they can be read by, for example, his new Spanish agent. Do you remember Consuela Martinez? You met her in London with Wickham." I did indeed remember the cool, dangerous-looking Spanish lady and her coldly calculating look.

"Yes, Wickham sent her to tail me, but instead, as she really works for us, she told me that Wickham was trying to recruit you for a mission in Spain." He gave a small laugh and fingered the gold crucifix hanging around his neck.

As the facts sank in I saw now why I had been hunted in London, and in that same instant I understood that as the agent was telling me all of this he had no intention of letting me live so that I could reveal Consuela's real identity.

"So it was you who had that man looking for me at Vauxhall and later…" I could not bring myself to mention my apartment, a memory I had been trying hard to forget for weeks now.

He seemed supremely confident, as though he was still playing a part on the stage, and spoke loudly so that his voice carried to the corners of the church.

"Yes, you are a hard man to kill, Mr Flashman. We nearly had you at Vauxhall, and then again when José cut the throat of your woman. You surprised me then; I confess you did. I did not think you would get the better of such a practised killer. But I promised you then that you were a dead man, Mr Flashman, and I keep my promises."

I am not a brave man. Most of my killing has been done either in fear or, occasionally, rage. I had killed the man I now knew as José in fear when I had seen that terrible gash on Jasmine's throat, but now, as I heard him boast of the killing, I felt a cold fury build in me. I looked again around the church and could see no one else. The priest apparently had no weapons and stood now just two feet away. But it seemed he had such contempt of me that he felt he could mock me with impunity. If he was alone and I was able to kill him then that could be my only chance of escape.

Still I hesitated, and while I moved my right hand slowly inside the folds of my coat I asked, "So Jasmine was killed on your orders?"

"Of course. We did not want the slut around as a witness. Anyway, why should you care what happens to a common whore?"

Those words were the impetus I needed for action. As he finished the sentence my hand closed around the butt of one of the pistols in my belt and then two things happened which, even though I did them, took me by surprise.

The first was that I heard myself snarl, "Because I loved her." In that second I realised what I had repressed until then: that she had indeed been my first true love, which was why I had felt such emptiness when she had gone.

The second surprising thing was that, without any conscious thought, I had whipped the pistol from my belt, cocked it, pushed it against the agent's chest and pulled the trigger. As my hand flashed out of my coat the agent had managed to announce its arrival with a high-pitched shriek of "Pistol!", but had otherwise made no move to defend himself. The impact of the ball smashing though his ribcage knocked him back and then he fell slowly to the floor. He was not yet dead but gasping and wheezing as blood spread across his vestments and dribbled from his mouth. The sharp crack of the gun had been slightly muffled by his clothes and the flame from the discharge had set some of them smouldering.

For a second I stared in shock at what I had done and then for another moment I dared to hope that I could get away. That hope was dashed as the door to the church burst open and two soldiers and a young Army officer burst in. As they did so I turned to see if there was another way out, just in time to see two more soldiers rising from behind tombs within the church with muskets levelled at me. They had been there all along but for some strange reason had let me kill the agent. That strange reason was revealed a second later when the curtain of the confessional was pulled back and from the dark recess within an elegantly dressed Army

90

officer moved forward with a pistol levelled at me. I am not sure if anyone has ever been stupid enough to flick the testicles of a mating tiger, but I imagine that the resulting look of malevolent danger would be similar to that which I experienced from this officer, who had sat calmly in the confessional while I killed the agent.

He was about forty and my height, and as he moved slowly forward with the pistol held as steady as a rock he smiled at me with utterly no warmth at all. In fact, his eyes looked at me in a way that reminded me of a shark I had seen caught in Gibraltar: they were cold and pitiless.

"Good evening, Señor Flashman. I must firstly thank you for disposing of Hernando. His reliance on theatrical costumes was becoming an embarrassment."

With that he stepped forward to the still-breathing Hernando, who watched him while fluttering one hand feebly at this chest. A flicker of flame had started to build around the scorch mark on the dying man's vestments, and delicately this new arrival reached out with his boot to press out the flame. Evidently he continued to apply weight to the dying man's chest as, with a final gurgle and a whimper, the eyes of the man I now knew as Hernando rolled back up into his head and he lay still.

"He was too well connected at court to be disposed of easily without questions being asked. But now he has been murdered by a British agent whom we have apprehended."

The stranger smiled at me and then, to the young officer now standing behind me, he added, "Search him." They patted me down and quickly found the remaining pistol but also searched all my pockets as though looking for something else.

When nothing was found the older officer said, "No despatches, Señor Flashman. That is disappointing. Surely you did not come all this way just to pray at our fine church?"

I finally managed to get my voice back. "Who are you?"

"Ah, forgive me. I am Colonel Abrantes. I am what you would call a liaison officer between Spain and our French allies. There are those within Spain and outside it who are resistant to change, Señor Flashman. They seek comfort in the old ways of nobility and decadence. In France they are pressing ahead with modernisation and innovation. My job is to remove obstacles to building a greater Spain. I do hope you are not going to be an obstacle, Señor Flashman."

And with that he nodded to someone standing behind me and I felt a massive blow on the back of my head and the world went black.

I only know what happened next because of Archie. As he sat in the dunes he watched me disappear into the maze of houses. Then a strange thing happened: a light flashed from the top of the bell tower. Being the smart lad that he was, he realised that this was a signal sent while the buildings hid the tower from my view and that he was possibly not the only one watching my arrival in town. Slowly he backed down the side of the ridge and then he silently worked his way along it. Sure enough, a hundred yards further on he found a soldier lying in the dunes watching the town through a telescope, with a shuttered lantern at his side and a musket, which had slid down the dune to near his feet.

In a moment the soldier was walking back to the beach and the waiting boat crew at the point of his own musket. A swift interrogation followed, which confirmed that I had walked into a trap organised by a Colonel Abrantes, who seemed to strike more fear into the soldier than a sailor standing over him with a cudgel. The boat was despatched to tell Cochrane of the situation, while brave Archie decided to go into town to see what was happening to me. The signal lantern was left on the beach so Archie could call for the boat's return.

Archie got to a darkened doorway overlooking the square just in time to see the exit of our party. There were now two carts outside the church. From the light coming out of the open church doorway he saw two soldiers holding the arms and legs of a person dressed in white with a black stain on their front who was swung into one cart and was clearly a corpse. Then he saw me being dragged out unconscious, draped over the shoulders of two soldiers, and deposited none too gently in the other cart. The cart with the corpse headed off in one direction, but the rest of the group headed out of an exit on the other side of the square.

Archie followed at a distance, and presently they came to the closest thing to a fortress that Estepona had on the outskirts of town. It was a tall, round stone tower, built to hold a cannon to protect the harbour and now surrounded by a high stone wall which created a courtyard around the tower.

I knew nothing of this when I came to in a round, dark room. I was cold and wet and realised that I had been brought around by having a bucket of cold water thrown over me. Instinctively I tried to move to protect myself from the shock of the cold water, but I found that I was bound. I was strapped to what seemed to be a low stool with a high back. My hands were tied behind the back of the stool and there were other ropes binding me to it about my chest and throat.

The room was lit by guttering torches mounted in wall sockets, and looking around I could see three other people in the room. Slightly to the left, and smiling at me coldly with his shark-like eyes, was Abrantes. To the right was a huge cove in shirtsleeves; he was grinning at me and holding an empty bucket. Looking around I saw another figure to my far right, an elderly, white-bearded man leaning against the wall, wearing what seemed to be thick black gloves that he had resting over his chest.

"Señor Flashman," said Abrantes calmly, "I know you came ashore with letters for the priest over there." He nodded to the old man. "You are already a dead man for the murder of Hernandes, but your death can be quick or it can be slow. Possibly, if you co-operate fully, I will be able to speak to the court and they may show mercy and spare your life in sentencing."

I thought back to my fears of being a galley slave just yesterday and realised, ironically, that this fate was the best I could hope for today. I looked into the colonel's eyes and saw little chance of mercy being shown there. I knew instinctively that as soon as I told him what he wanted to know, it would be curtains for poor Flashy. There was no chance of me even getting to trial, as the last thing he would want was the circumstances of Hernandes's death coming out.

I started to rack my brains for ways of buying time, but it was hard to concentrate as Abrantes continued:

"But, Señor Flashman, if you do not co-operate then your death will be very slow and painful. We have countless ways of extracting the truth. The Inquisition have been perfecting the art for centuries."

My mind started to fill with images of people being burned at the stake, a rack I had once seen in a museum and other instruments used to disembowel and castrate victims, and as I thought of that, I instinctively brought my legs together.

Dear God, this was worse than a nightmare. It is easy to read about those stiff-upper-lip johnnies who spit in the eye of their torturers and dare them to do their worst. But let me tell you, when you are face to face with a pitiless bastard who has limitless access to torture then your mouth is too damn dry with fear to find any spit. I would like to tell you that I came out with some off-hand retort, but right then I was genuinely speechless.

It didn't matter, as Abrantes went on: "Tell me, Señor Flashman, have you ever seen a garrotte?" I managed to shake my head. I had no idea what he was talking about.

"That is unfortunate as you are sitting on one." I positively yelped and pulled against my bonds. I did not know what a garrotte was then, but I was pretty sure that if Abrantes was keen on it then it was going to be a lot less pleasant than a sponge bath.

"Hanging can be so quick, Señor Flashman. If the knot is in the right place and there is a sharp drop then death can be instantaneous. A garrotte can kill much more slowly and give the victim time to make his peace with God as he dies. It is a simple device: the rope loop around your neck is tightened by twisting a pole in it behind the post so that your throat is crushed. Or we can simply stop you breathing for a while. My friend here is an expert in inflicting pain – shall we give you a brief demonstration?"

"No, no, I am sure it works fine, there is no need to demon–"

That was as much as I could gabble while twisting in my bonds and trying to get my chin in the rope loop around my throat to stop it crushing my neck. But it was no good: the grinning oaf who had now been revealed as Abrantes's torturer moved surprisingly quickly behind me, and out of the corner of my eye I saw him move round a bar and the rope tightened around my throat.

I have heard that a brothel in Kensington offers partial strangulation to heighten the sexual experience while another tart flicks at your balls with a feather duster. Well, being garrotted did nothing to arouse me. Assuming, dear reader, that you are not a patron of that particular bordello and consequently have not been strangled, I will describe the sensation. As the rope tightened, my neck was pulled against the post, forcing my head to look down, and then slowly the rope started to crush my neck. The feeling of powerlessness panicked me the most. I thrashed around on the little stool, tried even to get up, but couldn't with my neck in that vice. My hands flailed around behind the post, trying to find some of the torturer, but he was too canny for that. My breathing became constricted, but never completely blocked, and I remember hearing the rasping sound of my breath in my head and the creaking noise of the rope and post as I strained against them.

I am not sure how long it went on for. I tried to reason with myself that Abrantes would not kill me until he had the information he needed. But maybe I had a delicate neck or maybe the torturer would get carried away; he did not look too sharp. By now the lack of oxygen was starting to take effect and I began to feel light-headed and my vision was starting to go. I was just on the point of blacking out when I heard more creaking and the pressure around my neck eased.

I was brought back fully into the land of the living by another dousing of seawater. I wondered how many buckets of the stuff they had as I sat there, scared and shivering with cold – or it could have been fear; there was no way to be sure.

As I was still staring at the floor the torturer grabbed my hair and pulled my head back so that I was looking at Abrantes.

"So, Señor Flashman, you were going to tell me the location of the letters that you were going to give to the priest," he said, looking at me disdainfully as I coughed and spluttered from the choking and the dousing.

Time, I thought, I had to buy time. And then it came to me. "I buried them in the sand on the way into town. I had to be sure the meeting was safe before I handed them over. If you take me back there, I think I can find the space again."

I had no idea how long I had been unconscious, but if it was still night then perhaps Archie and the boat crew would be waiting on the beach for me. Maybe they could overcome Abrantes and whatever guard he took. Maybe I could escape.

Abrantes dashed my suddenly rising sense of hope. "If that is true, I had a man watching you come into town. He can recover the packet. Perhaps you are no use to me after all, Señor Flashman. What is the name of the agent who was to get the information?"

I remembered Wickham saying the agent was the priest's brother, and instinctively I looked across at where the priest lay. He had looked up at this question and was staring at me. I could see now that the black gloves he had seemed to be wearing were in fact blood-soaked rags. He had clearly been tortured, but evidently had not given away his brother.

"I don't know," I replied. "My mission was just to give the documents to the priest."

"Really?" said Abrantes. "No back-up plan, no other names or contacts? If the priest was not there, you were going to just sail home again, were you?"

Well, there was no back-up plan, which just goes to show what amateurs we were at the spying game back then. While

96

I knew the agent was the priest's brother, I had no idea how to find him. I would probably have had to ask around town if the priest had not been there, or if the priest had recently died, hope his brother turned up for the funeral.

Abrantes clearly did not believe me. "Show him the priest's hands," he said to the torturer, and immediately the priest began to whimper and try to edge away. The torturer dragged the priest across the floor and then started pulling away the rags, which were crusted with blood to the wounds beneath. The priest screamed and wailed piteously and I looked away, but as the first hand was uncovered I glanced back at it, and wished I hadn't. The fingernails were all missing, as was the smallest finger, and most of the remaining finger bones had been broken so that the hand looked like some swollen claw. It was clearly agony for the priest if the hand was moved, as the torturer was doing now for my benefit, with resulting shrieks from the old man.

"Stop it! Stop it!" I shouted.

I looked at that horrible, ruined hand and then down at my own fingers and knew with absolute certainty that when the time came I would tell them everything they wanted to know. In fact, I would tell them anything at all to avoid that pain, whether true or not.

I looked at Abrantes and he smiled in triumph at me. He knew I would break, but could not resist twisting the screw a bit more. As the torturer dragged the priest back to the side of the room he said, "Do you know that the most powerful tool for an interrogator is anticipation. You see something you fear and then are left to worry about it. In a few hours you are begging to tell your secrets. The good news for you, Flashman, is that the instruments he uses need to be red hot to cauterise the wounds as they are made – we would not want you bleeding to death before you have told us everything. You look cold, Flashman. Let us give you some warmth." Then, to the torturer, he added, "Light the brazier and put the instruments in it."

On the other side of the room I saw a metal brazier standing on a stone platform with what looked like charcoal inside of it with some kindling underneath that the torturer now lit. Then, from the stone below it, he picked up what looked like a knife, some flat metal rods and some shears and started inserting them into the sides of the brazier. He looked across and grinned at me. I knew that whatever I said they were going to torture me.

"Now," said Abrantes, "it is late and I need some sleep. We will be back in an hour or two, Flashman."

With that Abrantes and the torturer strolled from the room, leaving me still tied to the infernal garrotte with the whimpering priest and a brazier slowly warming instruments that were destined to leave me screaming in agony.

~~~~~~

Chapter 11

I have no idea how long we were left in that cell, but it was one of the most desolate periods I have experienced. At one point the old priest called out to me, "Be strong, my son. God is with us. He will give you strength." Well, I felt precious little strength at that point, I can tell you.

I sat there shivering with cold and fear, watching that damned brazier get hotter. After a while I could sense the heat coming from it and see heat shimmer above it. While the shivering from the cold might have diminished, I still trembled with fear when I thought about those instruments getting hotter in those coals.

Eventually the door opened again and in walked the torturer. With an evil leer at me, he walked over to the brazier and, pulling a cloth from his pocket to wrap around the handle, he pulled out a knife. He spat on the blade and I heard his spit sizzle in the heat.

"It looks like it ees time to send for the colonel," he said as he inserted the blade back into the coals. "You will soon be talking, Engleeshman," he added as he turned to leave the room.

As he went to walk through the door he grunted. I looked up to see why he had hesitated, and for a second I did not see it. Eventually, as his knees began to sag, I saw the small metal triangle poking out of his back – the end of a blade that he was now sliding off from onto the floor. The hand holding the blade wrenched it out of the body and into the doorway stepped Cochrane.

That single moment is why I will forgive every one of his annoying traits a million times over. The relief washed over me like a physical force, and if I was not already tied to a chair, I would probably have fallen down.

"Hello, Flashman. You were taking a bit of a while so we thought we had better come and get you." Cochrane smiled as he strode in, followed by four well-armed sailors. One untied me while two others went and helped the priest slowly to his feet. The fourth searched the room and found a trap door in the floor.

"It is very good to see you. My reception here was just about to warm up." I gestured to the brazier and the corpse. "And this character was hoping to persuade me to lead the singing."

"Good God," said Cochrane, using his handkerchief to remove one of the instruments, "are these torture tools?"

"Well, if they are nail clippers then they are dammed rough ones. They have broken all the fingers and removed all the nails from the priest's hands – careful with him, lads."

I was now able to stand and just wanted to get out of that room. A dull grey dawn light was visible as I walked outside. In the small walled courtyard that surrounded the tower the bodies of two Spanish soldiers lay by the gate and four more were tied up as prisoners.

"You didn't capture or kill a Spanish colonel by any happy chance, did you?" I asked as I saw the bodies.

"No," said Cochrane, following me outside. "Archie followed you into town and saw your arrest and only counted half a dozen soldiers, but there are likely to be more. I brought thirty of the crew in case we had to cut you out. Hello, what's this?"

Through the gate we could see several townspeople led by a fat man wearing a sash heading towards the courtyard. Cochrane went to meet them and the fat man immediately burst into a babble of fast Spanish. Cochrane looked to me for translation.

"He is the mayor of the town," I explained, "and he is asking if we have found their priest and if he is still alive."

Cochrane led the mayor to where the old man now lay, propped against the outside wall of the tower, being tended to by Guthrie, the ship's surgeon. One of the other visitors went with the mayor, who immediately burst into tears when he saw the priest and the blood-soaked rags that were being peeled gently back from his hands.

"Will he be all right?" I asked Guthrie.

"Oh aye, I dare say he will. His fingers will be a bit crooked, but if he gets over the shock of the last few days, he should be fine, and he looks a strong old bird."

The other visitor introduced himself in English. "I am the local doctor. I will look after the father when you leave. It will probably be best to hide him out of town in case the soldiers come back." The doctor looked down his nose at the mayor now crouched next the priest and blubbing apologies at him. "The mayor is embarrassed because the townspeople have for days been insisting that he demand the release of our priest from the soldiers. But he was afraid to do so."

Having met Abrantes, my sympathies were with the mayor. Any such demands were likely to result in the mayor getting a red-hot manicure too. Remembering my mission, I asked, "Does the priest have any relatives in the area?"

For a second the doctor looked at me strangely, as though I was implying that the priest was corrupt with an unofficial wife and children hidden away. But then, deciding that the question was genuine, he replied, "He has a brother who lives in Cadiz. We sent a message to him as soon as the priest was arrested as he has some influence with the military. But he has not yet arrived."

I realised I would have to get the message to the priest here and now; I could see more townspeople coming to the tower, including two carrying a stretcher.

I crouched down next to the priest, Guthrie and the mayor, who now seemed to getting a grip of himself. "Could you give me a moment alone with the priest? He was a great comfort when we were prisoners together and I would like to thank him."

Guthrie, of course, knew about my mission and smiled. He stood up and ushered the other bystanders and the mayor a few yards off to give us some privacy.

"Your brother is on his way," I said quietly. "The papers for him are hidden in a gap between the wall and the grotto for the Virgin at a crossroads in town. Do you have someone you can trust who can recover them for you?"

101

"I did not realise that you knew the papers were for my brother." The priest spoke softly. "When you said to the soldier that you did not know, I thought you were telling the truth. Thank you for protecting my brother." Even at a time like this, when his hands must have been in agony, the priest exuded a calm dignity. He added, "Yes, I can recover them. I know the place you mean."

I felt a need to be honest with this man. We had shared that cell and I did not want to deceive him. "I do not think I could have protected your brother if they had tortured me."

"I know. I wonder now if I could have been so strong if it were not my own brother I was protecting. But God gives us strength when we seek His help. Perhaps He heard your prayers and sent rescue?" The old man smiled at the thought. "Thank your friends for me. I would give you a blessing, but as you are Protestant and my hands are broken it would be painful and futile. But I do wish you and your friends well... as long as you do not prey on innocent Spaniards."

"Good luck to you and your brother," I replied, getting up.

The men with the stretcher and the doctor came forward to start moving the priest out of the courtyard, but he insisted on walking out without the stretcher and personally thanking Cochrane for his rescue on the way.

Cochrane came over to me afterwards. "I don't like priests: too much corruption when you can buy forgiveness for your sins. But that one has got some courage, I'll say that. Is your mission here done? I would like to get on our way."

As I opened my mouth to reply a bugle sounded.

"Ah, that does not sound good," said Cochrane, bounding towards the north wall and climbing on some barrels to see over the top.

I ran after him and was just in time to see a squadron of around sixty Spanish cavalrymen emerge three hundred yards away from out of the scrub to our north and ride down to the area of firm sand and shingle near the sea. I looked to my right to get my bearings, as I had been unconscious when we arrived and had no idea where the tower was. The sea was breaking on a beach two hundred yards to our right and there on the beach was the cutter that had brought the crew of the *Speedy* to shore and a handful of local fishing boats. The cavalry stopped close to the waves and seemed to be waiting for something.

"They are daring us to make a run for the boat," said Cochrane. "It would be murder. They would be among us with those sabres long before we could get the thing launched."

"Where is the *Speedy*?" I asked.

"Oh, she is hiding safe in the next bay, hidden behind some cliffs." Cochrane had got his telescope out now and was studying the cavalry. "They are grandly dressed; I cannot see them getting off their horses to hack at the gate with their sabres. No, they won't attack us here, but then we cannot escape with them there either."

Someone else climbed up on the barrels with us and I looked around to see Archie smiling at me. "It is good to see you back among the conscious," he said. To Cochrane he added, "What now, dear brother?"

"Take a couple of men and thoroughly search this place. See what is in every barrel, what is on top of the tower and what is in that underground room. If we have to defend this place, I need to know what resources we can use."

"Tell me, Flashman, the officer out there with the cavalry in the different uniform to the rest, is he the chap who was threatening you?"

Cochrane passed across his telescope and with a slightly trembling hand I focused on the troop of horsemen. Sure enough, Abrantes was there at their head. My nerves were struggling to keep up. Half an hour or so ago I had been tied to a garrotte with only the prospect of pain and torture to look forward to. Then I was rescued and all seemed well, but barely a few minutes later I was back in the soup, trapped by the very same villain as before. I confirmed that it was indeed the colonel. For background I explained how he had allowed me to kill one of his accomplices because Abrantes had found him an embarrassment.

"Good God," cried Cochrane. "You killed him? I never knew we had such a cutthroat in our midst."

I had neglected to mention how I had been provoked into the act; there seemed little point explaining now. I preferred to be thought of as a dangerous member of the ship's company, fool that I was.

A minute or two later Archie was back to report that the top of the tower held an old cannon pointing out to sea but no cannonballs. The room below the cannon held two barrels of gunpowder of dubious quality. The room below that was the ground-floor room I had been held in, but below that there was a very deep cellar, twelve to eighteen feet deep, that was partly flooded at the bottom and empty. Apart from the tower there was a small, empty wooden stable and a cookhouse that was filthy but had enough food to make a meal for a dozen men, and a small barrel of olive oil plus three barrels of fresh water. There were also assorted empty wine barrels scattered around the yard, including the ones we were standing on.

Well, I thought, if you can turn this lot of disadvantages into an advantage, I would like to see it. Aloud, I asked, "What will we do – wait until dark and then try to slip away?"

"Possibly," mused Cochrane. "Although they will have their men closer around the boats then and they may have carbines as well as sabres. We would lose a lot that way. Maybe we would be better trying to get men out in groups through the town at night, while they think we are still here."

With the courtyard wall ten feet high, only those with a barrel to stand on could see over it. Cochrane ordered the barrels to be evenly spaced around the walls and then the stables were broken down to produce planks that were laid on top of the barrels to produce a fire step behind the wall. He also sent a group of men up to lever the cannon on the tower round to the north. Without cannon balls the best they could do was load it with the powder and a bucket of shingle to provide a stone version of grape shot if the enemy chose to attack.

The cavalry showed no inclination to attack, however, and once they saw a run for the boats was not imminent, most dismounted and a few were sent off with messages. The reason for their relaxed approach appeared just before noon when more uniforms appeared further up the beach. First to appear was a file of around two hundred infantry, and then a short while later more horses appeared, pulling a cannon.

Up until this moment I had taken confidence from Cochrane's calm demeanour. I imagined that, come darkness, we would find a way of getting away, as I was determined not to fall into Abrantes's clutches again. But now we were outnumbered six to one, and it did not look like the enemy were going to let us wait until dark. They were just going to blast a hole in the wall and come charging in.

Even Cochrane looked at bit worried at this latest development. The problem, he explained, was that we only had six muskets from the captured soldiers. The other weapons we had brought were pistols, cutlasses and boarding pikes, which were fine for action in the close confines of a ship, but not ideal for a land battle. Archie had already returned to me my old pistols, which he had found in a search of the tower, but I thought they were of little comfort against the numbers we faced.

Knowing that the tower could be a target of the gunners, Cochrane had the two barrels of gunpowder taken outside. Initially he was going to shield them behind the tower, but when he saw their size, smaller that the big wine barrels, he hit on a fresh plan. He got the men to put eight inches of gravel from the beach into the bottom of two wine barrels and then put the gunpowder barrels on top and pack more gravel around them so that they became large gravel bombs. A couple of the gunners had brought lengths of slow match and fuse with them on the mission, thinking that some kind of demolition might be required. Lengths of fuse were cut for three minutes and five minutes, and the plan was to push these over the wall when a breach had been made, just before the enemy advanced into it.

Cochrane was convinced that the Spanish troops were not as resolute in battle as the French, and that if we showed strong resistance, they would not press home the attack. I pointed out that their officers would probably be more afraid of Abrantes than us, and he would certainly make them attack as he had unfinished business.

The Spanish gunners, in any event, were lacklustre. Their first three shots ploughed up three mounds of sand and shingle about twenty feet from the walls. But they soon got their eye in or their gun barrels warmed up and started knocking down the top of the wall in front of the tower and then the side wall of the tower itself, which seemed fairly thin. In no time at all the wall in front of the tower was down to just six feet in height and there was a gaping mouth in the tower wall opposite the breach.

With just one gun and leisurely gunners, there was normally a two-minute pause between shots, and in one of those gaps I explored the damage with Cochrane and Archie. We were standing in the ground-floor room where I had been held. I was pleased to see that one cannon ball that had smashed through the tower wall had also smashed to smithereens the garrotte.

"How deep did you say the cellar was?" Cochrane asked Archie.

"Twelve to eighteen feet with about six inches of water at the bottom."

"Excellent," cried Cochrane. "Remember those bug traps we used to build as boys? Well, we'll just build a giant bug trap for the Spanish. Get some men to get these floorboards up between firing; keep them whole as we will need them for the ramp. And if yonder cannon does not do it for us, lower the bottom lip of the hole in the tower wall so that we have at least a thirty-degree drop from the breach."

I had absolutely no idea what Cochrane was talking about, but Archie understood and was delighted with the plan. "With the cannon, the bug trap and the mines, we will see them off yet." He rushed off to get some of the men to help build this trap about which I was still none the wiser.

As we left the tower another ball slammed into the wall. I was struggling to share their confidence that something the Cochrane lads built as boys to trap bugs was going to serve here.

Initially it looked like there would not be much time to build their trap, as after a few more balls the gunners seemed to decide that the job was done. The wall opposite the tower now had a breach in it that was eight feet wide and the ten-foot wall had been lowered to four or five feet with a rubble ramp on either side for their infantry to climb up.

The crew worked furiously to pull up the floorboards and then lower the side of the hole in the tower so that it was several feet below the height of the breach. Cochrane also had several men roll out the mines and leave them hidden from the enemy behind the huge mounds of sand and gravel thrown up the early artillery shots. With each barrel a crewmember was crouching with a piece of burning slow match, ready to light the fuse and run back to the tower.

When the tower floorboards had been removed they were taken to the cookhouse, where they were liberally coated with cooks' slush or grease that had built up there in prodigious quantities. The planks were then inserted in the gap between the breach and the tower. There they gradually built up a solid platform, starting just below the lip of the breach and sloping steeply into the hole in the tower.

Throughout this construction I was continually looking over the wall, expecting to see the ranks of infantry marching towards us. But it took them an age to get organised and I got satisfaction from seeing Abrantes railing at his officers to get the men into a column. Well over an hour after the artillery had finished, the infantry finally looked ready. The cavalry had also remounted and resumed their former position close to the shore in case any of our men decided to make a run for it to escape the infantry.

107

I looked back to the town and about a hundred townspeople were watching from windows and the ends of streets. Given that word must have spread of what Abrantes had done to their priest, it was hard to say which side they wanted to win.

Trumpets now sounded from the infantry and Cochrane responded by asking Archie to send up a signal rocket.

"What is that for?" I asked.

"That is for my last surprise." Cochrane grinned. "Light the mines, muskets to the ramparts and get ready to catch the mine lighters as they come through the breach. I don't want them to be the first visitors to the bug trap." He was all energy now.

I had been doubtful of the effectiveness of the bug trap, but when the two crew members who had lit the mines stepped over the breach, they immediately lost their footing and would have fallen if they had not deliberately come in at the edges where friendly hands helped them down. Cochrane now had the planks doused liberally with the olive oil we had found in the kitchen to make them more slippery yet.

The infantry eventually started forward at a reluctant, slow pace. They must have seen we had been busy; maybe they had heard it was Cochrane, who was well known on that coast. But surely they knew that some reception was planned for them. The officer rode his horse at the head of the column and Abrantes, still shouting for them to go faster, rode at their rear. They marched in neat lines until they were within fifty yards of the tower. Then the old cannon at its top fired.

The gun had been depressed as low as it would go, packed with a double charge of the suspect gunpowder and a bucket of gravel, and the effect was devastating. The cannon missed the front of the column, which it had been aiming for; instead, the stones scythed into the troops several rows back. There was a chorus of agonised screams and a spray of blood could be seen above the column where the stones had hit. The officer shouted at his men to advance before the gun could reload and those at the front surged forward while the rest tried to work their way around their wounded comrades. A desultory crackle of our six muskets rent the air and then the Spaniards roared as they charged up the breach to bring death and destruction to those inside.

The first soldiers pushed on by those behind them stood no chance and were off their feet in seconds and sliding towards the trap. Weapons such as boarding pikes, while of little use in a normal land battle, were ideal now at close range to keep the Spanish troops off balance and on the ramp to the tower. The Spaniards had little opportunity to bring their long muskets to bear, and invariably when they fell the swinging musket tangled in the legs of those behind. At least twenty Spanish troops must have fallen into the trap with another dozen dead or dying who had fallen or thrown themselves off the sides of the ramp. Cochrane had concentrated his forces there so that the sides of the ramp were lined with well-armed men.

The Spanish, seeing so many men enter the courtyard, assumed that it was close to being taken and they surged forward again. But the men at the head of the column had heard the screams of those before them and were now climbing the breach more cautiously with muskets raised while a crowd of troops built behind them. As the next wave of Spanish troops appeared warily in the breach, a fusillade of pistol shots met them, including one of my own. Only one of the Spaniards managed to get a shot off and a seaman on the opposite side of the ramp from me spun away, wounded. Virtually all of the remaining Spanish infantry were now milling about outside the breach, those at the front being pushed by their impatient comrades behind. It was at this moment that there was a mighty roar as the first mine went off.

One of the tower cannon gun crew told me later that the explosion carved a huge swath through the attacking troops. By the breach we heard the crack of blasted shingle on the wall outside and then a new chorus of screaming. A bloodied corpse was blown through the breach and slowly slid part way down the slippery planks, leaving a trail of bloody stones. It was then that the Spanish troops must have noticed the second mine lying in the sand and realised that it too must be about to blow. They started to run away from the mine and then they kept on going.

I heard the screams and shouts and leapt onto the makeshift firing step that allowed me to look over the wall. The Spanish troops were retreating from us, many having dropped their muskets on the way. The course of the battle could be seen from the carnage, with a cluster of around twenty dead and dying soldiers fifty yards off where the cannon had fired and at least another forty around where the first mine had been. Many of these had been pulverised beyond recognition, but I could make out the Spanish infantry officer as his body was still partly astride the mangled corpse of his horse. Seeing that prompted me to look to the cavalry, who were still standing where they had started the battle but were now all staring inland at the defeated infantry running away and the bodies that they had left behind. This meant that they were not looking at the wondrous sight that I now beheld, as round the headland came a dowdy-looking, small, black ship with its gun ports open and its cannon already run out.

For Parker and his gunners on the *Speedy*, the tightly packed group of horsemen was an obvious target. With only forty crew on the ship to sail and fire the guns, Parker had ordered all guns loaded and run out ready immediately after Cochrane left with the landing party. From past experience he knew that when Cochrane sent the signal flare he would want the *Speedy* there as fast as possible and ready for anything. There were just two men on each gun to adjust the aim and fire, with the rest concentrating on sailing the ship.

Parker adjusted the heading of the *Speedy* so that the guns could bear on the horsemen and a ragged broadside rang out. Four-pounder guns might be puny against a battleship, but they are devastating on horseflesh. Where they hit they often ploughed through several horses. I saw one trooper have his mount literally eviscerated under him with a cannon ball bursting out of the animal's chest and then slamming into another animal while the trooper remained astride his mount as it slumped to the ground. In just a few seconds around half of a squadron of cavalry was turned into mangled horseflesh while the rest turned and fled after the infantry.

I would have watched them go but Cochrane brought me back to my senses by shouting, "Flashman, get your head down! The second mine is still to go off."

I ducked back down to find the courtyard full of activity. The gun crew on the tower had already announced the *Speedy*'s arrival and the destruction of the cavalry to the rest of the landing party and now it was all bustle to get away. The cannon crew were shinning down the outside of the tower on a rope as the internal stairs ended in the bug trap. Other crew members were tearing away the barricade they had put up behind the gate.

The second mine went off with a dull thump and some screams from the wounded outside. As the gate was cleared the men streamed out. Most went down to the beach and the waiting longboat, but a few went to the Spanish dead, probably to loot the bodies. Cochrane called for them to take muskets and cartridge boxes and hurry. We had only one casualty, a seaman who had taken a ball to the shoulder, and he was being helped down to the boats by his mates. I looked back and the ground in front of the breach seemed covered with Spanish dead and some wounded who were crying out piteously.

The last to leave the courtyard were Cochrane and Archie, who strolled casually. I tried to hurry them along but Cochrane insisted that he had never run from an enemy and would not do so now. The remaining infantry and cavalry watched us from the edge of the dunes but showed no inclination to interfere. One lone horseman, however, did ride forward. I could guess who it was and how furious he must be. I fervently hoped our paths would not cross again, a hope that turned out to be as forlorn as the group that first rushed the tower.

~~~~~~

111

Chapter 12

Given my earlier problems with seasickness, I have never been more grateful to climb aboard a ship than when I hauled myself aboard the *Speedy* late in the afternoon following the defence of the tower. After everything I had been through, I knelt down and kissed the deck, much to the amusement of the others – but the horrors that had awaited me in that brazier were still fresh in the memory and my relief at being back on a British deck was palpable. Cochrane was keen to put to sea and the crew rushed to get the anchor up and us under sail again while talking excitedly about what they had seen and done.

As we got underway I stood on the quarterdeck with Archie, looking back at the beach. The soldiers and cavalry survivors had come back down to the beach to start to help the wounded and a steady stream were being helped into the town.

"Poor devils, I almost feel sorry for them. They didn't really stand a chance," said Archie.

"You would not say that if it was your fingers that they were going to cut off with a hot knife."

"Aye, I dare say you are right. Before we left I opened the tower door to look into the bug trap. They were lying several deep at the bottom, but one of them even managed to get a shot off at me with his musket."

"They probably thought that you had some fresh torment ready to inflict on them. Perhaps they thought you would pin them to cards like bugs!"

It was the disparity in casualties that stunned and indeed delighted me. Looking at the beach and thinking about the men in the tower, we had killed or severely wounded at least one hundred and possibly one hundred and fifty of the Spanish. In exchange we had one wounded seaman who had been able to walk from the beach and whom Guthrie was confident would suffer no permanent damage. This turned out to be typical of many of Cochrane's actions. In

September 1808, commanding the frigate *Imperieuse*, he kept the whole French coast of the Languedoc region in alarm with coastal raids, tied up two thousand French troops needed elsewhere and destroyed a French cavalry regiment in a similar action to Estepona, and the only injury suffered was one crew member slightly burnt when blowing up a gun battery.

As a result, the crew loved him. He was daring and audacious, but always had tricks up his sleeves to keep them as safe as possible, and he brought them a steady stream of prize money. In contrast to his prickly nature with his superior officers, to subordinates he was inspirational. He led by example, knew all the crew by name and showed a genuine interest in their wellbeing. I once saw him using his sextant and noticing that a ship's boy was watching what he was doing. Most officers would have sent him about his duties with a sharp reprimand or worse. But Cochrane could see the boy's interest, and as little else was happening at the time, he called him over and spent half an hour explaining the basics of navigation. Carter was the boy's name, and he was sharp and eager to learn. I met him years later and he was a naval lieutenant then.

For my part, word quickly spread that I had despatched another enemy agent and that I had been facing torture when I was rescued. I was looked upon with renewed respect. I was no longer viewed as a passenger, but as a proven member of the crew. Given that they had been under no obligation to rescue me, and indeed I had not been expecting it, I expressed my gratitude as widely as I could. Once we were safely out to sea Cochrane granted a double-rum ration on my behalf and I gave the wounded seaman a gold escudo coin from Wickham's funds.

We were now patrolling north-east to Port Mahon in Minorca, which was the *Speedy*'s home base and where some of her crew who had made up earlier prize crews waited to rejoin the ship. If the first part of the cruise had been a nightmare, the second part was a delight. The winds were fair and the days warm for the time of year.

While the ship carried the usual barrels of salt beef and pork and ship's biscuit, these were often putrid or rife with weevils and so stores were often liberated from captured coastal traders or bought from local fishing boats. When no other ships were in sight Cochrane even allowed fishing by a handful of the crew to supplement the communal pot. As the tiny galley on the ship struggled to do anything but boil things, Cochrane had a brick charcoal pit made between the masts, well away from the sails, and in a huge, shallow dish he had liberated from somewhere we would fry shrimps, pieces of fish and shellfish. The cook would often add rice to make a dish he had learnt in Spain, and with a stock made in the galley from fish heads and other bits we would soon have a filling and tasty dinner. Some of the happiest nights I can remember were sitting on the deck of the *Speedy* with virtually the whole crew, apart from a regularly changed helmsman and lookout, with a bowl of rice and fish while we chatted under the stars.

The numbers around the pot dwindled over the next two weeks as we took two prizes and sent them ahead with prize crews. In both cases the captures were anticlimaxes. We were sailing along the Spanish coast and at night would try to get close inshore to cut off the escape of any ships visible in the dawn. Twice we spotted ship sails silhouetted in the dawn sky to the east and set off in pursuit. Approaching from the still-darkened west, we gained several leagues before we were even seen and by then it was too late to escape. In both cases they struck their colours before we had even fired a shot across their bows. I joined the boarding party for one of them as interpreter and the captain of the coaster had heard all about the 'diablo Cochrane' and crossed himself every time the name was mentioned. After the second capture we had barely enough men to sail the *Speedy* and so we set a course directly to Port Mahon.

Mahon turned out to be a deep, sheltered anchorage that had been in British hands for nearly a hundred years bar a couple of interruptions, with brief ownership by the French before the revolution and more recently by the Spanish. The governor then was another Charles Stewart, no relation of my London acquaintance but instead an irascible soldier who had led the forces that recaptured the island two years previously.

Cochrane had offered to return me to Gibraltar on his next trip and so there seemed no need to disturb the general. I still needed to check that the Spanish agent had completed his mission, but could do that in Gibraltar. Indeed, I was not sure if I wanted to return to England directly, particularly when I discovered that I had earned a good few guineas as prize money in my honorary midshipman role. Once on the *Speedy*'s decks, I felt secure and with as strong a sense of belonging as I had experienced since school. If more prizes were to be had with the ease of the recent ones then it seemed sensible to stay with my new friends and build up my cash at the same time. Wickham had, after all, told me to take my time coming back.

While Cochrane wrote the report of his latest cruise for the Admiralty, I sent a report of recent events to Wickham care of the War Office. Naturally I gave it some embellishment in my favour. I described how I had tricked the Spanish agent into revealing that Consuela was a double agent working for the Spanish. I wrote that I had killed the Spanish agent after he tried to pull a knife on me, the same story I had given the crew of the *Speedy*, and described my capture against overwhelming odds. I gave Cochrane full credit for the defence of the tower and subsequent destruction of the enemy forces, but implied that we had jointly planned my rescue in advance in case of need. It made damned good reading, and I was confident that it would earn me credit back home. I also wrote to my father, explaining that I was still on my diplomatic mission, that my first objective had been achieved but that my mission might take some time to complete. In the meantime, I told him, I was with a very capable naval escort. I added that I was also being generously paid for my work and was accruing prize money as an acting midshipman, so he was not to worry. As it turned out he was not worrying, but he did start thinking

115

about how he could spend my prize money for me as he had access to my bank account while I was still under the age of twenty-one.

I sent my report via Admiral Keith's secretary, a man called Mansfield, who was based at the naval headquarters there. He may have been a clerk, but I quickly realised that Mansfield wielded considerable influence. As in all walks of life, there are capable men who manage those beneath them and less capable men who delegate much of their responsibility to their juniors. Admiral Keith was evidently one of the latter.

Cochrane had previously told me that his first command was not originally to have been the *Speedy* but instead a corvette of eighteen guns called the *Bonne Citoyenne*. Mansfield's brother, also a naval lieutenant, happened to arrive from Gibraltar at the same time and the able clerk engineered his brother getting the *Bonne Citoyenne*, so Cochrane was relegated to the *Speedy*. Naturally Cochrane had railed against this decision and written directly to the admiral, although whether the admiral had got the letter remains in doubt. In any event, Cochrane earned the enmity of the clerk, and as the admiral invariably followed every recommendation that the clerk gave, this meant that Cochrane and the *Speedy* were rarely shown any favour.

Mansfield was damned offhand with me too when I arrived in his office to send my report.

"What does a crewman of the *Speedy* have to do with the War Office?" he asked imperiously as he looked at the address.

"None of your damned business," I replied sharply. "I carry diplomatic papers signed by the prime minister and my instructions do not include keeping naval clerks informed."

He gave me an angry glare, but that is the only way to deal with imperious underlings: give them an inch and they will take a mile, as Admiral Keith discovered to his cost later.

I strolled out of the headquarters feeling well pleased with myself. It was pleasant to be back on friendly shores

116

again and it did not take long to explore the town. Having killed the man who had arranged Jasmine's death, I felt strangely released, as though a debt had been paid, and for the first time since I left London I felt a strong urge for female company. As in any sea port, there were some rough-looking females hanging around the harbour and a couple of equally tawdry ale houses where, doubtless, women could be had, but I was looking for a more quality establishment.

I found it at the end of the main street: Madam Rosa's House of Relaxation and Entertainment for Gentlemen was just what I was looking for. Comfortable surroundings, a reassuring obsession with cleanliness and some of the prettiest girls I had seen in a long time. I chose a pretty young thing from Naples who was most obliging and I was in fine fettle all afternoon.

The visit also confirmed my suspicion that if ever you want to know what is going on in a place then the local whorehouse is the place to go. Most men will try to impress the girl they are with by imparting some bit of news or gossip, and most girls are expert in extracting information if it does not come willingly. I once suggested to Canning that the War Office set up their own whorehouse in every major European city and establish a system to get the resulting information to London. We would have had the best intelligence network the world has ever seen. I even offered to help set it up. What a job that would be: clean sheets and endless girls instead of mud, muskets and cannon fire. He just looked at me, appalled, when I suggested it and said that it was immoral. No vision, some of our ministers... unless the French have already done it and he was already under their 'pudenda'. It would be just like the French too.

In any event, from my friendly little Neapolitan I discovered that all was not well in Port Mahon. For a start, Cochrane was not making himself popular with his fellow captains, firstly by moaning about the size of his command and then by being so successful with it. Other captains felt he was getting more than his fair share of prizes, but why they could not go and get their own with their bigger ships

117

was beyond me. The town was dependent on whichever navy held the island, and it seemed friend Mansfield, as well as trying to run the admiral, was trying to run the town. He was on bribes and kickbacks from nearly every business. Madam Rosa's was one of the few places able to hold out as it had so many senior naval officers as patrons. My dislike of the man grew, and so for devilment I hinted that I had overheard him talking to a ship's surgeon about cures for the pox. I was sure that little gem would find its way back to Madam Rosa. As her livelihood depended on the cleanliness of the girls, with a bit of luck it would see him banned from the only good whorehouse in town.

After a few weeks' refit in Port Mahon, the *Speedy* put to sea again in mid-March 1801. She had reverted to her more conventional naval appearance as word of the disguise would have spread along the Spanish coast by now and it would not fool anyone. It felt good to be at sea again, and this time I did not feel seasick. The boat was more crowded, with the full complement of crew, but I was now used to my hutch-like cabin and stooping while below decks.

As Cochrane, Archie, Parker, Guthrie and I squeezed into the main cabin on the first afternoon we all felt right at home. The skylight was open and the ceiling was so low that when Cochrane stood up his head and shoulders protruded onto the deck; indeed, this was how he shaved every morning. Lunch was boiled crabs bought on the quayside that morning, served with butter, and was delicious. All was well with the world and we were not unduly concerned when the lookout called that there was a sail astern. There had been several other warships in Port Mahon when we left and we assumed that it was one of them. Cochrane ordered the recognition flags to be flown and poked his head through the skylight to check on their response.

We all went on deck shortly afterwards, and through telescopes could see that the ship following us was a powerful frigate. At least the naval types among us could. All I could see was some masts and sails on the horizon. For all I knew it could be a frigate, a ship of the line or the Isle of

118

White packet. Cochrane warned that it had not given any response to our recognition signals. As a precaution, he ordered more sail in the freshening wind in the hope of outrunning the stranger or losing her at night.

Twice more that afternoon recognition signals were raised by the *Speedy* and ignored by the ship on the horizon. At deck level you could still just make out the masts and some sail, but I went aloft to the main mast top, which is a platform above the yardarm, with Cochrane and Archie to get a better view. Needless to say, to get to the top the Cochrane brothers swung out, hanging over the deck to climb the futtock shrouds, while yours truly was more than happy to take the easier route through the gap known as the lubber's hole.

A sailing ship at sea seems like a living thing. When you are below in the cabins at night there is a constant creaking and groaning from the timbers as they move through the waves, which, once you get used to it, is quite comforting. The noises develop into rhythms and regular sounds, and in my case I found that they very easily lulled you to sleep. But it was only when you climbed the mast that you got a sense of the power that drove the ship. There was a constant whine and whistle of the wind through the rigging and the ropes themselves often vibrated with the strains and pressure they were under.

I had been up to the mainmast top before; it was a large platform roughly a third of the way up the mast. I felt reasonably secure standing on it, holding a rope for support and staring back towards the sails in our wake. I could see little more than from deck level, and Archie and Cochrane persuaded me to go higher to the much smaller top above the main topsail. Cochrane went first and carried on right to the mast head while Archie guided me up. The ratlines or rope ladders were near vertical now, and the higher we got, the more pronounced became the movement of the ship as the bow surged up over the waves.

Eventually I reached the upper top where another sailor waited to help me climb up on it. At this height the relatively benign movement of the deck below pushing through the waves translated into a swing of around thirty degrees either side of horizontal. Various topmen scampered about the rigging with casual ease. They were greatly amused to see a terrified newcomer in their midst and one evil bastard called out, "'Ave you seen the view of the deck from there, sor?" Like a fool, I instinctively looked down and then shrank back in horror to gales of laughter from the topmen. The deck looked tiny from up there, and as the mast swung about in the waves there were moments when we were not over the deck at all but over the sea instead. Half-hugging the topmast like a long-lost friend, I stared aft and this time could make out the dark shape of a hull beneath the masts. Archie lent me his telescope, but holding it one handed, as I refused to let go of the mast, I only got fleeting glimpses of the enemy ship as it passed the lens.

Getting down from the upper top was even harder than going up, especially getting off the top itself, as I could not see where I was putting my feet, but eventually I was back on deck. The ship behind us, which Cochrane was now convinced was French, looked more distant. We had on as much sail as we could carry and we seemed to be maintaining the distance with the ship behind, but dinner in the crowded cabin that evening was a tenser affair than lunch. We were going as fast as we could, and while we did not change course, the hope was that the horizon would be clear in the morning.

Come dawn most of the crew were on deck, straining their eyes astern. Sure enough, as the light spread across the horizon, the sails were still there.

Cochrane was convinced that they would give up sooner or later if we could maintain the distance. If not, we would change course to a friendly port like Gibraltar. That plan came apart along with our main top gallant yard just after midday. There was a crack as it broke and the sail started flapping uselessly in the wind. The crew did what they called 'fishing' to repair it, which is binding a cord tightly around the break to hold it together and straight. While the repaired yard arm would take some sail then it would not take as much as it did before without risking more damage.

We were still moving on at a fair old clip, but over the hours it was clear that the chasing ship was gaining. As the sky started to darken for the second night, instead of just the top sails being visible from deck level, virtually the whole of the masts could be seen now and, with a telescope, glimpses of the hull.

Again, Cochrane was unconcerned, and he ordered an empty water barrel and some rocks from the ballast to be brought on deck. It was a moonless night, and as complete darkness was achieved an item was lowered over the side. Then all lights were extinguished over the ship and the course was changed by ninety degrees from south-west to the south-east.

There was a lot of cursing and banged heads that night. You don't realise how useful a lantern in a passageway is until it is not there. Even after having spent some weeks on the ship I found myself ducking too early for a beam and bringing my head up again exactly underneath it. Concussions aside, we did not get much sleep, and again, everyone was on deck just before dawn.

As the sun came up most of us would have given a week's pay to see what was happening on the French frigate at that particular moment. The French would have spotted the problem with our main topsail the previous afternoon and seen that they were now gaining on their prey. They would have ploughed on through the night and sensed that that they were getting closer still. They may even have had their bow-chaser cannon loaded and ready for a ranging shot at dawn. Imagine their confusion then when, as the sun crept over the eastern horizon, they discovered that the stern light from the *Speedy* that they had been tracking all night was in fact a lantern nailed to the top of a weighted barrel that was bobbing about in an otherwise empty sea.

~~~~~~

Chapter 13

On the *Speedy* we were jubilant that the horizon was clear.
The crew, and to a degree even I, began to look upon
Cochrane as some sort of magician who had a trick to get us
out of any scrape. It was a confidence that was soon to be
sorely tested. In the meantime Cochrane decided to continue
upon the south-easterly course, away from the coast of
Spain, our usual hunting ground, towards Malta. He
reasoned that with the disguised frigate we had encountered
before and now the one that had stalked us from Port Mahon,
the enemy were making a determined effort to track down a
ship that had been a prodigious thorn in their side. It would
make sense to cruise in a new area for a while and come
back when their guard was lowered. He also admitted that he
was curious to see Malta, and the rest of the crew were also
interested to see the island that had until very recently been
ruled for 500 years by the Knights of St John. Napoleon had
tricked his way into the harbour and captured the island in
1798, but just a few months ago the island had willingly
come under the protection of the British.

We had a good mooring in the harbour of the capital,
Valetta, and planned to stay there for a week while we
resupplied and made repairs. While other captains may have
had to worry about press-ganged sailors deserting the ship,
in the *Speedy* there were no such concerns. The crew were
making more prize money than they had ever known and so
shore leave was allowed for all. Cochrane, Archie and Parker
spent much of their time in the dockyard sorting out repairs
to our damaged rigging and I was left to my own devices.

In many ways it was not the ideal time to visit Malta as a
tourist as the island had undergone so much change in the
last two years. First it had been captured and looted by the
French of anything valuable and transportable. Say what you
like about the French, but nobody loots better than them. In
the Peninsular campaign I remember seeing a marching
column of French infantry cross a battlefield and loot

countless dead without even breaking their stride. When I looked at the corpses later I saw pockets cut open and hat linings ripped; there was not even a pinch of snuff left behind. Most of the Knights of St John had left and this devout island had seen churches plundered, priests exiled and papal jurisdiction abolished. The Maltese rose in rebellion and the French army retreated to Valetta where they were besieged with the city's civilian population for over a year. Evidence of that siege was still visible when we arrived. Many people looked painfully thin, and with the exception of fish, food was still in short supply.

One thing that was not scarce, though, was luxury accommodation. Many of the knights had left behind them large palaces and some were still being maintained by their staff as guest houses. I exchanged my half share in a cupboard on the *Speedy* for a huge palatial bedroom with a four-poster bed surrounded by ornate wall and ceiling frescoes. The canny housekeeper Signor Camperini had managed to hang on to most of the furnishings by letting rooms in the palace out to the French in the past. With the fellow guests I had use of a library, a games room and even a private chapel, although the priest had gone and the only cross left was made of wood. The palace had its own vegetable garden and had kept its cook, so we had good meals each day too.

For entertainment the usual seaman's pleasures were also in short supply. The Knights of St John were required to make a vow of celibacy, and as a result they did not marry, but invariably they and their retinues took mistresses with enthusiasm. These women circulated far more frequently than wives, and as a result the girls on the island were rife with the pox. Indeed, the French general defending Valetta during the siege had sent all the prostitutes out into the countryside as infection rates for his own forces were so high. Things must have been bad if a Frenchman sent the whores away. The other typical entertainment of sailors was gambling, often with cock fights or bull- and bear-baiting. But in Valetta during the siege they had eaten every bull, donkey, cat, dog and even the rats to stay alive, and so this entertainment was lacking too. I did hear that one tavern had a bout between a rat and a squirrel, which attracted a large crowd of gamblers. The squirrel won, if you are interested, which is surprising as I would have bet on the rat.

So you would think, in such benign surroundings, where even wine and ale were in short supply, it would be difficult for Cochrane to put himself in a position where his life faced more mortal danger than any other point in his career. You would probably be even more surprised to learn that it was me who saved him.

Being in the middle of the Mediterranean, Malta was also home to a huge range of different nationalities that had come to support the Knights of St John, for trade or as a refuge. These included North Africans, Spaniards, Neapolitans, Russians, Greeks, Venetians and freed Turkish slaves. Another group was French émigrés from the revolution who were proud as peacocks and had arrived just after the British occupation, doubtless hearing that palaces could be bought cheaply. One of these aristos had decided to hold a fancy dress ball in his new palace and he had invited the captains of all the naval ships in the harbour as guests.

Now while Cochrane may have the cunning of a fox in battle, in social situations, to be blunt, he has the wit of a weevil. Rejecting the idea of appearing like a wigged and powdered fop as most of the other guests were likely to do, he hit upon the less-than-cunning plan of going to the ball dressed as a common seaman. He doubtless raided the foc'sle for authentic kit, and when he arrived at the ball with everyone else in bewigged finery, not surprisingly, he was refused entry.

His upbringing as the son of a penniless Scottish noble meant that he was always sensitive to slights from other members of the aristocracy, and this situation brought out the worst in him. He waved his invitation and demanded entry, and when they told him that such costumes were not permitted, he loudly accused the French royalists of slandering British sailors and insisted he could come in any costume he chose. The French officer who acted as master of ceremonies came to the door and reached for Cochrane's collar in order to drag him out of the ante room. Cochrane responded with a powerful punch to the royalist's nose and a stream of obscenities, spoken in French so he could be sure the royalist understood the insults. An angry melee ensued with Cochrane felling more guests with his fists until some burly guards came and dragged him away.

When it was discovered that Cochrane was an officer and the son of an earl as well, the French officer demanded satisfaction for his swollen nose. Cochrane, still in a temper, agreed to a duel behind the castle ramparts at dawn the next morning.

The first I knew of this was later that evening. After hearing about my palatial accommodation, Archie had taken his own rooms in the same palace, and we were playing chess in the library when Parker burst in with the news. Archie was appalled, but I thought there must be a way out of it.

"Can't he apologise?" I asked.

"God, no!" cried Archie. "He has struck an officer. A verbal apology won't serve. The Frenchie can demand to take a cane to Thomas and he would never submit to that. Anyway, the challenge is accepted now, and if he tries to get out of it, he would be seen as a coward."

Duelling was, and as far as I know still is, governed by the Code Duello, a strict set of rules written in the last century governing how duels should be fought and in what form any apologies should be given. While duelling had been made illegal or was officially discouraged in the Navy and elsewhere, it was accepted that gentlemen would care more for their honour than the law on these occasions.

The situation became worse when Parker told us that this particular French officer had killed a Maltese gentleman in a duel just the previous month. The two of them were wringing their hands in despair and looking upon Cochrane as though he was already dead. I saw instantly that I would have to take charge, and as these two were so wrapped in honour, I would have to keep things to myself. For the Flashman family are no strangers to duels, and the rumours surrounding the death of my Uncle John showed that we are not all strict adherents to the Code Duello.

Parker was already designated as Cochrane's second in the duel; it was frowned upon to have a blood relative as your second and Parker was also the more senior officer to Archie. As the challenged party, Cochrane had the choice of weapons, and I told Parker that I would bring the pistols and be the loader. Parker must have sensed I was up to something for he warned, "Their second will be watching you load, Flashman, and will soon spot any tricks. If it is not a fair fight, it would be murder, and you could be hanged."

"Don't worry," I reassured him. "It will be a fair fight and their second can check all he wants."

The two of them left to comfort Cochrane in what they thought would be his final hours while I set to work.

Uncle John Flashman had been challenged to a duel while I was a boy for sleeping with another man's wife. Being a typical Flashman, he viewed codes of honour more as guidelines and had no intention of dying in the encounter. He appointed a timid man who could easily be intimidated as the loader and then set about making a hollow pistol ball. The pistol ball looked like any other, but when fired, the thin lead shell shattered and the scraps of lead caused little damage. Uncle John intended for his opponent to have the hollow ball while he had a solid one and was doubtless planning how he could console the man's widow.

The flaw in Uncle John's plan was that his loader was even more terrified of the deception being discovered and his being hanged for murder than he was of what my Uncle John could do to him. As a result, he panicked at the last minute and loaded two solid balls and John was killed. The foiled plan was hushed up within the family, but my father fired the hollow ball at a tree and confirmed that it would have worked.

Given that it was midnight when Parker and Archie left, I had around six hours to find a set of duelling pistols and make two hollow pistol balls to fit them in a strange city I did not know.

My first stroke of luck was Signor Camperini, whom I asked for help. There are many characters in history that have played small, seemingly insignificant parts, but without them the world would be a very different place. One of those is Camperini, who helped me save Cochrane's life that night. Without him, all of the subsequent achievements of Cochrane could have been lost. So if you are reading this in Chile, raise a glass to Signor Camperini for your subsequent liberation from the Spanish with Cochrane's help.

I had an urgent need for some duelling pistols and some thin sheets of lead, all in the small hours of the morning. The duelling pistols were surprisingly easy to acquire as there was an excellent set in the palace that Camperini was willing to loan for a guinea. When he found out who the protagonists were, he said I could have it for nothing if Cochrane killed the Frenchman, as the Maltese killed in the previous duel had been a friend of his. The pistols were beautiful, smooth bore with silver and gold inlay on black ebony wood. The barrels were finely engraved and the hammers were also of silver. They were packed in a velvet-lined walnut-wood box and had all the usual accoutrements such as powder flask, bullet moulds and cleaning tools. In the middle of the box, between the two recesses for the pistols, were two other recesses with lids that each contained four pistol balls.

The lead sheeting was harder to get, but Camperini sent a boy to a local blacksmith with one of my dwindling supply of gold coins to buy some. Despite it being one o'clock in the morning, the blacksmith was sufficiently intrigued to bring it himself, which turned out to be fortunate.

In case you are ever trapped into a duel and need to make some hollow pistol balls, I will explain how it is done. First you cut a lump of soft wax from the top of a candle and roll it into a ball. Try it in the bullet mould for size; there should be roughly a tenth of an inch gap between the wax and the mould. Next get your lead sheet and check it is no thicker than a tenth of an inch. This, it turns out, is rarely the case, and so if yours is double that thickness, it helps to have a burly Maltese blacksmith on hand who can beat yours thinner. Cut the lead into small circles and, using a wooden spoon handle, hammer the lead discs into both sides of the pistol ball mould. The mould is like a set of steel pliers with a ball-shaped mould instead of pincers. Put the wax ball in one side to ensure that the ball retains its shape and then squeeze the two sides together. This is a lot easier said than done, and again, a burly Maltese blacksmith is handy here.

By now we had decamped to the kitchen to avoid being seen by other guests and the blacksmith put the mould in the fire to soften the lead and make a smooth join; this also caused the wax to melt away. After a bit of touching up with molten lead and filing for a smooth finish, the first ball took us about an hour and a half. But we were getting the hang of it then and we made a further three balls in just two hours. The duelling pistol box then had four solid balls in the right recess and four of the hollow balls in the left one. Both Camperini and the blacksmith seemed to be under the impression that Cochrane would be getting a solid ball in his pistol and the Frenchman a hollow one. They chortled darkly in Maltese, presumably about the imminent death of the Frenchman who had killed their friend. I did not have the heart to tell them that as the Frenchman had the first choice of weapons, we would have to put a hollow ball in both.

It was around two hours before dawn when we finished and I decided to take the pistols to the *Speedy* and join Cochrane's party when they set off for the duel. Just as I was leaving, Camperini came rushing up with a small folding table.

"What is that?" I asked.

"You are the loader. You must have a table to do the loading on."

So, looking like some travelling salesman with a pistol case under one arm and a small folding table under the other, I set off for the ship. It was a sombre and silent place when I got there. The crew that were still aboard had heard about the

128

duel and, despite the hour, a number were on deck, waiting to wish Cochrane luck when he set off. I was going to go below but Parker stepped out of the shadows and explained that Cochrane wanted to be alone.

He looked at what I was carrying. "Are those the pistols?"

"Yes, a good set. I have borrowed them from the palace where I am staying, at no charge if Cochrane kills the Frenchman."

There was silence as Parker mulled over the alternative and then, to confirm this train of thought, he asked, "Are the barrels rifled?"

"No. I thought that would be best, especially if the Frenchie is a crack shot. What is his name, by the way?"

Parker thought for a moment and replied, "I am not sure. It sounded like the Comte de Pimpleface, but it surely cannot be that. Flashman, why in God's name do you have a small folding table under your arm?"

"The chap who runs the palace I am staying in assured me that loaders in duels must have a table to load on. I don't know; I have never done this before."

Conversation continued in this inane manner for some time. Archie and Guthrie, the surgeon, joined us and we discovered that none of us, including Cochrane, had been remotely involved in a duel before. As we chatted we kept glancing at the eastern sky at the increasing dawn glow that was appearing on the horizon.

As the light started to spread across the sky we heard the hatch get thrown back and Cochrane appeared on deck. He hesitated when he saw us and then came over. His face seemed pale and strained and, looking at Parker, he said, "There are some letters in my cabin if... if anything happens." Then, looking at the rest of us, he forced a smile and said, "Come on then, let's get on with it." With that he strode to the gangplank to lead the way with several of the crew shouting good luck to him as he went across.

We made a strange group as we set off through the town to the ground behind the castle ramparts. Cochrane, tall and thin, striding alone at our head, Parker, Guthrie and Archie just behind, whispering to each other, and Flashy, the salesman, bringing up the rear with his folding table and case of samples.

When we arrived we found the French party already there. The comte strode off to one end of the field when he saw us so that he would not have to be close to Cochrane. I did not understand French rank markings, but from the braid on his uniform he seemed to be a middle-ranking officer. He was aged in his mid-thirties and had a haughty, proud bearing. His second approached us and introduced himself as Lieutenant Gaston, and another, more senior officer stepped forward; he was acting as master of ceremonies. He formally asked both seconds if their dualists were determined to continue and received affirmative answers. Cochrane then set off to the opposite end of the field with Archie for company, leaving Parker, as Cochrane's second, and the French Lieutenant Gaston to oversee the loading of the pistols by yours truly. Guthrie also loitered nearby.

"Ah, I see you 'ave brought a leetle table – 'ow quaint."

You take an instant dislike to some people and Gaston was one of those for me. He smirked as I set the table up in the middle of the field between the two protagonists. I thought that even if a table is not the normal thing, having brought it, I might as well use it. I put the pistol case on the table and opened the lid. Immediately Gaston stepped forward and picked up one of the pistols. He checked the flint and the hammer action and then he looked down the barrel.

"Ah, I see. It ees not rifled. We 'ave rifled pistols we could use."

"No, thank you, these are the pistols we will be using," said I, frostily.

"I theenk you 'ope the major will miss with these smooth-bore guns, yes? Well, I will watch the loading like... 'ow you say... watch you like a falcon."

Well, that was all I needed. I was already feeling nervous about what rested on me in the next few minutes. I had been hoping that the seconds would just chat among themselves and leave me to get on with it. But I had only picked up the powder flask before the Frenchman was on me again.

"I want to inspect the powder." He reached forward and I gave him the flask. He poured some powder onto his hand, rubbed it between his fingers, smelt it and then daintily put out his tongue to taste it. Then he wrinkled his nose up and spat it out in disgust.

"Thees powder is old. It is degraded. It ees no good. You theenk with this old powder and old smooth-bore pistols that you save your kapitan? *Non*, I inseest that we use our powder... and I theenk our powder measure too."

In truth I had not even looked at the powder until now, just shaken the flask to check that there was more than enough to load the two pistols. Both of the seconds were now looking at me reproachfully as though they had caught me out in trying some trick. Parker even murmured to me, "I warned you, Flashman."

Well, if they thought they had caught me on one trick then maybe they would not look so hard for a second. So I tried to look a little crestfallen and grudgingly conceded that we could use their powder. A silver flask and a powder measure were brought over. The French powder was very finely ground and black and even I could see that it was of vastly superior quality. I carefully poured out full measures and tipped them down both barrels. I could guess what was going to happen next and so I deliberately opened the right hand recess containing the solid balls. On cue the frog leaned forward.

"I would like to check the balls."

He reached down and took one from the recess, felt the weight of it in his hand and then held it against the end of one of the muzzles to check the tightness of the fit. For a horrible moment I thought he would drop it down the barrel and I would have to think of an excuse to get it back, but to my relief he gave it back to me. Now I needed a distraction so that I could switch the opened recess to the one containing

131

the hollow balls. I looked up at Guthrie in mute appeal and, bless him, he came through.

"Have ye got your own surgeon here?" he asked in his gruff voice and Gaston looked across and pointed out a gentleman huddled in a cloak a few yards away with some other French bystanders.

It was all the time I needed to swap the two lids so that now the hollow balls were exposed. I reached down and picked one up, but to my alarm I felt the lead shell give way against my fingertip; with Gaston now watching me again, he would be bound to notice a gaping hole in the ball as it went into the pistol. Thinking fast, I pretended to fumble the ball and it dropped into the grass at my feet, out of view. I reached forward and, even more gently, took a second ball and dropped it into the muzzle of the first pistol. Using the ramrod, I ensured that the ball was gently resting on the powder but, clenching my jaw and giving a little grunt of exertion, I gave the impression that I was ramming it down hard. I then did the same with some wadding to stop the ball rolling out. Despite my apparent exertions, as far as I could tell the delicate hollow ball was still intact at the bottom of the barrel. I then did the same for the second pistol and, having put a pinch of powder into the frizzen of each gun to catch the spark from the flint and carry it to the powder charge, they were ready to fire. I held the barrels of both guns so that the butts were pointing to Lieutenant Gaston for him to make his choice.

Both seconds took pistols and carried them to their respective duellists, who were now walking to the centre of the field to meet with the master of ceremonies. As the non-combatants gathered together in the centre of the field to watch, the master explained that, starting back to back, each duellist would take ten paces and then turn. They could fire when the master dropped his handkerchief. The master took several paces back, out of the firing line, pulling a big white handkerchief out of his pocket. He gave the order to start pacing and both men, with tense, pale faces, set off. It all happened so quickly: in a few seconds the allotted distance was reached. They turned side on to their opponent and raised their weapons. The handkerchief dropped.

They fired instantly, and despite the large puffs of smoke emitted from each barrel, it was immediately apparent that both men had been hit. I watched in horror as Cochrane staggered back and fell, clutching his chest, while the Frenchman had a leg buckle underneath him and also fell to the ground. How could this have happened after all my hard work?

Both sets of supporters ran to their respective duellist. Cochrane was tearing at his clothes to see his chest, but by the time we reached him he was laughing in relief.

"Damnest thing. I felt the ball hit me in the chest, but the ball does not seem to have got through my clothes."

"Oh, thank God!" cried Archie, and he threw himself at his brother, hugging him tightly. Guthrie and Parker both looked at me, but Cochrane, pushing Archie away, was looking at the Frenchman, who now had his surgeon leaning over him.

"I must see to the count," said Cochrane, pulling himself to his feet and starting towards the prostrate figure. When we reached him the count was wincing in pain as the surgeon probed a wound on his thigh.

"How are you wounded, sir?" asked Cochrane, looking concerned.

"It is just a flesh wound," responded the surgeon. "The ball seems to have broken up as there is just a piece of it in his leg."

"God be praised!" cried Cochrane, now full of energy and life. "Now that honour is served, sir, I would apologise for striking you. I should have anticipated that my costume could cause confusion." So having just risked his life to avoid giving an apology, Cochrane now freely gave one, although now at least his opponent could not demand he be whipped under the Code Duello.

The wounded Frenchman, however, ignored the apology and asked, "'Ow are you milord? You clutched your chest?"

"Oh, I am fine," breezed Cochrane, "the ball was stopped by my clothes."

The Frenchman's eyes narrowed in suspicion. "What trickery ees this? One ball breaks up and another ees stopped just by clothes. This ees not right."

Everyone stopped talking. Glancing around, I became uncomfortably aware that in this ugly moment, everyone was looking at me. Well, attack is the best form of defence and I knew just whom my target would be.

"I agree," I said loudly so all could hear. "There must have been trickery. Your man checked the balls were sound but he insisted on using his own powder in the guns. I checked our powder last night," I lied. "It blew a hole in a barn door at twenty paces. His powder," I pointed at the astonished Gaston, "does not seem capable of blowing a hole in a waistcoat at the same distance."

"But... but..." gasped Gaston, searching for the right words in English.

I did not give him the chance to say more, but reached down to pick up the count's pistol. Waving it at Gaston, I added, "Perhaps it was you who wanted to protect his officer. Perhaps you thought that mixing soot and ash with the powder would weaken the charge and make both appear to miss. We both checked the balls, but only you checked the powder."

With that, I strode away with dignity, well, at least until I had to pick up my little table and pistol case and resume my salesman appearance. As I left them I heard the wounded Frenchman ask Gaston what he had done. Gaston was insisting that the powder was good and offering to burn some there, but it was too late. The English party was now making its way triumphantly from the field, some with their suspicions of French duplicity confirmed. Cochrane and Archie went on ahead, talking loudly together about the astonishing turn of events, but Guthrie and Parker fell in alongside me.

For a moment no one spoke and then Parker hesitantly asked, "Flashman, those pistol balls. I saw you show him one set, but I noticed you loaded from another set. Was the powder really bad?"

I grinned. "Bearing in mind your obligations as a second under the code and your honour as a gentleman, are you really sure you want me to answer that question?"

"No." Parker smiled. "On reflection, I think ignorance would be best. Here, let me help you carry your little table."

Editor's Note: The duel really did happen as described and both Cochrane and historians have been puzzled at the lack of serious injury when both participants were shot by their opponent. Flashman's account solves this mystery. I have not been able to find other accounts of such hollow balls being used in duels, but if there were flaws or bubbles in the lead when the ball was cast it could break up on firing and so detection of this sharp practice would be difficult.

~~~~~~

Chapter 14

We set sail from Malta a few days after the duel incident and I for one was pleased to see the island fall astern. I had been harbouring the fear that the much maligned Lieutenant Gaston would be seeking satisfaction from me over the claims I had made about his gunpowder, but all parties seemed keen to forget about the incident. Cochrane thanked me for my help at the duel, and if he had any inkling of what I had really done, he showed no sign of it.

The weather was warmer now. It was late April 1801 and life was good. We captured a small ship off the coast of North Africa with a cargo of exceptionally good wine. We met local fisherman and bought fresh fish. One of the crew even managed to catch a huge tuna fish, which was big enough to feed the entire crew for one night. We often spent our evenings sitting under the stars around the cooking pot, sharing tales and our thoughts of the future.

For the other officers, their futures were set at the mercy of the lords of the Admiralty. If they were lucky and diligent then they should progress up the ladder. Cochrane was all too aware though, that he did not have many friends in the Admiralty. He had been court-martialled less than two years ago for insubordination to a pompous first lieutenant in an admiral's flagship. The court had cleared him, but the Admiral had admonished his behaviour and sent a report to the Admiralty and to the First Sea Lord, Lord St Vincent, who was a stickler for discipline. He had captured more ships in the Mediterranean than anyone else over the last twelve months, but they had been mostly small ships that had given up without a fight. He had no patron to promote his achievements among senior officers. I remember one night he said wistfully that he would have to do something really spectacular so that they could not ignore him. I really should have paid more attention to that comment, for if I had known the sort of thing he had in mind, I would have abandoned ship at the first opportunity!

For my part, I knew that my time with the *Speedy* must soon come to an end, but while I was enjoying myself with some of the truest friends I had ever known, it was hard to tear myself away. The fact that I was not eating into my savings but earning money from our prizes and my honorary midshipman's pay was a bonus. Archie tried to persuade me to sign up to become an official midshipman like him and join the Navy properly, but I knew enough about the service to know that the life could be brutal in other ships and with other captains.

We headed back to our old hunting ground off the Spanish coast and were soon doing what we did best, taking prizes. When we did come across an enemy ship, all Spanish, the sight of the *Speedy* and its legendary devil captain Cochrane was enough to ensure a rapid surrender, with the only shooting being the shot across the bows. Three ships were taken in that manner, with prize crews put about to take them back to Port Mahon. The crew of the *Speedy* had thus depleted to fifty-four, just over half of the original complement of ninety men. One more prize, declared Cochrane, and we would head back to base to count our prize gold.

The morning of the sixth of May 1801 dawned like many others we had experienced on that Spanish coast. We were then off Barcelona and the previous day we had given chase to a couple of small Spanish gunboats that had put into the city's port. We had stayed in the vicinity, hoping to find a prize when the usual early morning mist cleared.

We were all on deck that morning. It was chilly without the sun and I remember being wrapped up in a big boat cloak to keep out the cold. We had learned from long experience that with our size and speed this was our best chance of the day of getting close to a prize. Sound travelled far in the mist and so everyone knew to be as quiet as possible. On the hour we did not sound the normal ship's bells but instead strained our ears for the sound of someone else's.

Cochrane paced the deck in his normal energetic manner. "There is something out there, I can just sense it," he whispered. "One more decent prize and then we head for home."

A seaman came padding quietly from the front of the ship and whispered to Cochrane, "Jarvis in the bows, sir, thinks he heard bells to the west."

In the opposite direction from the coast. This would have to be a ship. Demonstrating the exceptional degree of trust between officers and men on the *Speedy*, without a moment's hesitation Cochrane ordered the course changed to be more westerly. He turned to Archie. "Go up the mainmast, Arch, and tell the lookout to be extra vigilant for any mast tops that might appear over the top of the mist to the west."

The tension began to build in the boat now, and when the trailing edge of my boat cloak pulled over an empty bucket with a clatter, I got glares from crewman and officers alike.

When the summer sun burns off sea mist on that coast, it does so quickly. For hours from dawn you shiver in a thick, damp mist and then the heat of the sun must build up to a critical point where it burns the mist off in just a few short minutes. That is what happened on that morning.

First Archie came speeding down the rigging to report that there were three mast heads to the west. He was not certain but he thought they looked more like a warship's than a merchant's. As he was reporting this news we began to notice that the sun was burning down through the mist, which was splitting into tendrils. Whatever the ship was, it would soon be revealed, and if it was a warship we would be revealed to it.

"Three masts," whispered Parker to Cochrane. "That is going to be a sizeable ship. Should we beat to quarters?"

"Yes, but do it quietly and don't run the guns out yet."

Many of the crew were within earshot when the order was given and immediately the deck sprang into action. While there was no drumming or shouting, the noise that broke out compared to the previous silence was tremendous. Down below on the gun deck there was a loud clatter as partitions were broken down and the decks cleared. The

138

wheels on the gun trucks squealed as they were unlashed and pulled back from their gun port to load, ready for running out. The powder boys were running frantically to and fro from the magazine with powder charges, and other gun crew were gathering shot, wadding and priming boxes. The gun ports had to be opened briefly to make room to use the rammer to push the charges home down the barrel, but were then closed again.

As I stood, redundant, on the deck with nothing to do but keep out of the way, I had a bad feeling about what that ship could be. Since I had been on the *Speedy* the Spanish had sent two frigates looking for us; could this be another? The gun boats we had seen the day before had also acted strangely. They had not been escorting anything, and instead of disappearing at the first sight of us, they had waited until we started to chase them and then stayed just out of range all the way to Barcelona. It was as though they were acting like decoys to get us here. Now here we were, exactly as they seemed to want, with a mystery ship bearing down on us. It is easy to be clever in hindsight, but long before we saw it I was sure that the mystery ship would not turn out to be a fat, full, toothless merchant ship. What I could not have predicted in a million years was the insane events that would follow.

Cochrane, with his telescope to his eye, was straining to get the first glimpse of the owner of the three masts, but a hole appeared in the mist, revealing it to everyone on deck at the same time. To our north-west, heading in exactly the opposite direction to us, was a huge Spanish frigate.

"The *Gamo*, thirty-two guns," Cochrane announced calmly.

The ship was huge. It was four times the size of the *Speedy*; our mast heads were barely above their poop deck.

I turned to Cochrane. "I hope to God that you have a trick up your sleeve to get us out of this."

"Oh, I have, but you won't like it." Cochrane smiled and then looked up at the weather vane. The wind was coming from the south, meaning that to escape in that direction we would be sailing close into the wind and making little progress. The frigate had a big lateen rig on its stern mast, which would doubtless be better than our mizzen sail at sailing into the wind. With its longer range guns it could blow us out of the water without us being able to touch her.

"We need to get to the other side of her," Cochrane said, half to himself. However, it did not look like the *Gamo* was going to give us the chance. Her crew would all have heard about the *Speedy* and her devilish captain, Lord Cochrane, who had a trick for every occasion. They may even have been on a mission specifically to find us.

A few hundred yards before we were about to pass, at a distance well out of the range of our guns but well within the range of theirs, their gun ports were flung open. Sixteen big guns rolled out of their port side facing us and the big Spanish battle ensign flag broke from their stern, fluttering over the sea behind them. A gun boomed, putting a shot across our bows. Their intention was clear: heave to or be blown out of the water.

Cochrane was, however, ready, and having spoken to the ship's boy with his well-used flag locker, the flag of the United States ran swiftly up the mast. "Come on, lads, cheer and wave at the gallant allies of the United States like the good little Yankees you are. Bring up the men from the gun deck too. They haven't got the range so they may as well be on deck to add to the confusion."

Within seconds the deck was full of capering seaman cheering and waving at the Spanish ship. Cochrane, conscious that every officer with a telescope on the enemy's quarterdeck would have it trained on him, reached into his coat pocket and took out a letter, which he unfolded. He walked to the rail and, keeping his cocked hat over his distinctive red hair, he waved the letter at the Spanish ship in one hand and pointed to it with the other as though it was some important declaration that he expected the Spanish to know about.

"What is that?" I asked, walking over to him and waving my own hat in the air at the frigate.

"It is a letter from my uncle Alexander, but to them it could be anything."

The frigate was directly opposite us and if they were going to fire, it would be now. I stared at the sixteen black dots pointing out of the gun ports, expecting to see them flash with flame and death. They stayed black dots, and even without a telescope you could see men arguing and debating our identity on their high poop deck and the flash of telescopes as they studied us. Their certainty that we were the *Speedy* had been replaced by doubt. While they must have known Cochrane used false flags, the United States was friendly to the French and Spanish alliance and there would be repercussions if they attacked an American ship. They must also have wondered what paper the American captain was waving at them. At a time when news was carried on horseback, those on the front lines were often the last to hear the news. Had America declared war on the English or had France made peace with the English, including their Spanish allies? They had to make a decision, to fire or not.

Then, just as things hung in the balance, they saw that the little ship was changing course so that it would sail close to their stern. It was inconceivable that such a tiny ship would attack them. It must be so that its crew could shout the news contained in the mystery document. And so the Spanish held their fire. If it was Cochrane, whatever trick he tried they were confident that they had the speed and firepower to turn the *Speedy* into matchwood.

On the deck of the *Speedy*, Cochrane was explaining the same facts to his crew but with a remarkably different conclusion. "We can't outrun them and from this range we can't out-gun them. We are so small compared to them that the last thing they will expect is for us to attack. But that is what we are going to do."

For a second I thought I had misheard. Had he said 'attack' when we had fifty-four men and they must have had over three hundred men and marines aboard. (Three hundred and nineteen, as it turned out later.) We would be outnumbered more than six to one, assuming we weren't blown apart before we could reach them. I must have been gaping with astonishment, and I wasn't the only one.

Cochrane talked calmly and confidently as though he were proposing a summer walk. He ignored the stunned looks amongst his audience and continued: "Listen, lads, you know as well as I do that the Spanish do not hold up well in a fight. We must have captured at least thirty of their ships now and not one has shown serious resistance. We fought their army too, and they fled and let us escape. The Spanish are rotten: their officers are too proud to fight and the men are not willing to die just for the glory of their officers.

"We have them off balance now, as they do not know who we are. We are going to keep them off balance. When we go past their stern, we'll put up the battle ensign and give them a broadside down the length of their ship. They won't be expecting that. Then we'll pull in tight on their leeward side. The wind will help us angle our guns to fire up through their decks at close range. Look how high their guns are; they will not be able to aim down at our decks."

"But what do we do then?" I asked. "They will still blast us when we try to get away."

Cochrane looked at me with a wolfish smile and I realised that I had not yet appreciated the full horror of his plan.

"Why, we board, of course. They won't be expecting that." He paused to beam at us and then laughed. "Look, by then they will know it is the *Speedy* and they know that I have more tricks than a box of monkeys. We will have kept them off balance. They will think that it would be suicidal for us to attack them unless we had some tricks up our sleeve, and so they will be looking for a trap."

"Do you have some tricks up your sleeve?" asked Archie, sounding concerned.

"Of course," said Cochrane airily. "Look, lads, have I ever let you down before? I tell you, we can take this ship. Our small size is not a disadvantage, but an advantage, for we will be below her guns. We can pound her with impunity. When we get aboard they will be weakened and frightened

142

of whatever tricks we have in store. They will be looking for reasons to back off and we will give them some. You are the *Speedy*, the terror of the Spanish on this coast. Think, lads, if we take this ship, we will be the talk of the fleet. You will never again have to buy a drink in a naval town when you tell them you were on the *Speedy* when she took the *Gamo*. Think of the prize money too, lads, for she will make us all rich."

In romantic novels everyone huzzahs at this point and runs off to the guns, but on the deck of the *Speedy* there was a second's silence as every man there absorbed the enormity of what Cochrane had just said. He was asking us to take on massive odds in a death or glory attack. I suspect that everyone there, like me, was weighing up the alternatives and realising that there weren't any. We were committed to the attack from the moment the *Gamo* emerged from the mist. It was that or being taken prisoner, and as we were viewed as virtual pirates by the Spanish and after the attack at Estepona, we could expect little mercy. I remembered with a chill that Abrantes awaited me if I was taken prisoner.

A flicker of concern started to cross Cochrane's expectant face; he must have wondered if we would take on this insane challenge. But before he could say any more it was the big seaman Eriksson who broke the silence:

"I don't want to die chained to a galley or dangling from a rope so I say we attack. We either die like Vikings with weapons in our hands or we become heroes that men will talk about for years."

"Fight like Vikings!" someone shouted in agreement, and suddenly we were all cheering and, so help me, I was joining in as enthusiastically as the rest.

Perhaps in the same situation now, in my old age, I would think more about trying to talk my way out of being a prisoner, but I doubt it. The dagoes are proud as Lucifer when they have prisoners and they treat them like dirt. There would be little chance of any mercy there. Having fought with them in subsequent years in Portugal and Spain, I also now know that Cochrane was right in saying they don't hold up well in a fight. In both their army and navy there is a huge social gulf between the officers and men. The officers, often nobility, generally feel that actual fighting is something for the lower orders to do. They rarely condescend to even speak to a common soldier or sailor, and they expect obedience as a birthright. The men, on the other hand, have no wish to die for officers they don't know or for reasons they do not understand, and they often look for an excuse to give up. Why, at Talavera a whole Spanish regiment broke and ran at what they thought was the sound of a single musket shot. Look it up; it is in the history books now. A whole Spanish regiment guarding Wellington's right flank broke and ran, stopping only to loot the British baggage in their escape. What the history books don't tell you is that it was not a musket shot but a loud horse's fart that set them off, and I should know as I was sitting on the horse at the time. But that is another story.

We were close enough to the stern of the *Gamo* to see faces now. Whether they recognised Cochrane (for I saw someone pointing at us and shouting) or whether it was the renewed cheering that alarmed them, I don't know, but suddenly they went on the attack. A broadside from the great frigate crashed out, but it was too late. We were already past their stern-most guns, and in any event the range had not been adjusted from when they first sighted us and so the balls went high and wide. It brought Cochrane back to the task in hand, though.

"Right, gun crews, double-shot the port guns and run out. Fire as you bear and rake their stern. Topmen, man the braces. I want to go tight round their stern."

The deck was alive with activity as we only had a hundred yards to go before we would be level with the stern of the frigate. Looking up, I saw the United States flag coming down to be replaced by the big, white Royal Navy battle ensign.

From the back, the *Gamo* was even more intimidating than from the side. The stern rose up in a huge and ornately gilded shape overhanging the rudder and housing the doubtless luxurious officers' quarters. I had noticed that the gun deck of the *Gamo* did not extend all the way to the rear of the vessel as it would in an English warship, probably to avoid disturbing the cabins when they cleared for action. As we had been level with her stern, this had helped us avoid the first broadside. Now, I looked anxiously for stern chaser guns that would be able to fire at virtually point blank range as we crossed their stern, but none were to be seen.

A crowd of Spanish officers and some of their marines appeared at the stern rail to watch as the *Speedy* pulled round the back of the ship. Puffs of smoke appeared as the marines opened fire, but to no effect. They evidently expected us to try to escape in the opposite direction, but the *Speedy* heeled in the wind while making the turn, pointing the guns upwards. One by one the little four-pounder guns spat out their double loads of shot. At short range the effect was devastating. At least one set of balls smashed through the stern rail, sending iron and splinters into the men standing at it. We subsequently discovered that this killed both the captain and the boatswain. Other balls crashed through the huge stern windows of the rear cabins and then proceeded to smash their way down the crowded gun deck, bringing more death and destruction.

The gun crews moved to quickly reload their guns. The one advantage of such small weapons was that they were much easier and quicker to load and train than the twelve-pounders that formed the main armament of the frigate. Having crossed the stern of the *Gamo*, the course was changed to sail alongside it on the leeward side. Cochrane kept as close to the big ship as possible as we gained on it to move close alongside. The front of the *Speedy* moved past the shattered wreckage of their stern, which literally towered above us. As we moved further alongside their starboard side, another broadside crashed out. Their balls parted ropes and burst through the foremast mainsail, but otherwise passed harmlessly overhead.

As we gradually got level with the big Spanish ship, Cochrane moved closer still so that our rigging became entangled with theirs. Our little broadside crashed out again and at point-blank range you could see splinters flying where the balls smashed through the enemy planking. Again the Spanish fired their guns, which were now directly overhead. You could hear a tearing sound as the balls tore through the air, but apart from some more holes in sails and broken cordage, no damage was done.

This was my first, but sadly not my last, sea battle. You may see them in paintings and try to imagine what they are like, but nothing prepares you for the noise and the smoke. While our guns went off with sharp cracks and relatively small puffs of smoke, their cannons boomed out literally just above our heads and sent out plumes of smoke across our decks. You could hear the cries and shouts from the crews of both ships, and now there was a crackle of musket fire from marines on their deck and I saw one of our sailors go down, hit in chest, and be swiftly taken below.

The worst part of most sea battles is the long wait as formations of slow ships move to engage, but in this battle we barely had time to think before the guns started and the time flew by. The only damage we were taking was from some Spanish marines who were shooting down onto our decks. I heard a second man scream, but did not see him as quickly the smoke became too thick, leaving them firing blind.

So began one of the craziest hours of my life, for that was how long we stayed pounding the *Gamo* with our little guns from just a few feet away. Only half of the crew were involved in firing the cannons and many of the rest of us got muskets from the store. While Cochrane paced the quarterdeck in open view, I was happy to crouch behind a bulwark and take shots at where I knew their deck to be. I have no idea whether I hit anyone, but it gave me something to do.

The rigging of the two ships was intertwined, but as our lower sails and rigging were gradually shot away we got a grappling hook caught in their bows. This was tied to a capstan so that we did not fall behind and could move our ship up and down the length of theirs. We were well aware that if the Spanish were able to stand off and blast us then the tables would be turned.

As our shots tore up their decks and theirs went over the top of ours, the Spanish decided that the easiest way to resolve the battle would be to board the *Speedy*. However, I could clearly hear the orders being given in Spanish on the nearby deck to prepare for boarding and I warned Cochrane. We slackened the bow rope and moved a few yards away from the *Gamo*. Thus when they came to board there was a gap between the two hulls too big to jump. They stood peering through the smoke, looking for the *Speedy*'s deck and seeing a dark mass at their rail. We gave them a fusillade of musket shots while they hesitated. Twice more they tried to board; twice more we did the same thing. They lost a few men each time, mostly to muskets, but one man tried the jump and fell, screaming, into the sea.

After an hour Parker sent one of the younger midshipmen up from the gun deck to report that they were starting to run low on ammunition. Some of the guns had been triple-shotted and the light guns could be fired nearly once a minute, so they were getting through balls at a fast rate. The passage of the battle was also taking us closer to the Spanish coast and the gunboats that we had seen the previous day had come out to watch but had so far not interfered. We could not sail away; it was time to bring things to a conclusion.

I saw Cochrane give some orders to Parker for the midshipman and the boy's astonished reaction. I could not hear what was said, but Cochrane laughed and repeated the orders and sent the boy on his way. Having learnt a lesson from our hearing the Spanish bellowing for boarding parties, he called down to the deck and shouted that we should get ready for the second stage of the plan. We all knew what this meant and my guts started to churn. It was one thing to take pot-shots from the relatively safe deck of the *Speedy*, but we now had to climb across the gap between the two moving ships and up their side, to be met with well-prepared Spanish sailors and marines at odds of six to one.

The boarding party started to gather on the main deck where they exchanged muskets for cutlasses, boarding pikes and other weapons more suited to close quarter fighting. Cochrane called out encouragingly to the group: "Wait for the command. A few minutes energetically employed will decide this matter in our favour."

I noticed that our guns had stopped firing. We would need the gun crews for the boarding party but they did not appear on deck. I was standing next to Eriksson, who was hefting his favourite weapon, a mighty Viking-style war axe. I was planning to stick close to him when we boarded, as it would be a brave Spaniard that got close to the big Dane. I had two pistols in my belt and a cutlass in a hand that was trembling with apprehension. The only comfort was the fact that the group of seamen around me, while tense, seemed confident and determined. This small comfort was about to be taken away as Cochrane called me over.

"Flashman, I don't want you to join the boarding party." He shouted this as another salvo of enemy fire crashed out above us. For a moment I felt relief wash over me, and then a second later a slight feeling of hurt, as though I had been excluded from the crew. I thought perhaps I would be needed to man the wheel of the *Speedy*, but then I saw that Guthrie, the surgeon, was already there. But Cochrane was not planning to leave me out of the fun.

"Don't look so upset, Flashman. I have special plans for you. Right now the Spanish are probably waiting for us to try to board, but I have a diversion planned. In a few minutes Parker will take the gun crews up over the bows to attack their reception committee in the rear. I have told them to black their faces up and yell like banshees when they attack. They will signal when the Spanish reception committee has been distracted and then the main boarding party will attack until the Spanish colours are hauled down."

"You seem confident that they will haul down their colours," I said, now very worried that he was overconfident.

"That is where you come in, Flashman: I want *you* to haul them down."

"What?" I was thunderstruck. Surely he did not expect me to fight my way through a Spanish crew and then hold them off while I hauled down their colours on my own?

"It has to be you, as it is not in accordance with the rules of war. If asked, I can honestly say that none of the ship's officers or crew were responsible."

"But how can I do it? They will cut me to pieces!"

"It will be easier than you think. All attention will be focused on the black-faced devils coming over the bow and then the main boarding party. You will need to climb up the stern and, when I give you the signal, three blasts on my whistle, haul down their colours. With luck most will throw down their weapons and surrender before they realise that their officers did not give the order."

This seemed to be optimism of the highest order, said so casually that it made hauling down the flag of an enemy's battleship sound as easy as picking an apple. I felt suddenly a massive weight of responsibility as I at last understood that Cochrane's whole plan for capturing an enemy frigate seemed to depend on the delicate reed that was the courage and fighting ability of one Thomas Flashman Esquire. We were doomed.

But before I could say anything, not that I could think of anything to say, we were both distracted by an astonishing sight. Coming out of the forward hatch were around twenty men looking like chimney sweeps with black hands and faces but white spaces around their eyes. They were armed to the teeth.

We had pulled our bows level with theirs earlier with the rope attached to the capstan, and with a wave, Parker led his men over the side and into the bows of the *Gamo*. If he encountered any resistance there, he dealt with it quickly and quietly. Some of the main boarding party now slackened the capstan so that we began to slide back down the *Gamo* until our stern was level with theirs.

As we listened for our black-faced crew to charge across their decks, I looked at the rest of the pitifully small boarding party that was waiting on our main deck. Amongst them were our two younger midshipmen, aged twelve and thirteen, who were armed in the regulation manner. All they held in their hands were naval dirks, daggers to you and me, with blades about eight inches long. Maybe arming them in this way was some callous naval tactic to instil courage in sailors. For what man will shirk when a small boy is willing to fight alongside you armed with nothing more dangerous than a fruit knife? Well, probably me, for one, if I could get away with it.

Christ, I have had letter openers that are more lethal than those dirks. I went to one of the weapons chests and rummaged about. I found the old rapier sword I had discarded on my first day aboard and a small pistol. A cutlass would be too heavy for a boy, but the light rapier would serve. I told them both to put their dirks in the belts and gave the rapier to the tallest and told him to use it only as a stabbing weapon. The twelve-year-old, who was a scrawny runt and yet to fill out, got the pistol, which I checked was loaded and primed.

This sounds like kindly old Flashy helping the pups, but in truth it was also to keep me occupied because by then I was in a hell of a funk. If I had been standing, waiting, doing nothing, I think my nerve would have broken. Sure, I was not with the boarding party that would meet the Spanish onslaught, but they at least had comrades around them. I had to enter that towering vessel on my own, and likely with the lives of all of us resting on my efforts.

The Spanish would have noticed that we had stopped firing and must have expected us to try boarding. They were probably gathered on the main deck and may have been wondering what the scraping sound presaged as our ship slid back down their side. As they stared through their own gun smoke at the *Speedy*, they can't have been expecting the black-faced banshees that charged them from their own bows. Parker's small band of men were outnumbered more than ten to one, and after the initial attack they retreated to the bows where they could not be outflanked, drawing the enemy away from the side. One of the black-faced crew must have pulled a bosun's call from his pocket and gave the whistle for piping the captain aboard. Cochrane took the cue and led the main boarding party over the rail.

From my position far below on the main deck of the *Speedy* I could not see what happened next. Cochrane had been worried about being repulsed at the rail, which is always the hardest part of boarding, but the black-faced diversion had done its work and I saw the thirty members of the main boarding crew climb up the side of the *Gamo* and disappear without loss to their number. While Cochrane should have led the charge, it was the massive Eriksson that managed to get on the enemy deck first, and I heard his massive below of "Vikings!" and then a blood-curdling shriek. I am pretty sure that I saw a fountain of blood up above the rail, which, from the angle I was looking at, must have meant that someone was near decapitated by the mighty axe that Eriksson was carrying. That was the last distinct sound I heard before the melee dissolved into a mass of shouts and cries.

Guthrie and I now stood alone on the deck of the *Speedy*. A pitched battle was raging yards away, but we were in an oasis of calm as none of the Spanish on the *Gamo* were paying attention to us.

Guthrie looked across at me and shouted above the noise of screaming and yelling from nearby, "What has he got you doing?"

"Oh, nothing much," I shouted back. "Just hopping across to this enemy frigate and hauling down their colours when they are not looking."

Guthrie laughed. "Is that all? He wants me to send across the marines."

"The marines? But we haven't... Oh, never mind... Will you give me a leg up?"

Suddenly I felt resigned to the insanity of the moment. The die was cast; there was nothing I could do but attempt to pull down their flag. If I succeeded, we had a chance, a slim one in my opinion; but without it, three hundred men would surely never willingly surrender to fifty. With Abrantes and death waiting for me if we failed, I had nothing to lose.

The great stern of the *Gamo* towered over our own quarterdeck. The extensive gilding, which started at my head level, would probably have made it easy to climb even without the alterations that our guns had done as we passed. It would be easy to haul myself up into the great stern cabin through the ornately carved windows, but I could not see how I could get up to the quarterdeck, which overhung the cabin on all sides. I looked up again and nobody from their deck was paying attention to us. Guthrie put a loop of rope around the wheel spokes and came over. I put my cutlass in my belt with the pistols, to free my hands, and he helped me haul myself up.

After a moment's climbing I was at an opening to the lower deck and risked a look inside. This was the gun deck level and the guns were mostly abandoned by the crew, who had joined the fight on the main deck. Those left were the dead and dying, and there seemed to be plenty of those. At such a short range even our small-calibre guns had wrought a devastating effect, and there were holes and torn planking and splintering everywhere I looked. But I was exposed, hanging on to the outside of the ship, and I climbed quickly further up to the windows of the great cabin above. A quick look to check the coast was clear and then I pulled myself inside.

The only occupant was dead. Judging by the gold on his uniform, he had been the captain, and judging by the luxury of the fittings, this was his cabin. The body was lying on a sturdy oak desk, which had the remains of several chairs around it. To illuminate the desk, above it was a broken skylight.

Suddenly I was aware of a voice muttering quietly somewhere close by. I crept to the door, which was slightly open, and saw another outer cabin. There in front of me was a young priest, kneeling over three more corpses, all officers by the look of them. Beyond him was another door, slightly ajar, that led out onto the deck. Well, you can't kill a praying priest, at least not from behind, and so I pulled a pistol from my belt and, holding the muzzle, hit him hard behind the ear with the butt. He fell over the corpses with a slight groan and was still. I crept forward to the outer door.

I looked down on a scene I will never forget. The deck was crowded with men, heaving and jostling with each other but with absolutely no order apart from in two areas. In the bows a row of black-faced men was just visible, fighting a crowd of Spanish sailors. I had a clearer view of the larger boarding party on the main deck. They had carved out a triangle of deck that they were defending vigorously, while staying together so that they were not overwhelmed. If we had been up against skilled fighters such as French infantry, Mohawk Indians or even Mrs Pargetter's sewing circle, we would not have stood a chance, but a second's glance showed you that Spanish heart was not in the fight. They made no attempt to rush the boarders and seemed content to contain them. When Eriksson burst from the group to make a rush at them, they literally fell over themselves to get out of the way.

As I watched I saw Cochrane break away from the fight and run back to the rail. "Now, Guthrie, send over the marines."

Guthrie ran over to the hatch in the *Speedy*'s deck and bellowed down it: "Now, marines, now is your time… Yes, both companies… Go!"

From the deck above my head I heard the voice of a Spanish officer who clearly spoke English translating for his fellow officers. "He is shouting about marines, they have marines, they are sending marines across." The reply was obscured by three sharp blasts on a whistle.

By Christ, I thought, this is it, and I turned back to the stern cabin. I had seen only one way onto the quarterdeck and the flag, and now I had to take it. Getting back to the desk, with a whispered apology, I rolled the captain's body onto the floor. It hit the deck with a sickening thump but he was beyond pain now. Then I looked amongst the wreckage of the chairs for one that still had four good legs. I put that on the desk and quickly climbed up. Standing on the desk, I poked my head up through the skylight.

Three officers stood on the quarterdeck. Judging from the braid, one was a senior officer and the other two more junior lieutenants. They were all standing at the quarterdeck rail, surveying the fighting below and, from what I could hear over the noise of battle, arguing furiously over the possible existence of the marines. I looked around. I could see the rope holding the battle flag just a few feet away. It couldn't be this easy, surely. I stepped up onto the chair and climbed over the broken glass onto the deck. Still I had not been noticed. I moved back drew my sword and quickly cut the halyard that kept the huge silk battle flag in place and, putting my cutlass back in my belt, started hauling the lowering rope down as fast as I could.

There was a flaw in Cochrane's plan. He had been looking at the great flag from down on the main deck, and as soon as it showed signs of downward movement, he pointed this out to the Spanish about him and demanded their surrender. They might not speak English, but they knew what a lowered flag meant and many threw down their weapons. Others looked in surprise at their officers on the quarterdeck... who in turn stared round in astonishment at the complete stranger brazenly lowering their flag.

The two younger officers both sprang forward while drawing ornately decorated swords from their scabbards. I let go of the rope and drew my cutlass again, unsure whether I should grab the flag rope and dive overboard, or defend myself. The nearest officer made up my mind by adopting Position One as taught by my French fencing master. With the memory of Eriksson's voice in my ears, I rushed forward three steps and combined a huge swing with the cutlass to bash away his blade with a colossal kick into his bollocks that lifted him off the ground and put him instantly out of the fight.

The other attacker was nearly on me, but I moved around his fallen comrade, whose body was now between us. The second assailant looked a more competent swordsman: he swished his blade confidently and moved lightly on the balls of his feet as we circled the groaning body. His eyes were locked on my arms and sword, trying to anticipate my moves like a good swordsman, but in truth I had no great moves that would serve against a skilled opponent. My foot stumbled over the fallen sword of his comrade, the toe of my right foot underneath the blade by the hilt. It gave me an idea which would probably not have worked had the senior officer not helped me out.

"Never mind him, get the flag, the flag!" shouted the officer still at the quarterdeck rail. We both instinctively glanced at the officer who had now pulled out a pistol and was pointing it at me. My assailant then quickly risked a quick glance round to look at the flag, which was now draped over the stern rail of the ship. It was the distraction I needed.

Everything happened at once. My right foot flicked the sword lying across my instep into the air and towards the face of my assailant. He glimpsed the metal coming towards him out of the corner of his eye and instinctively his blade swept round to meet it. I pounced forward in a classic lunge, stepping as I did so on the fallen assailant, who groaned and moved under my foot. The standing assailant realised that my hand was not attached to the first sword but instead to another cutlass blade that was now lunging forward to his exposed side. I would have got him, but the Spanish officer under my foot moved and put me off balance, and so instead of a firm hit my cutlass blade just scored a deep cut down his side.

But now I was overstretched and the standing assailant grinned in triumph as he started to swing his blade down toward my neck and shoulders. Off balance, there was no way I could recover in time to block the stroke, and not for the first time since I met Cochrane I was convinced I was going to die. Then, inexplicably, the swordsman's face grimaced and he was falling and dropping his weapon. I looked up and saw that the senior officer's pistol was smoking and there was a look of horror on his face. Standing

155

on the opposite side of the assailant from my sword cut, he must have assumed I had run his comrade through. He had fired at me and, from around eighteen feet away, missed and hit the lieutenant instead.

The lieutenant was now on his hands and knees with my sword cut down his right side and a bullet wound in his left. The senior officer was still staring, frozen at what he had done. I advanced on him with my blood-stained sword pointing in his direction. "Tell your men to surrender," I said.

With his sword un-drawn at his side, he looked beyond me at his fallen officers and at the flag that was now fully lowered and at risk of falling into the sea. But still he seemed to hesitate. I was now just six feet away and, closer to the rail, I could see that while many of the Spaniards had stopped fighting and were staring towards the officer on the quarterdeck, there were still pockets of continued combat with shouts and the ring of steel on steel and the occasional bang of a pistol. We were still massively outnumbered, and I remembered Cochrane's words about keeping them unbalanced and realised I had to bring this to an end quickly.

With my left hand I pulled out one of the pistols, cocked it and levelled it at the officer's head. "Last chance," I said in Spanish. "Tell your men to surrender."

As he stared down the black muzzle of the pistol that a slightly trembling hand was pointing in his direction, the officer seemed to come to his senses. He turned back over the rail towards his crew and ordered them to drop their weapons. There was a reassuring clatter of metal on wood as weapons fell to the deck and men still fighting were pulled apart by their comrades.

I stood covering the officer, but out of the corner of my eye I could see Cochrane and Eriksson pushing their way through the crowd on deck towards me. They bounded up the ladder to the quarterdeck. Cochrane took in my blood-stained sword and the two lieutenants now lying prostrate on the ground and pounded me on the back. "Well done, Flashman, well done indeed." He stepped up to the rail and shouted down at the *Speedy*'s crew, "Disarm them and get them down into the hold, quickly now."

I glanced across at Eriksson, who looked like something from a nightmare. He was covered from head to toe in spatters of blood and his arms and his great war axe were covered in gore. There was a wild look in his eyes too. He was in a killing rage. You see it sometimes in battle: a man finds a wild exhilaration in killing and wants to kill, kill, kill without thought for anything else. A man in a killing rage is worth ten men in battle, not that I have ever experienced the feeling, although I did come close once at a debate with some liberals at the Reform Club.

Eriksson hefted his axe at the remaining Spanish officer still on his feet and snarled at him as though daring him to give some resistance. But the officer was staring at the big Dane in horror and he swiftly offered his sword in surrender to Cochrane, who accepted the weapon and did not offer it back.

I looked down onto the main deck. The crew of the *Speedy* were busy pushing the Spanish towards the hatch to the hold none too gently, but given the numbers involved, it would take a few minutes to get them all below. It turned out that there were two hundred and sixty-three unhurt prisoners who were being managed by a fraction of that number.

Archie and some of the boarding party were busy manhandling one of the big carronade guns around so that it would cover the hatch if there was any sign of trouble. For the most part, the Spanish allowed themselves to be herded below. Only one group showed any sign of resistance, and a shout and wave of the axe from Eriksson at the rail beside me seemed to persuade them to think better of it.

The Dane was starting to calm down now and he clapped me on the shoulder, grinning and gesturing to the wounded officers on the deck behind us that were now being helped up by two of the crew. "You haff fun here, yes? You have Viking blood, I think." He gestured across at Cochrane, who was shouting for a crewman to go back to the *Speedy* to get a spare white ensign to fly on the *Gamo* to show she had been captured. "He one lucky bastard," said the Dane thoughtfully, which was as succinct and accurate a summary of the *Gamo* action as I ever heard.

By a mixture of bravery, trickery and some would say insanity, on the sixth of May 1801 the tiny brig *Speedy* had captured the huge Xebec-class frigate *Gamo*. I know it sounds unbelievable – it does to me and I was there – but it is a historical fact. The casualty figures bear out my recollections too, for our losses in the boarding action were just one man killed and four wounded, including poor Parker, who was in a bad way having had a sword through his leg and musket ball in his chest. We had lost two other crew, killed during the exchange of broadsides, one by musket fire from the enemy deck and one by some falling rigging block shot away from the mast. Four seamen had been wounded in that part of the battle too, so our total casualties were three seamen killed and one officer and seven seamen wounded. In comparison, the *Gamo* had lost their captain and boatswain and thirteen seamen, and forty-one were wounded.

It was an astonishing achievement and, in the views of many, the best single-ship action of the war. Only someone with the creativity of Cochrane would ever have thought it was possible, but it could only have been achieved against a demoralised crew such as those we had seen on Spanish boats. Cochrane was right about something else too: I never have had to buy myself a drink in a naval town when they knew I had served on the *Speedy* when she took the *Gamo*.

As a curious footnote, my exploits in that battle have just recently been preserved for all time in oils. One of those scrawny, young midshipmen, a boy called Rickets, has obviously done well for himself and commissioned an artist called Clarkson Stanfield to paint the battle as he recalled it. I saw the painting recently at the Royal Academy, and you can clearly see me on the Spanish deck, hauling down the Spanish colours while a Spanish officer comes at me waving a sword. Some old trout also at the viewing told me that the person hauling down the colours was Rickets himself. I put her right, as you can clearly see that the person pulling down the colours is a man, not a boy.

Editor's Note: The central part of this painting has been used as the cover for this book, but the original can be viewed at the Victoria and Albert Museum or on various websites. The person hauling down the Spanish colours is clearly visible and indeed does appear to be a man rather than a boy.

~~~~~~

Chapter 15

As it turned out, capturing the *Gamo* brought a whole new set of problems, not least the two hundred and sixty-three unhurt prisoners who at any point would realise that they had been tricked and that they vastly outnumbered their captors. To deter any uprising, Archie got the big carronade covering the hatch and loaded it with grape, and until we reached Port Mahon a seaman with a smoking slow match stood next to it.

The battle had taken us in clear sight of the Spanish coast and a handful of Spanish gunboats sailing in the vicinity that watched what was happening but did not attempt to interfere. Had they tried, we would have been hard-pressed to hold both ships while keeping the prisoners in check. We now had just forty men left to sail both the *Speedy* and the *Gamo* away from the Spanish coast. The *Speedy*'s rigging was shot to pieces and so initially she was put in tow to get both ships out of sight from land. There was even talk of abandoning her and just returning with the *Gamo*, but Cochrane wanted to sail her home with the *Gamo* towering over her as his prize.

When the horizon was clear, the men set to work to repair the rigging on the *Speedy* and we divided the crew. The wounded and twenty men including the surgeon were left on the *Gamo*, with Archie taking command. I was on the *Gamo* too, acting as interpreter when required. Cochrane and the remaining crew stayed on the *Speedy*.

The senior Spanish officer gave his parole not to help the prisoners retake the ship and was allowed on deck. The officer he had shot seemed to be recovering and the senior officer now seemed anxious to please and even asked if he could have a certificate from Cochrane to prove he had done his duty during the action. Cochrane would not hear of it, as he held the Spaniard in contempt for his poor defence of the ship, but I promised the officer that he would have his certificate if we all got safely back to Port Mahon. We did too, and so I drafted a certificate to say that he had "conducted himself like a true Spaniard", which Cochrane signed with amusement. The officer seemed delighted with the certification, and years later Cochrane told me that he had discovered that the officer had used the document to help secure further promotion in the Spanish navy.

The journey back to Minorca took several days, but the weather was kind and despite various scares and alarms we kept the enemy sailors in the hold. Each morning there was funeral service for Spanish wounded who had died, but Guthrie managed to keep most alive. Thoughts began to turn to prize money as we got closer to home and every man there began to calculate what the *Gamo* would be worth to a prize court. As a warship she would be worth perhaps ten thousand pounds, and the damage we had made could easily be prepared. Prize money was allocated in eighths with the admiral getting one eighth, the captain two eighths, the able seamen two eighths and the remaining three eighths were divided among the other officers and non-commissioned officers in order of seniority. As there were so few of us this would give everyone a very handsome sum. Even an honorary midshipman like me could hope for several hundred pounds. But for Cochrane the bigger reward was that he was likely to be given command of the *Gamo* and with a bigger, more powerful ship he could bring the Spanish coast to a virtual standstill.

Our entry into Port Mahon was a proud moment with the little *Speedy* leading the way with her prize looming over her, flying the naval ensign above the Spanish flag to show she had been taken. The guns of the fort fired a salute and congratulations were shouted from other naval ships in the anchorage as we passed them.

However, if Cochrane thought that this incredible feat would gain him promotion and recognition within the Navy, he underestimated the power of the enemies he had within the service. Cochrane's senior officer was Captain Manley Dixon, a man who did not get a share of the *Speedy*'s prize money and who greatly resented the wealth that 'his lordship' was accruing through his actions. Over forty ships

161

of assorted types and sizes had then been taken, and mixing with the officers of other ships I heard dark murmurings that Cochrane was more interested in prize money than prosecuting the war. This was just jealousy; officers on larger ships were often on blockade duty without the opportunity to take prizes. But with seamen on the *Speedy* already earning more than some junior officers on other ships through prize money, the arrival of the *Gamo* and its potential for further wealth for the *Speedy*'s crew soured the sense of congratulation for many.

Certainly Manley Dixon received Cochrane with perfunctory courtesy when he presented his written report of the engagement. This was to be submitted to the Admiralty and would normally be supported by a glowing endorsement of the action by the commanding officer with a recommendation for promotion or recognition such as proposing captaincy of the prize.

Cochrane was seething after the meeting. "You could straighten a bent ramrod by shoving it up his arse," he growled to me as he walked away from the naval headquarters. " 'Your lordship is to be congratulated' was all the starchy bastard said. He didn't even offer me a drink."

Cochrane was right to be concerned. In addition to Manley Dixon, Mansfield, Admiral Keith's all-powerful clerk, was now venomous in his hatred of Cochrane, as I had discovered when I called at his office to see if there had been any letters. "Only three killed, eh? Well, they can't have put up much of a fight. Don't spend your prize money just yet, Flashman – prize courts can come to strange decisions." He was walking with a slight limp and I later discovered from the girls at Madam Rosa's that once the suspicion arose that he was suffering from the clap, they had insisted that he have a dose of mercury treatment before he was allowed back in the establishment. As the only alternative was some rough seamen's whorehouses that would almost certainly give him the clap, after much raging and threats he reluctantly agreed to see the local doctor. He was convinced that Cochrane had started the rumour as the *Speedy* had been in port when it started.

There was a letter from Wickham congratulating me on the success of my mission, which seemed like a distant memory now. There was also one from my father saying that he had heard from Castlereagh that I had done some good service, and asking when I was coming home. The old man said he was proud of me and I remember being quite touched as I didn't think I had given him cause to say that before. My father also mentioned in passing that James and Emily were expecting a baby, and from the due date given it seemed that Dr Graham's electric bed might have worked after all.

While we didn't know it then, Manley Dixon and Mansfield had already started to wreak their vengeance. Manley Dixon's covering letter to the Admiralty with Cochrane's report was a bare three lines long. While it described the capture as 'very spirited and brilliant', what it did not say spoke greater volumes in the convention of such things at the Admiralty. Mansfield then sat on even this for a whole month before sending it, as they had reason to hope that Cochrane would not be around much longer.

With *Gamo* under assessment for a prize court to consider its future, the *Speedy* was restored to its full crew to await the outcome. Initial hopes that this would be a quick affair and that the next voyage would be in the larger ship were soon dashed when new orders arrived for the *Speedy*.

When a man as cocksure and confident as Cochrane looks worried, you know you are in trouble. He looked worried when he summoned me to the tiny stern cabin of the *Speedy* for a council of war. Already there was Guthrie, and Archie, who was now acting lieutenant as Parker was ashore in the hospital recovering from his wounds. Without a word, Cochrane handed me his written orders to read. After the usual pleasantries and preamble at the start of all formal orders, I saw that we were to proceed to Algiers where we were to represent to the ruler called the dey the illegality of his cruisers having taken a British vessel. This capture had been in retaliation of the British taking an Algerian vessel running a blockade. We were further to 'remonstrate with him and warn him of his future conduct, impressing the power of the Royal Navy that could be brought to bear'.

If intimidating an enemy potentate was required then with two full frigates and a ship of the line sharing the harbour with us at the time, the *Speedy* would appear a poor tool to use. I asked the obvious question.

"Why are they sending us?"

"Because they are hoping we won't come back. Their galleys and prisons are full of European and American sailors who have been captured and now many are getting ransomed. Five years ago the Americans paid the dey a million US dollars to release one hundred and fifteen sailors whom he had held in prison for over ten years."

"A million dollars!" I was staggered that the new republic could afford such a sum.

"It must have been around a fifth of their total government budget and they paid annual tributes after that too. I heard that the Americans are trying to get their privateers organised to make a navy to protect their shipping as a navy would be cheaper than paying tributes. But whatever they do now, their earlier generosity has given the Algerians the idea that big money can be made by hostage taking."

"But they wouldn't attack a Royal Navy ship, surely?"

"They might if it looked weak and they thought that they could get away with it. The Navy is stretched blockading the coast of France and Spain. We wouldn't pay them a million, but favours could be done."

"You are forgetting who the demands would be sent to," interrupted Guthrie. "Any demands would probably come here, and Manley Dixon and Mansfield would be in no rush to respond. They could even claim that the *Speedy* had been lost at sea and leave us to rot."

I could not see that happening. If the Algerians did not get a response from Port Mahon then they would try Gibraltar or elsewhere. Sooner or later our captivity would come to the attention of the Admiralty, although what efforts they would take to secure our release remained doubtful. I could not see them paying a ransom; it would make it open season on British merchants for every Barbary pirate. But the whole Barbary Coast of North Africa was full of pirates and to take them on we would need forces that we could not spare while we were also fighting France and Spain.

"Can we refuse to go?" I asked.

"Only if we want to be court-martialled and disgraced," replied Cochrane. "No, we must go and be strong and assertive representatives of Britain. On no account must we appear weak, but we must show the utmost tact and diplomacy."

This last phrase hung in the air and I knew that two others around the table were thinking the same thing: if tact and diplomacy were required then Thomas Cochrane was not your man. Oh, he was fine with the crew and subordinates, but he had immense pride when dealing with his superiors and seemed oblivious of the offence he caused. Eventually Archie broke the silence.

"Much as I love you, dear brother, tact and diplomacy are not your strong suits."

"Wait, though," said Guthrie. "We have a diplomat in our midst with papers signed by William Pitt, no less, certifying that he is carrying messages for the British government."

"Hold on," said I. "Pitt is not prime minister any more and I am just a courier, not a diplomat. Look at me: I am not twenty yet; no one is going to believe that I am a diplomat."

I had started that day with little other concern than which of Madam Bella's delightful distractions I would visit that evening, but now, like a persistent bailiff, trouble had found me again. We were being asked to face down the most fearsome pirate king in the Mediterranean. Of course I could have refused and jumped ship, but having just made my father proud for the first time in my life, I was damned if I was going to go home in disgrace. More importantly, despite the worries of the others, I simply could not believe that any Arab pirate leader would be stupid enough to take on the might of the Royal Navy. He must know that to do so would sooner or later see the visit of our fleets and his destruction. Finally, after all we had been through, I felt a strongly loyalty to the ship and the crew. We all knew that the ship's cat would make a better diplomat than Cochrane and I could see that using my diplomatic papers was the only ace we had. Cochrane had saved me at Estepona, and now I could do him a favour in return – and unlike the duel, this time he would know about it.

After initially looking a bit hurt Cochrane was suddenly all for the scheme. "We can fig you up to look like a diplomat, and as for Pitt no longer being prime minister, they will probably never know, and if they do, we say that Addington's government has fallen and Pitt is now back in power. Yes indeed, the *Speedy* will be far more believable as the conveyance of a diplomat rather than as a threat with its puny armament. We are turning a disadvantage…"

"Don't say it!" the rest of us chorused together in response.

From then on all was activity, particularly with regards to my attire. My best coat and breeches were sent ashore to be cleaned and pressed in the local laundry. Because we wanted to keep our preparations away from prying eyes at the naval headquarters, which would doubtless stop anything that improved our chances of success, I sought the help of Madam Bella. She and the girls were able to make me a pale-blue silk sash to wear over one shoulder and some old and battered ostrich feathers were adapted to make a feather trim to a new cocked hat that was bought for our endeavours. They even used some gold thread to embroider some oak leaves around the lapel of my jacket when it came back from the laundry. Trying out my new full fig in front of them, which was supplemented by my restored and polished rapier, they all agreed that I could pass muster. I just hoped that the dey would be as easily impressed.

Work had been underway to smarten the ship too, with the gun ports freshly painted black to stand out against the cream stripe along the hull that was also repainted. All brass was polished and the decks holystoned to a shining white.

New flags were bought from the ship's stores, and Cochrane and Archie both had their best uniforms laundered and any holes patched. The boat crew were given fresh matching shirts and trousers that would not have looked out of place on an admiral's barge, and the longboat was given a new coat of white paint.

We set sail late in the afternoon on the day after the orders were received and headed almost due south. After an unremarkable four-day voyage with favourable winds we arrived off Algiers. We had been intercepted the previous day by two smaller and faster Algerian vessels, one of which had sped on ahead to warn of our arrival, while the other stayed to shadow us out of range. Finally the coast of North Africa appeared and then we could make out a bay and the city of Algiers. We moved slowly towards the anchorage, which was crowded with a forest of masts. Through the middle of it stretched a stone-built jetty leading to a small island in the bay where there was a lighthouse on top of a fortress with three tiers of guns guarding the entrance. Looking around, I saw every type of vessel from Arab-built dhows, lateen-rigged ships and oared gun boats to what looked like captured ships of European build. One of them was probably that of the captured British merchantmen, but it was impossible identify which.

We considered whether to fire some guns in salute to the dey and it was a lengthy debate. Did a dey warrant the twenty-one-gun salute of a monarch, and how common were gun salutes in Algiers? With at least two other fortresses we could see surrounding the anchorage that were likely to have their guns trained on us and swarms of boats all around us, would they think we were attacking? In the end we decided to dip the flag in salute and leave our guns loaded and ready just in case.

To the amusement of the crew, I prowled around the deck in my new finery, trying to look important, as I knew we would be being watched from both the surrounding ships and the shore.

A launch weaved through the harbour traffic directly towards us. In the stern sat a turbaned grandee in richly decorated clothes, contrasting strongly with the tattered rags of the oarsmen who I realised must be slaves. They hooked on to our chains and the turbaned fellow sprang lightly up the side of the ship and onto the deck with the practised ease of a seaman. He paused to cast a very appraising eye around the deck before hawking and spitting on our spotless planking. "Why are you here?" he asked arrogantly.

"We have an emissary from His Britannic Majesty's Government with a message for the dey," said Cochrane, gesturing at where I stood, looking as imperious as possible at the stern rail.

The visitor looked at me and gave a grunt of contempt. "Anchor there," he commanded, pointing to a spot in the centre of the harbour that must have been comfortably in the range of at least fifty shore guns from the citadel and surrounding forts. Without any further comment, the stranger dropped back into his launch and was rowed away.

With a chill, I realised that we were now well past the point where we could go back. I had been shocked at the contempt shown to us by our visitor and began to wonder if my earlier confidence that the dey would not dare to offend the British had been misplaced. We moved to our anchorage in virtual silence, and when the anchor was let go the running of the chain and hawser sounded ominous. I would be damn glad when we weighed that anchor again. I remember making a promise to myself: if we got out of there without harm then I would make my way back to England. I should have made enough prize money, especially with the *Gamo*, and sooner or later Cochrane's luck would run out.

We were close inshore now and a swarm of hawkers' bumboats crowded around, selling fruit, flatbreads, decorated knives and all manner of other goods. One swarthy native was even trying to sell the services of an incredibly fat woman who was sitting at the front of his craft and waving demurely at the crew. They would never get her through a gun port I thought it would take six men to haul her on deck, not that she was worth the effort.

As I surveyed the scene I was conscious of other eyes on me and so I borrowed a telescope, rested in it the ratlines and studied the shore. The town was dominated by a huge fortress and citadel on some high ground near the harbour. Walls ran from that around the town as far as I could see and at three other points around the harbour there were heavy gun emplacements where large gun muzzles could be seen poking out of embrasures. In short, it was clear that we would not be leaving here unless the dey was happy to see us go. I scanned the harbour front and the first thing to cross the lens was a coffle of chained slaves being driven along. Each was carrying a large sack-wrapped bundle over his shoulders. Some were definitely European in origin; I saw ginger hair and blond amongst the group. My lens rested on a huge blond man who must once have been the size of Eriksson. Now he was almost skeletally thin, but what shocked me most was his face: it was completely expressionless. He was a broken man, and even when one of the overseers lashed at him, he barely flinched. If they could do that to a man like Eriksson, what could they do to the rest of us?

We had another visitor that afternoon and to my surprise it was an American. James Leander Cathcart was only thirty-three when I met him, but already he had led an extraordinary life. He had been born in Ireland, emigrated to America at the age of eight and by the age of twelve was serving as a midshipman on an American privateer during the revolutionary war. He was captured by the British and was held in a prison hulk until he escaped, after a three-year internment, in 1782, still only aged fifteen. When he was eighteen he was captured by Barbary pirates from Algiers on an American ship bound for Spain and he was a slave in Algiers for eleven years. During this time, by a mixture of good luck and cunning, he was able to work his way up to eventually becoming a chief clerk to the dey and he helped negotiate the release of himself and his fellow American

169

prisoners for the huge million-dollar settlement. After such an experience wild horses would not have been able to drag me back to this forsaken coast, but here he was acting as an agent for the American government in negotiating with the Barbary states.

Cathcart climbed aboard, looking a mixture of European and Arab (I suppose this helped him move freely in both worlds) and also very comfortable in the heat, especially compared to me in my thick woollen uniform. He wore a European shirt and waistcoat but baggy Arab pantaloons and Arab slippers. Cochrane welcomed the stranger aboard and we retired to the shade of the tiny main cabin. Cochrane apologised for the small confines of the room but Cathcart just laughed. "Why, sir, this cabin is a palace compared to many of the places I have stayed in." He then went on to talk about some of his extraordinary captivity in Algiers. After some weeks of rough usage by his captors he had been purchased in the slave market by the dey for use in the palace gardens. There he had looked after wild animals such as lions and leopards, and while he had been half-starved, he was not as badly beaten as many of the other slaves in Algiers. He described how, while hungry, they had to tend the dey's fruit trees and vines, but if they were caught eating the fruit, they received a severe beating on the soles of their feet called a bastonading. With so many nerve endings on the sole, the pain was intense and could leave a man crippled. Cathcart spoke from experience of the pain as he had been bastonaded several times and once lost several toenails in the punishment.

Cochrane asked, "Is it true your government paid a million dollars for the release of the American prisoners?"

"Aye, I had to help with the negotiations and the dey's opening demand was two and a half million dollars plus two fully equipped frigates. The talks took years, and by then we had lost a good number to plague and other diseases."

"Is there still plague in Algiers?" I asked. This was a question that had worried us all about our destination as we knew it had been rife six months ago.

"Oh, it comes and goes, but it is not so bad at the minute. So you need an interview with the dey?"

We explained our mission and Cathcart listened quietly and then explained the political situation in Algiers. "The old dey I served is now dead. A man called Mustapha Ali was voted to be the new dey, but he preferred to be the hasnagi or prime minister. The old hasnagi was promoted to be dey, but the real power is with Mustapha Ali, who is at the moment friendly to us. He is a good man and is not as corrupt as the other officials. That does not mean that he will release the British sailors; they were taken in retaliation for the capture of an Algerian vessel. The best that you can hope for is an exchange of prisoners in due course. But in the meantime your visit will show that they have not been forgotten and it might get them better treatment."

This was good news, but Cathcart went on. "The new dey will not take kindly to warnings about piracy. The Algerians have been living on piracy and kidnapping for generations; it is their way of life. He relies on pirates for his support and cannot afford to do anything to stop them. You must treat him with respect; if he feels insulted in front of the court he will have no choice but to retaliate to save face. I can speak to Mustapha Ali and help to arrange an interview with the dey if you want my help."

"Your help would be much appreciated," said Cochrane. "I am grateful given you have cause to hold ill will toward Britain as a result of your past associations with us."

Cathcart laughed. "I have spent nearly half my life in captivity. But for the years I was in the stinking British prison hulk, I was at least treated like a man and an honourable prisoner of war. Here I was treated like an animal. Of the twenty-one men I was captured with, nine died of disease, including one who went mad. I will do whatever I can to help those poor wretches, whatever their nationality."

Cathcart departed and we hoped to get an interview the next day, but instead every day we got a message saying that the dey was unable to see us but would hopefully see us the

171

next day. We rigged a sail over the mizzen yard to provide shade over the quarterdeck, but there was little breeze and it was baking hot as we sat around waiting on the dey's pleasure. Several of the crew bought powerful arrack spirit from the hawking boats and when Cochrane found two of them drunk to insensibility it was the only time I saw him threaten a flogging. The heat and the pressure of the waiting were getting to him.

After six days Cathcart finally wrote to confirm that the interview would be that afternoon. His note said that he would come and escort us and warned us not to go ashore without him.

Just after midday Cathcart appeared again, this time in a larger and more impressive launch and accompanied by a liveried servant of the dey. Cochrane and I were ready and waiting, already sweating profusely in our full uniforms. As we climbed up the steps of the dock from the boat a large crowd awaited us, and while we could not understand them, it was clear that they were hostile. They started shouting, waving sticks, and some stones were even thrown, but the dey's guards were on hand and laid into them with whips to push them back. The guards closed around us and we were marched off through the streets.

"They are taking us past the prison of the galley slaves," warned Cathcart quietly. "They are trying to intimidate you. Do not show pity to the prisoners or they will beat them harshly to demonstrate their power over them."

We could smell the prison before we saw it; the stench was appalling but the reason only became clear as we rounded the corner. It was a big, stone, two-storey building with what looked like some better rooms on the first floor. But at ground level there were some dark and dingy taverns for guards along one side and then some long, barred rooms that were full of prisoners looking painfully thin and dressed in rags. As soon as they saw us a pitiful wailing began with shouts for help in English, French and Spanish and a lot of other languages I did not understand. I glanced at them but, mindful of Cathcart's warning, I tried to show no emotion and kept my eyes ahead. As we walked around the corner of the prison building we saw that it also accommodated a row of cages that contained more of the dey's menagerie: I counted four lions and two tigers lying asleep. They were lying on more straw than the prisoners enjoyed and had lumps of meat in some of the cages. I saw twenty or thirty rats feeding on the meat and running between the cages and the prisoner's barracks, which were separated from the creatures by more iron bars. The combination of smells from human and animal dung left in the heat with rotting meat and all the flies and rats was enough to make you gag, and both Cochrane and I pulled handkerchiefs from our pockets to cover our mouths and noses.

Before we could move on we were held back by our guards as a group of prisoners were driven across the street in front of us. Most had the lost look of the blond giant I had seen a few days ago, but one man, seeing our uniforms, called out in English, "I am Pierre Auclair. I was in the French legation here. I beg you, for pity's sake, to get word that I am here to the French..."

He was interrupted by the swinging sticks of the guards, who sent his fellows cringing into a corner of the yard, but Auclair was knocked down and dragged into the centre of the yard.

"I fear you are about to witness a bastinarding," said Cathcart quietly. "Don't interfere or you will just make things worse."

A stout eight-foot pole was brought into the yard by one of the guards and I could see that there were two ropes attached to its middle. As soon as he saw it, Auclair began raving in French, but the guards grabbed his feet and began tying his ankles tightly to the pole so that it rested above his insteps. Then two of the guards took the ends of the pole and hauled it up to chest height, leaving Auclair half upside down and with the soles of his feet pointing at the sky. Two more guards stepped forward now with canes and began to take turns in lashing the soles of Auclair's feet as hard as they could. The man was screaming in agony and I looked at

Cathcart, who was wincing as the blows landed as he must have remembered taking this punishment himself.

After a few moments Cathcart shouted angrily to one of our guards and reluctantly they began to push on past the group still punishing Auclair. I discovered later that a hundred lashes was a typical amount, but feet could be left bleeding and crippled lumps of flesh with as many as five hundred lashes.

As we walked past the building next to the prison, which turned out to be a hospital, one more horror awaited us. From one the ground floor windows an arm shot out between some bars and a woman's voice called out in Spanish, "I am Maria di Silva from Colares, Portugal. Please tell me you have come to rescue me. Kill me or rescue me, but please God, do not leave me alive here another day."

I was shocked and turned to Cathcart. "They have women prisoners here too?"

"Oh yes, far fewer than men, but when they capture women prisoners on ships they are held for ransom, or some are sold as wives or concubines. They are not worked as slave labour, but as you can imagine they are used in other ways."

I looked at the poor creature in the window. I could just make out a shadowed face and dark hair in the gloom, but then one of the guards lashed his whip at the window and the woman screamed and the arm disappeared.

"Could we get her out?" I asked.

"If she is pretty then her price will be tens of thousands of dollars. Do you have such an amount? You should focus your mind on getting yourself out, Mr Flashman," said Cathcart, which brought me up sharp to remembering the danger we were in.

After a few further minutes walking down those hellish streets, with beggars yelling entreaties and pirates shouting abuse through the cordon made by our guards, we eventually reached the gates of the citadel and the palace beyond. Suddenly we left the noise of the streets behind and found ourselves in a pleasant courtyard offering peace and

174

tranquillity with a crystal-clear fountain in its centre. We were not allowed to rest there, though, but led through a door guarded by two huge guards with polished axes over their shoulders into a large, cool anteroom. It was beautifully decorated with tiled mosaic patterns over the walls and a high, domed ceiling. In the middle of the room were low stools and a table and Cathcart gestured for us to sit while a servant came forward with cups of thick, sweet coffee. It was quite refreshing and when I finished my cup it was instantly refilled. Cathcart explained that the coffee pourer, called a caffeegie, would normally fill my cup three times and when I had finished I should leave some coins in the cup. The money would then be passed to the dey, who usually made a small addition and then divided it twice a year among the captives for their support. All visitors were expected to make donations according to their rank and the cups were of solid gold and inlaid with jewels to show off the wealth of the dey and encourage generosity. I reached into my purse and found I had three of the large gold coins left from the money Wickham had given me. Thinking of the poor wretches we had seen on the way here, I dropped all of them into my cup. The caffeegie smiled and took the tray away and we were left on our own.

Half an hour passed while Cathcart told us of palace life in his time here and then a chamberlain came for us and led us down a gallery lined with more guards armed with either polished axes or huge scimitars, both types of weapon seeming to be the size used by an executioner rather than a soldier. Each of the men eyed us with an insolent look as we passed and a few hefted their weapons as though they would relish the opportunity to test them on our necks. At the end of the gallery huge doors were thrown open and we entered the dey's audience chamber.

The room was half filled with courtiers in robes and turbans. Conversation stopped as we walked in, and as people turned to stare at us the looks we got were decidedly unfriendly. Two more guards came up alongside us and marched us towards a large, ornately dressed man sitting cross-legged on an elevated couch at the far end of the room. At three different points on the journey the guards growled something at us and Cathcart told us to *salaam* to the dey as he had shown us how to do previously.

The contrast between the dey and his courtiers was striking. The courtiers were mostly lean, hard-faced men with daggers and swords in their belts, and they glared at us as though they would cut our throats without a second thought. The dey, on the other hand, had his plump frame covered in rich silks and cloth of gold. When I got closer I could see that he was also wearing makeup with some rouge and black lines around his eyes. On the floor in front of his stool sat two young boys, naked but for some kind of gauzy pantaloons and with trays of sweetmeats and wine that they could pass up to their ruler. With disgust, I noticed that the boys were also wearing makeup, matching that of the dey.

We came to a halt before this *exquisite* like schoolboys before the headmaster. He said something in Arabic to an interpreter standing nearby, who barked rudely at us, "What do you want?"

Well, this was it, this was my moment to play the diplomat. I needed to impress him with the power of Britain but also not push too hard to avoid causing offence. I brought myself up to my full height and withdrew from my pocket the paper signed by Pitt confirming that I was a diplomatic courier. "I am a messenger from the prime minister of King George the third of Great Britain and Ireland," I said self-importantly. The translator loudly converted my words for the dey and the surrounding courtiers. "He has instructed me to…"

The translator interrupted at the prompting of the dey: "We hear your king has gone mad."

The courtiers who had heard the dey instruct the translator laughed. I did not want to get into a debate on my monarch's sanity and so I pressed on: "He has recovered and both my king and prime minister were perfectly sane when they asked me to very respectfully point out that the recent capture of a British vessel by Algerian ships was not entirely in accordance with the law." I paused to allow the translator to catch up but saw the dey's face darken as he heard the final words. I quickly hurried on: "I am sure that this must have been some misunderstanding or oversight…"

The dey was talking to his interpreter again while glaring at us. His voice rose to a shout and there was no mistaking his anger or that of his courtiers, who were also starting to raise their voices at us.

The interpreter was speaking again: "The dey says how dare you speak to him of the law when your country has taken an Algerian ship also illegally." The dey was still talking and the translator hurried on: "He says that he should put you and your crew in the darkest prison until our vessel is freed and returned with our crewmen."

Several of the courtiers were cheering this suggestion and one was even waving a fist at us. I looked around the room and saw only hostile faces in the crowd. The guards, with those massive axes and swords, were starting to move forward in anticipation of being required. I looked round at Cathcart, seeking help, but he just mouthed "Keep calm" at me and glanced at someone over my shoulder.

Suddenly the noise fell away as a man stepped forward from the side of the room. He was an urbane-looking man with a closely cropped beard and simple but elegant robes. He moved with a sense of quiet confidence and power, and from the way that those around us, even the dey, fell silent, I guessed that this was Mustapha Ali, the prime minister. He surprised me by speaking English with the translator now working for the benefit of the dey and the audience.

"We would put you into our prisons as His Highness says but for the fact that we respect the British government. I am sure the capture of our vessel was also a misunderstanding or oversight and that it will be released. Is that not correct, Ambassador Flashman?"

I nodded eagerly. "Absolutely, we just need to sort out the confusion and return both ships and crews to their rightful owners."

The prime minister paused and looked at Cochrane and I with a smile of mild amusement playing across his face.

"I find it curious that you, Captain Cochrane, were chosen to help reprimand any nation for an act of piracy." He walked to the audience and touched a man on the shoulder. "This man, Hassan, is one of our best captains and he has taken four ships in the last year, and this man next to him has taken just one, but a large Portuguese merchant ship. Tell me, Captain Cochrane, how many ships have you captured with your little ship in the harbour?"

Cochrane paused, not sure if telling the truth would save or condemn us, but like me he suspected that this wily newcomer already had a good idea of the answer and so he answered honestly. "I think it is around forty-five ships." There were gasps of amazement when this number was translated.

"And tell me, Captain, were any of these ships from the port of Algiers?"

"No, they were all French or Spanish boats." Again there was a murmur from the audience, who were beginning to realise that there was a master of their art in their midst.

The prime minister smiled again and continued: "And your most recent capture, Captain, I believe it was the Spanish Xebec-class frigate, the *Gamo*, of thirty-two guns, which you also captured with that little brig in the bay, is that correct?" The prime minister seemed remarkably well informed and again there seemed little point in denying it.

"Aye, that is so, with fifty men against a crew of three hundred and twenty." Cochrane could not help crowing about the achievement and it gave the opportunity to warn about the fighting skills of his men. "I have a full crew of one hundred at the moment," he added. Again the translation caused murmurs of astonishment from the audience.

"Quite so, Captain. Do you wonder why I know so much about your prize?" As we did not reply, he continued: "It is because your admiral's office has just sold it to us."

Well, I have been bandy smacked with astonishment quite a few times in my life, but to discover that the people

178

who had sent us to remonstrate with a pirate kingdom had at the same time sold them a new warship to help in their piratical endeavours was literally unbelievable. But the prime minister has more shocks in store yet.

Cochrane was also clearly struggling to comprehend the situation. "Let me be sure I understand you, sir. You are telling me that while I have been sent here to discuss, er, recent events, my superiors have sold you a Spanish frigate as a prize?" His voice was tightening in anger and I could tell that he was on the verge of exploding with rage.

The prime minister now looked almost apologetic. "That is the case. Your admiral's office also warned us in advance that you would be visiting with unwelcome news and even made a point of hinting that you would not be greatly missed. They then sold us the *Gamo* for just five hundred pounds as though they were expecting some sort of favour in return."

"Five hundred pounds!" whispered Cochrane in disbelief. He had been hoping to get a prize value of twenty times that amount.

"They wanted you to hold us as hostages... or kill us?" says I, getting to the more pertinent point. My God, I knew Cochrane was unpopular but this was ridiculous. "It must have been Mansfield," I muttered to Cochrane.

He was reaching the same conclusion, for he suddenly exploded. "That spavined, spineless, cocksucking, treacherous bastard. Gives my prize away and then plots to get me killed. I'll rip his balls off with my bare hands, I'll tear the lying tongue out of his head, I'll... I'll kill the little fucker." There are few men more eloquent than a cheated Scotsman.

The prime minister waved away the guards who had rushed forward, not understanding the tirade and thinking that he was threatening the prime minister or the dey. He smiled again as he continued: "With such a prospect in mind, Captain, you will be pleased to hear that we do not intend to fulfil their expectations of us and have you kidnapped or

179

murdered. I received word this morning that the *Gamo* is on her way. I wanted to have this reassurance before we met."

My mind was spinning. I had been so angry at Mansfield that it had not occurred to me that we would be kidnapped or murdered after the prime minister had divulged the plot. While Cochrane had raged, a cold fury had built up in me. How dare some bloody clerk play games with our lives like this? Who did he think he was, and more importantly how could we pay him back? Revenge is a dish best served cold and I was racking my brains for a solution.

"A letter of thanks."

They turned to look at me in puzzlement and I realised that I had said it out loud. "Can I suggest, sir," I said, "that you send a letter of thanks to our admiral? I would, however, respectfully recommend that it would be best sent directly to Admiral Keith in the Bay of Aboukir, off the coast of Egypt, where he is with his fleet. It would be particularly helpful to spell out how exceptionally generous he has been in forgoing virtually all of his share of prize money, and please do also thank him for his warning of our arrival."

The prime minister laughed. "I can see how this would pay back your, er, 'spavined friend', but how would it benefit me?"

"If you inform his lordship that his generosity has prompted you to agree to an exchange of the Algerian ship and crew for the British ship and crew then he will take you up on it to get some face-saving benefit from his unintended largesse." I was not sure of the value of the Algerian crew and ship compared to ours, but surely with a frigate thrown into the balance the prime minister would find the proposal acceptable.

"You are indeed a diplomat, Ambassador Flashman. I will consider your proposal. And now your mission is complete, I suggest that you return to your ship and take your leave."

We *salaam*ed our way out of the room and gave our thanks to Cathcart, who was staying in the palace to conduct other business. As we had left the court on friendly terms, the guards with their huge axes and swords walked respectfully behind us rather than around us as before. A fat, gaudily dressed court chamberlain led the way, and with him in front and the palace guards bringing up the rear, the crowds kept well back when we emerged onto the streets. We returned the way we had come, and as we approached the hospital I looked up at the window but the woman was not to be seen. But rounding the corner we found Pierre Auclair lying curled up in the dust, whimpering in agony. Two of the guards who had punished him sat nearby in the shade.

Cochrane and I had not spoken since we had left the palace. We were both boiling in anger but did not want to talk in front of the chamberlain, who may have been able to speak English and report back to his masters. I don't know about Cochrane, but I had felt defeated and betrayed during the encounter with the prime minister and now my temper was up and I was looking for a target. Before I knew what I was doing, I snarled at the guards in the shade, "Pick him up and bring him with us." The guards, seeing the palace chamberlain and the palace guards standing behind us, assumed we had the authority of the court and moved to obey, one of them swinging Auclair up over his shoulder.

The fat chamberlain's hands fluttered in front of him. "You no permit for this," he shrilled.

Cochrane reached down and started to draw his sword a few inches. "Yew'll do exactly as he says or I will chop off your balls if ye still have them." He spoke quietly but with unmistakable aggression.

One of the palace guards, sensing trouble even though he spoke no English, now stepped forward, moving his huge executioner's sword down from his shoulder and standing between Cochrane and the chamberlain. It was a standoff and everyone looked to the chamberlain to make the next move. Only now was my brain catching up with my anger as I realised what I had started and what the risks were in this town where European life was held so cheap.

The chamberlain glanced from the broken prisoner to the foreign 'ambassador' and naval captain and then to the guard, now glowering over us with his rock-steady sword. Finally the chamberlain made up his mind and, muttering something to the guard with Auclair over his shoulder, he turned and continued down the street. We hesitated and the guard carrying Auclair moved to follow him. Our sword-wielding guard stepped back and our slightly elongated procession now proceeded down to the docks.

"Flashman," muttered Cochrane, "the next time you feel like picking up some waif, try to do it when some big, hairy bastard with a huge bloody sword is not standing behind me." He grinned at me and continued: "Still, it is good to get something out of this trip, even if it is a moth-eaten frog."

Chapter 16

Our boat crew were resting at their oars in the anchorage, just out of range of any stones thrown by the mob on the harbour front. This crowd dispersed when we appeared with our palace guards and the boat was rowed quickly back to the steps to collect us. Auclair was laid in the bottom of the boat and as he realised that he was leaving with us he started sobbing in relief. As soon as we were back on the *Speedy* we weighed anchor and caught the end of the ebbing tide to get out of the bay. We wanted to be away and out of range of the harbour guns before news of our extra passenger reached the palace. The fortresses stayed silent as we slipped away and we all felt a surge of relief as we got out into the open sea. None more so than Auclair, who had been left behind when the rest of the French legation was freed earlier in the year. Guthrie tied some boards around his feet to act as splints and bandaged them carefully so that they would heal straight and undamaged.

That evening, as the sun set in the west, a sail appeared on the horizon to the south. It looked like the Algerians had sent a ship after us. But it was only a small vessel that was no threat and so we shortened sail to allow it to catch up. The next morning the wind slowly lightened until we seemed to be moving no faster than a slug on sand. The Algerian had come to a halt too, half a mile away, and had lowered a boat to reach us. With nothing else to do, we lowered a boat and met them halfway. They had a message from the prime minister, who wrote to say that he would send a letter of thanks to Admiral Keith along the lines we proposed. He suggested that it might be best if we took our time to get back to Port Mahon to allow events to take their course.

This suited us: we were in no hurry to get back either. In fact, over dinner that night Cochrane revealed that he was planning to leave the Navy entirely. "What is the point of staying in?" he exclaimed. "I could capture an admiral's flagship in a laundry woman's bumboat and they still would not give me any recognition. Aye, they would probably try to get me killed that much harder. There is talk of peace coming and as soon as it is signed I am giving up the Navy. I have a mind to go into the House of Commons and root out this corruption at its heart."

"Are you sure you have the temperament to be a politician?" asked Archie tactfully with a grin tempting the corners of his mouth.

"Ye mean am I a windsucking fatwit that spends his time seeking enrichment at the expense of the public purse? Of course not. I am going to stand as a radical and pledge to remove all vice from government, and the Navy and dockyards in particular."

"But you will never get elected," I said. "You need the patronage of someone who owns a seat or a lot of money to buy one of the rotten boroughs. No one in power will help you get a seat as they all have an interest in maintaining the status quo."

"Stop your worry. I have a plan." Cochrane grinned. "So my disadvantage is that I have no money and the voters in the rotten boroughs are corrupt and greedy and will vote for whoever pays them the most, is that correct?"

"Yes," we chorused, wondering how he would turn this into an advantage.

"Well, I am going to stand in a rotten borough on an anti-corruption platform and offer voters nothing at all."

"Then you will get barely any votes at all," I said, puzzled as to why he thought this would work.

"Ah, but after the election I will go round the few voters who did vote for me and give them double what they would have got voting for the winner. Then I will sit back and wait for the next election."

"Sorry, I still don't get it," said Archie.

"At the next election the voters will remember that I paid double to my voters. They will need to weigh up the certainty of an amount from those offering cash to the potential of double from me. As they are greedy, I reckon I will get enough votes to be elected."

184

Well, I doubted it at the time, but that is exactly what he did a few years later. He turned the voters of Honiton, one of the most notorious rotten boroughs, into a laughing stock when they voted him in on the second election. Of course his political career was a disaster as he made enemies faster than a clean dog gathers fleas and he ended up being framed for a stock market fraud and disgraced, but that is for another time.

I will spare you the detail of that cruise, as it followed the same pattern of many of the earlier ones. We intercepted a British ship headed for Port Mahon and sent via that vessel a very brief report on our mission to Algiers, not mentioning the letter going to the admiral. We then sailed along the Spanish coast, getting close inshore at night and trying to cut out prizes in the dawn. We fell in with another naval brig, the *Kangaroo*, under a captain called Pulling who seemed a decent sort, and soon between us we had a fair armada of prizes. We had no wish to have men guarding prisoners and so captured crews were allowed to row for shore in the boats and in one of these boats we put in Auclair, who continued to profess gratitude for his rescue. Eventually, running low on ammunition and supplies and with our crew spread thinly over the various prizes, we could delay no longer and turned back to Port Mahon.

There were a number of naval ships in the harbour but no sign of the admiral's flagship. The *Speedy*, *Kangaroo* and their flotilla of prizes were anchored in the roads. As the anchors splashed into the water, boats were launched from the vessels to take crew members ashore. Cochrane and I were among the first to land and we walked the short distance to the naval headquarters. We strode into Mansfield's office, deliberately not knocking first, to find he was not there. Instead there was a timid-looking man who looked nervously at us from behind the desk.

"Who are you?" asked Cochrane brusquely.

"If it please your lordship..." The man tugged nervously at his forelock. "I am Benton, the new admiral's clerk."

185

"What happened to Mansfield?" I asked, hoping he had not escaped his just desserts.

"The admiral had a letter, sir, from some foreign gentleman, sir. 'E was mighty upset about it, sir, and 'e sent me aboard a frigate here, sir. The frigate was ordered to take Mr Mansfield and bring him to the admiral, sir." The man paused and then whispered in a scandalised tone, "They was to bring him in irons, sir."

"Excellent," I said happily.

Cochrane asked sternly, "I trust you have orders to sell any more prizes we bring in at the proper price rather than give them away to foreign potentates?"

"Oh aye, sir, the admiral was most insistent that he wants all decisions re. the sale of prizes referred to him. He's written to Captain Manley Dixon the same, sir."

We picked up our mail and went away well pleased. For all the Church's talk of piety and turning the other cheek, there are few things more satisfying than seeing someone who has crossed you getting paid back in full. Especially when it is some jumped-up little clerk who has done his best to get you beheaded or thrown in some stinking foreign jail. I only had one letter and I recognised the hand as my father's, so I put it in my pocket to read later as I saw that Cochrane had a more impressive letter with the Admiralty in London's seal on it. I will save you the stream of profanities that erupted from my friend as he read it.

"I am being turned down for promotion after I captured the *Gamo*. Can you guess why, Flashman?"

"Did you pass the port the wrong way at the celebration dinner afterwards or serve the wrong cheese?" I was resigned to any madness from the Navy now, but the real reason was still a surprise.

"No, I have been turned down because the number of my own men killed in the action was insufficient to support the application. Lord St Vincent has turned down Parker for promotion too. This from a man who earned his earldom in an action where Nelson took all the risk and casualties and only one man was killed on Vincent's flagship during the battle. Dammit, I am going to write back and remind him of that fact and assure him that I will do better killing my own men next time."

"You can't do that. You will never get any favour from him again."

"Pah, what is the difference from now when they try to get me killed or imprisoned? Perhaps I will give the miserable old bastard apoplexy and he will die and be replaced by someone with more sense."

The irony was that both St Vincent and Cochrane were similar characters. They were both proper seamen, both wanted to fight corruption in the Navy and both were as stubborn as a menopausal mule. Thus having got off on the wrong foot, they could never recognise any credit in the other. St Vincent had joined the Navy at fifteen as an able seaman, although the family had money to help him in his early career and he finished as admiral of the fleet. He was a harsh disciplinarian, but he did implement some reforms before he was brought down by the same people with vested interests in corruption that would later end Cochrane's political career in disgrace.

We consoled ourselves with wine that night and had a splendid dinner with Archie and Guthrie, during which I told them that I had decided to return home on the next mail boat. This time no one tried to talk me into staying in the Navy. There was a sense among us all that the happy days of cruising and effortless prize taking were coming to an end.

I thought back. I had been with the *Speedy* for over six months, but I felt I had truly grown in that time. Cochrane's extraordinary confidence in his own abilities enabled him to have great confidence in those around him, and we all strived unconsciously not to let him down. That, I think, was his secret: he brought out the best in those around him. I had changed greatly from the nervous young man who had joined his ship. We had escaped from two powerful frigates and captured a third. I had helped capture around twenty different prizes over that time, I had shot a spy, been captured in espionage then rescued, withstood threats of torture and a siege, and faced up to a foreign pirate king. The man who somehow found the courage to climb on the *Gamo* and haul down its colour and to bluff guards into handing over a wounded prisoner was very different to the boy who had been frightened in Vauxhall Gardens.

This is not to say that I had been transformed to Flashman the Brave: most of those acts had also involved preserving my own precious skin. They were also largely against the Spanish, who were the least effective enemy I have ever known, and I have known a few. Fighting is hard work, and Spanish men are the laziest I have encountered. They can get fired up into a passion but invariably they will take a nap before doing anything about it and then put off any action until the next day. I have stood with Wellington and a whole British Army in the Peninsular waiting for the Spanish to get out of bed and join an attack that was supposed to have happened at dawn. They arrived at noon, long after the French had made their escape.

To be fair, the Spanish women were different. When I served with the Army in Spain later in my career, only six wives per company were allowed to accompany the troops from England and be officially on the strength. The rest were left at home with no means of support, and so lotteries were held to decide who could come. A full-strength company was around eighty men, and so many soldiers found Spanish women during the years they served on the Peninsular. These Spanish wives were tough, often living with the Army out in the open. They had to submit to Army discipline and perform washing, cooking and other duties, and many gave birth and raised children as they followed their men around the country.

I remember one tight spot when we were defending a village against an attack from French dragoons. The women with us were busy reloading muskets from the dead and passing them up to the survivors on the ramparts. Some young girl, who had found herself a widow just hours before, was loading for me in the room below and passing the weapons up to where I lay on the roof. Part way through the action I heard a scream and looked down to see the green-jacketed body of a dragoon impaled on the bayonet of a musket she was holding.

One of the most shameful things I saw was when the British Army disembarked from Bordeaux at the end of the Peninsular campaign. They only took six wives per company back to England, leaving all the others with their children on the dockside, again with no means of support. Provosts drove weeping men onto the ships and weeping women and children off the docks. Some men had already risked hanging by deserting to be with their Spanish wives, and some found the money to come back to them. But others, such as those with wives in England, never saw these families again.

~~~~~~~

Chapter 17

If I thought that my decision to leave the *Speedy* would
result in a safer life then I was wrong: fate showed that it had
more tricks in store. Bizarrely the first of these related to a
house move by Cochrane's immediate commander, the dour
and resentful Captain Manley Dixon. He had been given a
reprimand by Keith for the Algiers affair and had no love for
us. He had recently been offered the use of a large villa on
the island by a merchant who had also acquired the lucrative
rights to run the mail packet ship to Gibraltar. The only
slight drawback for this merchant was that he did not own a
ship. To maximise his profits he hired the cheapest boat he
could find, one that had been condemned by its previous
owner. I discovered this when I stepped aboard it some days
later to start my journey home. It is true that rats do leave a
sinking ship. I saw several swimming in the water as I went
aboard and I would not criticise their judgement. Part of the
handrail came off when I hauled myself onto the deck. There
was a strong smell of rot and decay about the ship, which
had a marked list to starboard. Four seamen seemed to be
continually working the pumps and the jet of water going
overboard showed no sign of diminishing. This was all while
it was in a calm and protected bay; what it would be like in a
rough sea did not bear thinking about.

The thought of sailing to Gibraltar in this old bucket did
not fill me with joy, and I was just contemplating seeing if
Cochrane would be able to get me to Gibraltar instead when
I saw him being rowed to the mail boat. The *Speedy* had just
been relegated to mail boat escort ship by Manley Dixon,
doubtless in return for a discount in his rent. Cochrane was
ordered to take the mail from the mail boat in case it sank on
the journey and return it just outside Gibraltar so that the
merchant could claim the generous payment for the mail
concession. Cochrane was, of course, livid at this further
insult, but I struggled to share his rage as I hurriedly grabbed
my things and returned to the seaworthy *Speedy*.

Weighing anchor, we set sail to travel down the Spanish coast to reach Gibraltar. It was a longer route but it gave more chance of further prizes. Cochrane admitted that he hoped the longer voyage would give the mail boat more time to sink, depriving the merchant of his fee, but it doggedly wallowed in our wake.

Early one evening, just past Alicante, we spotted a small fleet of merchant ships anchored in a bay and turned towards them. As soon as they saw the predatory *Speedy* heading in their direction, the crews ran their vessels aground on the soft sand to avoid capture. We were under orders to escort the mail without delay and had already stretched them with the longer route; although we could argue that keeping close to the coast was a precaution to help the mail boat should she start to founder. But with the ships beached we would have to wait hours for the tide to turn to float them off and then send a landing party onto a hostile coast at night to carry them away. It would be a clear breach of our orders, but Cochrane could not leave the enemy targets untouched.

Leaving the mail boat waiting nervously offshore, we sailed into the bay and anchored opposite the beached ships so that we could bring our guns to bear. It was now close to dusk, with the sun setting on the hills behind the ships, and we could see lanterns as the crew hurriedly removed possessions from the little ships and then ran up the dunes for shelter.

If you want to learn how to fire cannon then a helpless and static target is a great way to start. So, taking the opportunity, I joined one of the gun crews and we started a pleasant evening of target practice. I have since fired thirty-two pounders and other big guns and they are exhausting beasts to load and lay to a target. The little four-pounders on the *Speedy* may have lacked weight of shell but they were easier to aim and accurate at that range. With Cochrane and Archie spotting the fall of shot and calling corrections to aim, we blazed away.

It was just getting hard to see the ships in the growing darkness when a fire broke out on one of them which illuminated our targets. The fire burned steadily for a while on just one ship when suddenly there was an explosion and a huge billow of flames which quickly spread to the other ships. One of the vessels had been carrying oil and now the ships burned like massive lamps with a light that would be visible across many miles in the darkness. We ceased fire – our work was done – and weighed anchor. The light from the fires made it easy to see our way out of the bay in the darkness and even helped us find the mail boat when we were in open water, ready to continue our journey down the coast.

We had been able to see the glow from the flames for most of the night and had been well pleased with our work. But as the first light from the dawn spread across the sky from the east we saw that we had not been the only ones watching the glow. There in the east three large sets of masts could be seen heading in our direction.

Trouble comes in various guises but rarely has it been more catastrophically misidentified. In his defence, the light was poor, but Cochrane's confident assertion that these were "Spanish galleons from South America" seemed more hope than probability to me, as surely these would have put in at Cadiz or another Atlantic port. If a treasure ship had tried to sail through the straits then every available ship from the Barbary Coast and Gibraltar would have been on it like hounds on a stag. Both Archie and I expressed doubts, but with his usual monumental confidence Cochrane assured us that he was right. With what turned out to be suicidal stupidity, we therefore turned towards the three mystery ships.

As the light slowly spread across the sky, all eyes were turned to the three sets of sails as they gradually grew over the horizon. Looking back at the coast, I saw a plume of black smoke now climbed into the sky over the bay with the beached ships, and clearly the newcomers were coming to investigate the source of the fire. Head on is the hardest angle at which to identify a ship, or cluster of sails above the horizon, as these were when we first saw them. Even when the black lumps of the hulls came into view there was still uncertainty over what they could be. Only Cochrane was still confident that they could be Spanish ships from the Americas, and he joked that to keep St Vincent happy he would have to kill nearly all the *Speedy*'s crew in capturing them to justify promotions for the survivors. It was a prophetic prediction.

With the sun rising behind them in the east we were able to see the three ships long before they could see us in the darker western sky. But as the sun climbed higher they eventually spotted the *Speedy* and the mail boat in our wake, and spread out to make sure we did not escape. The shapes of two of them lengthened to go either side of us while one came straight on. From the side views we saw that they had three long, cream stripes down their sides. They were battleships, ships of the line.

Before we could begin to entertain hopes that they might be friendly, a French battle flag broke from the stern of the leading ship. I looked across at Cochrane and he stared, aghast, at the ships for a few seconds. They were well spaced out and, on their new courses, would trap us against the land with no room for escape. The single broadside from any one of them would be able to smash us to smithereens.

That moment was one of the few occasions when I think I have seen Cochrane genuinely scared, but within a moment he was back to being himself, calculating angles and options to get us out of the trap we had sailed into. The French were upwind of us but the winds were light; our only hope was to outrun them. Orders were shouted, and we changed course away from French. Within moments the crew were racing about the rigging to get every stitch of canvas she could carry stretched to catch every gust of wind we could. Other crew were unlimbering the massive oars called sweeps that could be used to move the ship when there was light wind or none at all. We had four sweeps on each side, each manned by four men who strained to give the ship extra purchase in the calm sea.

Despite our efforts, the French ships started to gain on us. Their masts were three times higher than ours and caught more wind.

"We need to lighten the ship to go faster," shouted Cochrane. "Throw the guns overboard."

"But we will be defenceless," said Archie.

"We are defenceless now against the guns they have on those ships; our four-pounders will not scratch them but their weight is slowing us down. Throw them overboard, and anything else heavy we can get rid of. If we don't, it will all be on the sea bed and us with it in an hour."

That got the men moving. Within seconds a stretch of bulwark had been removed and the little cannons were being unlashed and run through this new gap in the rail. More items followed: the heavy iron stove, the bricks we had cooked with on deck, all the cannon balls and powder, all but a handful of the fresh-water barrels. These were followed by spare anchors and chains and boxes of biscuit and furniture, spare spars, rigging and everything not required to just sail the ship as fast as possible right now. By reducing the weight of the ship we would ride higher in the water and this would give us less drag in the sea and more speed. But it was a desperate effort as we would only raise the ship a few inches. I looked over the stern rail. We were leaving a trail of floating boxes, furniture and stores, but they were moving astern at a painfully slow pace.

The crew were still scouring the ship for things to throw overboard. They had even formed a chain to remove some of the ballast stones from the keel of the ship. This would make the boat lighter but more unstable. The only things that were stopped from going over the side were the last cases of the excellent wine that we had captured off the African coast months before.

"Wait!" cried Cochrane, seeing them being carried out of the hatch. "We might as well be fortified for the battle ahead. Give a bottle to each of the crew." Then, seeing the first of the sailors to get one about to knock the top off the bottle against the side of the ship, he called, "Belay that. Get

Barrett to open them properly. There is no need to drink broken glass. Treat that wine with respect."

Barrett, the cabin steward, appeared and was soon opening the bottles as fast as he could while muttering that to waste such wine on the crew was putting pearls before swine. Between swigs of wine the crew carried on at the sweeps and a steady stream of ballast stones splashed over the side. We had nearly one hundred crew aboard as we had taken no prizes on this trip and so the men were rotated regularly to stop them getting tired and slowing down. Looking over the side at the receding trail of debris in the water, we did seem to be moving slightly faster than before. But when I looked astern at the French ships spread out in our wake, they seemed to be gaining on us still, especially the one at the front, which was the furthest out to sea.

"There is a gap opening between their first and second ship," murmured Cochrane to me quietly. "If we wait until the front ship is level with us and then tack towards them, we might just get away. We will be upwind of the first ship then and it will struggle to get back."

The third ship was well astern, keeping close to the coast in case we tried to escape that way; it was the second or middle ship that worried me, as it was heading almost straight in our direction.

"What about that one?" I asked, pointing at it.

"We have to hope that their gunnery and seamanship are poor," said Cochrane grimly. He tried to brighten the mood by adding, "Their navy has been blockaded in port for months and so they can't have had much sea time recently."

I looked him in the eye. I was no seaman, but even I could see that the French ships were moving well and had spread out sensibly to trap us. They were well managed, and I did not doubt that their guns would be used handily as well.

Cochrane's shoulders sank slightly in resignation. "Well, it is the best chance we have, but I'll grant you, I would not wager a widow's pension on it."

I returned to the stern rail. Several times while sailing with Cochrane I had thought we were doomed, but he had always got us out of it. But each time he had always been confident, with plans up his sleeve. This was the first time that I had seen him genuinely lost for ideas in front of the enemy. The odds against us were enormous and many other captains would have struck their colours already, but the crew, including me, had come to expect Cochrane to have a plan for all occasions at sea. To see him bereft of cunning schemes was a shock, a bit like seeing your father being thrown from a horse, someone whom you thought was infallible showing that he was human like everyone else.

The crew sensed the change in mood too. As they finished throwing the ballast overboard there was little to do except watch the approaching French ships and Cochrane pacing futilely about the deck. One of them, a gunner called Jarvis, approached me holding his open bottle of wine. For a moment I thought he was going to offer me a draught of it, but then I saw that in his other hand he held a pen and ink and a piece of paper and that the bottle was empty.

"Beg pardin, sir," he said hesitantly, glancing across at Cochrane, who had stopped to listen. "I am sure your honours will do your best to get us out of this but, well… it does not look good. I was wonderin' if you would be so kind as to help me write a note for my Judy that I can put in this 'ere bottle and hope it finds a friendly shore if things go bad."

I glanced across at Cochrane. Some captains would have had the man flogged for such defeatist talk. He just smiled and nodded. Jarvis was around forty and had probably been at sea since before Cochrane was born. The old sailor knew long odds when he saw them and Cochrane, who valued their skills as seamen and gunners, knew that they could judge the situation as well as he.

"Certainly. What would you like to say?" I replied.

As all the cabin furniture had gone overboard there was no point going below and so we sat down on the deck to write. Jarvis had never written a letter as he could not write, and so he dictated to me what he wanted to say and I drafted the letter, which I read back to him. I can't remember the wording exactly after all this time, but it went something like this:

To my dearest Judy,

We are about to go into battle against three French battleships and so I am getting this letter written in case I do not return.

Use the prize money that you are going to receive to buy an inn. Buy one on a main road a good thirsty walk away from any other inn. Make sure it is out of range of the pressgangs so Tom and Mark are not taken for the Navy. Don't let them go for the Army either. I may be taken prisoner, so don't marry again unless you know I am dead.

The romantic fool was going to end his letter at this touching note, but I asked him a bit about his wife and then added the following.

You have been a good mother to our boys and I know you will bring them up strong and true. I am proud of them and of you as my wife these many years and I want you to know that I love you dearly. I will be thinking of you all in the hours ahead and I trust that God will somehow find a way for me to hold you all in my arms again.

He had been embarrassed to say such things himself for an officer to write, despite the dire circumstances. But this obviously hit the mark, as when I read it to him he welled up, murmured his thanks and went away with his letter, cuffing the tears from his eyes. My reward for this good turn was a steady stream of seamen with bits of paper that they wanted to send to loved ones. This group included one sailor with two bottles, one for a girl in Port Mahon and one for a girl in Portsmouth.

In other circumstances I might have resented becoming a seaman's scribe, but in this case I was glad to do it. It took my mind off those approaching banks of guns. On days with light winds such as that one, I have seen brave men crack as they spend hours watching those wooden walls of death creep slowly towards them across the ocean. I suspect that many of the seamen wrote the letters for the same reason. They must have known that there was little chance of a letter

197

in a bottle in the Mediterranean finding its way to Portsmouth, Leith or London, and especially Kingston, Jamaica, as one optimistic top man was hoping. Planning and dictating the letters just gave them something to do.

I was brought back to our perilous situation when Cochrane gave the order to tack to the east and cross the French line. I got up from the deck and looked across the sea to find that the leading French ship was now level with us and about a mile away. The middle ship was still heading towards us. Cochrane hoped to cross the bows of that one and the stern of the leading ship and thus miss both of their broadsides, but they were bound to react to our move. This was proven a few moments later when the side of the leading ship disappeared behind a wall of smoke. A fraction of a second later we heard the boom of their broadside across the water and even the whistle of a few balls. But at that range we would have been unlucky to have been hit, and sure enough, water spouts from balls hitting the sea sprang up in a wide area around us.

As soon as they had fired, the first ship started to turn towards us so that we would have to pass their guns again. A few moments later the bow chasers of the second ship opened fire and then the front-facing guns on the first ship followed suit. From then on we were under constant fire, and without guns to fire back ourselves, we felt like ducks in a duck shoot. Some of the men went below for protection, but the big twenty-four-pound balls could smash through our sides if they hit us and create a storm of splinters in a confined space. Others, like me, preferred to stay on deck.

They say that you can see the arc of a cannon ball if it is fired directly at you and there was one moment when I thought I saw a black line flash across the sky. I ducked and a second later there was a water spout in the sea a hundred yards behind us. They were getting the range, though, and our first casualty was a top man who screamed as a ball parted a line in the rigging. He fell and hit the side rail with a sickening crunch and then bounced over the side like a rag doll. He floated in the sea face down and appeared to be dead. I suppose that all of the crew who looked at him must have wondered if his end had been quicker and more merciful than the one that awaited them.

Signal flags were flying between the French ships, and when they were both half a mile away they turned again to present their broadsides. There was nothing we could do to avoid the barrage and I was still debating in my mind whether it was better to crouch behind the wooden sides, which could splinter, or remain standing when I heard Archie murmuring an ironic version of the grace we said before each meal: "For what we are about to receive, Lord, we are…" His final words were drowned out by the roar of the broadsides and at that moment sixty iron balls weighing around twenty-four pounds apiece were screaming towards us from the two French ships.

Many of the balls would have missed, but this time more than enough found their targets. In a single second the deck was transformed into a maelstrom of hell. The planks beneath my feet bucked with the impact of iron into the ship. I heard screams below as balls smashed through our side. Above, more ropes were parted and blocks and other bits of rigging were crashing to the deck while a topsail yard was smashed in two with the sail torn and useless.

In the second it took me to realise that I was unhurt I also took in the carnage that had turned the deck into a charnel house. At least one ball had smashed through the rail and sent a shower of huge splinters into a group of men standing on the main deck. I moved to help but was then frozen in horror at the sight of one corpse lying tangled in the scuppers, evidently thrown across the ship by the impact of the ball that had taken off its head. I was about to move on when I recognised a tattoo on the man's arm. It was Eriksson, the huge Dane who had so terrified the Spanish on the *Gamo* and who had spent hours teaching me how to fight. I looked around and saw the great axe that he liked to have with him in battle. Only minutes before I had heard other seamen ribbing him over the fact that it would be useless in this battle, and they were right. Far from defending himself, Eriksson would never have even seen the thing that had killed him instantly. I was about to move on when I remembered something Eriksson had told me about warriors only entering the Viking heaven of Valhalla if they died with weapons in their hands. While he spoke as though it were legend, I always thought that the Dane secretly at least half believed in the old Norse gods. I picked up the axe and pressed his lifeless fingers around its shaft. It was the least I could do: his advice had already saved my life once and was to do so several more times in my life.

The screams of the wounded brought me back to the needs of those who could still be saved, and nearby was another seaman covered in blood but very much alive. I moved over to him. There was a wound in his chest but the more immediate need was a wound in his neck which he was trying to stem with his hand as blood spurted out of it. As he could not see his own neck he was making a poor job of it, but I could see where the blood was coming from and reached forward and blocked the gap with my finger. I looked round and shouted for Guthrie.

"I'll be with you in a minute," he replied.

The man I was helping was starting to shake with shock and he looked at me with wide eyes. The whites of his eyes looked stark against the blood and grime spattered across the rest of his face. It was only when he gasped "Thank you, sir" that I realised that the man was Jarvis, the first sailor for whom I had written a letter just an hour ago. He looked in a bad way and not for the last time in my life I struggled to find words of comfort.

"Hello, Jarvis, you just hang in there. You will be all right. Guthrie will be along in a minute to help. Here, hold my other hand."

"I'm dying, aren't I, sir?"

"You have taken some wounds, but you know what Guthrie is like – he is a top sawbones and he will be here in a minute. Don't give up, you hang on, think of…" Here I struggled to remember his wife's name amongst all the others I had written to. "Think of Judy and the boys, think of running that inn with them. Imagine all those travellers passing by, drovers with flocks to sell you meat, soldiers and sailors with stories to tell. What would you call the inn?"

"It will be a good house, sir," he said, his voice already faint. "You would be right welcome to come and visit."

At last Guthrie came over and knelt down on the other side of Jarvis. Gently he reached forward and with a sharp knife cut down the front of the seaman's shirt and pulled the sides back. I nearly retched: there was a huge splinter sticking out of his chest; it was a wonder he had survived this long.

"It is okay, Jarvis. Look at me now and it will soon be over." As he said this Guthrie reached across and removed my hand from Jarvis's neck and the blood once more began to pump from the wound. As his lifeblood spread across the deck I felt his grip on my hand slowly slacken. He murmured "Thank you, sir" but it was unclear to whom he was talking as he was staring between us and then, with a shuddering gasp, he died. Battles at sea can be strange things: one moment death and destruction and then moments of calm. For me it was quiet as Jarvis died; there were still cries and shouts from around the ship but I just remember putting his hand back on the deck and thinking of that bottle floating in the sea astern.

Guthrie had moved on to someone else and I realised that I needed to pull myself together. I stood up and looked about us. The two French ships had returned to their original courses, straight towards us to close the range further before they fired again. Surprisingly we were still showing a good turn of speed despite the damage to our rigging. Back on the quarterdeck Cochrane was calling commands. The gap we had been aiming for originally would now involve sailing between the broadsides of two French ships, which would be suicide, but we were maintaining our course. Their bow-chaser guns now crashed out again but did little damage.

With just a few hundred yards to go before we would have sailed down the broadside of the leading ship, Cochrane put the helm hard over and we sailed across their bows. The French tried to react and put the warship's helm over to match our move. There was a mighty roar from their guns, but the ship had turned quickly, too quickly for their gunners, and much of their next broadside seemed to boil the sea with splashes directly in front of us. Enough of the guns, though, did find their target, and these seemed to be firing chain shot which tore through our rigging. Yards and sails were torn to pieces, and while Cochrane again tried to change course to pass behind the front French ship, the *Speedy* was sluggish to respond.

The first French battleship was already frantically reloading and we were close enough to hear the shouts of their gunners from inside their hull. The second French ship would soon be in point-blank range with their broadside. We were wallowing in an area that would be covered by both ships and either one of them could destroy us completely. We had barely any sails left, no guns and we were facing three French men-of-war.

Cochrane had one final look round for some new tactic, but seeing no escape, he moved swiftly to the stern rail and cut the halyard holding our flag with his sword. He hauled in the flag himself while shouting at the helmsman to heave to and point her into the wind. "That's it, lads," he called as brought the yards of silk inboard. "There is no point going on. We would all be killed for no purpose. The French will treat us better than the Spanish." He looked distraught and his voice cracked slightly as he added, "I am proud of you all." With a tear welling in his eye, he disappeared to his cabin to gather up any papers, orders and the mail and throw them overboard in a weighted bag.

That was the end of the *Speedy*. One minute we were desperately trying to escape and the next we were a captured prize. Even though none of us had been able to see a way of escaping for the last few hours it was still a shock to find that we had been caught. I think all of us thought that somehow Cochrane would find a trick to see us clear as he had so many times before. While Guthrie and some of the others tended to the wounded, Archie and I just stood stunned at the realisation that it was over. We were now prisoners of war.

~~~~~~

Chapter 18

The lead French ship, which turned out to be called the *Dessaix*, sent a boat over full of marines to secure their prize and to return with the *Speedy*'s officers.

I took care to carry my diplomatic papers and packed my other possessions in a kit bag and then, casting a last glance around her tiny, blood-stained deck, we climbed down the side of the *Speedy* into the waiting long boat. Guthrie had been left behind to look after the wounded and so there was just Archie, Cochrane and myself. The younger midshipmen, or snotties as they were known, were also left on the *Speedy*.

I don't recall anyone speaking on that trip; there really was not anything to say and I think we were all lost in our own thoughts. We were to be prisoners of war until we were exchanged or the war ended. There had been talk of an imminent peace when we were last at Port Mahon and so we may not have a long captivity. Cochrane was doubtless thinking of the loss of his first command and the court martial that would automatically follow when he was released. I, on the other hand, was thinking of Jarvis and thanking my lucky stars that the splinter storm that had killed him had missed me. Suddenly I had a flashback of my father talking about the battle of Marburg. He was right: on land and sea, war can be a bloody random business.

Once aboard the French warship we were treated with respect. Cochrane formally surrendered his sword to the captain. He was a tall, thin Frenchman called Christie Palliere, who to recognise our brave resistance, refused it. We were required to give our parole, or promise that we would not interfere with the running of the ship or try to escape – not that there was much chance of that – and we were then given the freedom of the ship and some bunks in the officers' quarters. The sinking mail boat was also captured by the third French warship and a reluctant prize crew put aboard.

Palliere told us that he had been given special instructions to look out for the *Speedy* but was surprised that a ship so small had caused the Spanish so many problems. That first evening in captivity Cochrane calculated that during the thirteen months that he had been in command of the *Speedy* he had taken or retaken upwards of fifty vessels, captured one hundred and twenty-two guns and taken five hundred and thirty-four prisoners. Not bad considering its previous captain appeared unable to catch a cold, never mind a ship.

The British fleet had blockaded the French in their ports for many months and we had been told that their lack of sea time would make their ships less efficient as their sailors had less experience of being at sea. These ships had recently slipped past Gibraltar from their Atlantic ports, but to my novice eye they seemed very capably manned. Cochrane was also impressed: he pointed out that the French sails were cut differently to the British ones. They had a greater expanse of flat canvas exposed to the wind compared to the bellying sails of the British. He told me that this meant that the French could sail closer to the wind and faster. The French clearly had not been wasting their time in port but working on improving their ships.

After a short cruise down the Spanish coast lasting just two days we arrived in Algeciras, a port on the Spanish coast across a large bay from the British-held port of Gibraltar. We were marched off the ships towards the citadel that overlooked the bay. The Spanish were jubilant that the harassment of their coast by the *Speedy* had been brought to an end, and there was more than one clout from musket buts from our Spanish guards to speed the crew on its way. The crew were marched down into the dungeons while the officers and I were housed in a large room in one of the towers. While the French and Spanish were allies, we had all felt more comfortable being prisoners under the French tricolour than under the red and gold flag of Spain. The Spanish had many scores to settle with the *Speedy*. Palliere, the French captain, had assured Cochrane that he had given orders that we were to be viewed as prisoners of the French and that he would check on our welfare, but this would only last while he was in port, and that did not look like it would be too long.

The main British fleet in the region was the one under Admiral Saumarez, which had been blockading the Spanish fleet in Cadiz. The French had sailed around them to pass through the straits of Gibraltar and into the Mediterranean. The British Navy now had a dilemma: they could not afford to have a group of powerful French warships loose attacking shipping around their main port of Gibraltar, but if Saumarez moved to attack them he would release the Spanish fleet in Cadiz. The problem for the British was clear from our prison cell, which had a window that overlooked the bay. The port of Gibraltar was clearly visible just six miles away. The three French warships were powerful enough to capture any shipping they wanted. Gibraltar was effectively closed until the French were destroyed or driven away.

Cochrane, Archie and I spent our first night in captivity debating what the British would do. We did not have long to wait. The *Speedy* had been captured on the third of July 1801; we arrived in Algeciras on the fifth of July; the British attacked on the sixth.

Cochrane had been invited by Palliere to join him for breakfast on the *Dessaix* that morning, leaving Archie and I gnawing on stale bread in our cell and wondering what we were missing. Suddenly we heard trumpets sounding the alarm and men running and shouting around the fortress and so we rushed to the window to see what was happening. It is the only time I have ever watched a battle from prison, which meant that I could enjoy the spectacle without feeling any obligation to join in. The battle also promised our liberty, for if the British raided the port then we were bound to be freed either in an exchange of prisoners or from British sailors capturing the citadel. As the British fleet rounded the headland we were hopeful that we would be enjoying tea and muffins with Governor O'Hara that afternoon.

The British fleet comprising ten powerful warships was more than a match for the French,. Their aim was to capture the French ships and carry them back to Gibraltar as prizes. But Admiral Linois, in command of the French, was equally determined that his ships would not be carried across the bay if he could help it. Using boats and anchors and winches, the French started to haul their ships close inshore so that they could work together with the shore batteries and defend the anchorage. We watched the French hauling away from our window as the British fleet gathered for the attack. To our delight, the French managed to run all three of their ships aground with their sterns facing the enemy. They would have wanted to swing them around so that their broadsides could cover the attack, but could now only fire with their stern chasers. As they could not fight from the ships, the French admiral then sent boatloads of his gunners ashore to man the Spanish gun batteries.

With a westerly wind and strong currents in the bay, the British struggled to make their way into the anchorage, having to sail past it to the north and then sweep back down the coast. The first two British ships tried to anchor opposite the harbour and pound away at the French ships. The shore batteries, particularly those manned by the French, gave a strong return of fire and the British were forced to slip their cables. We watched in dismay as one by one the British ships fired into the anchorage before being dragged away by wind and current. Eventually one British ship, the *Hannibal*, turned to sail directly into the anchorage. It seemed determined to sail between the French ships and the shore to capture at least one of them, unaware that the French ships were aground.

The *Hannibal* went aground herself bow on to the broadsides of the French ships. The remaining French gunners, now that they had a target they could aim at, took up the challenge with gusto and blasted the *Hannibal* with everything they had. The shore batteries joined in and we watched with horror as the brave, if reckless, ship took terrible punishment while able to do little to defend herself. The rigging was shot away, the decks were covered in wreckage and broken spars, holes were blasted through the bulwarks and eventually, after more than a third of the crew were killed or wounded, the commander of the *Hannibal*, Captain Ferris, struck his colours.

The rest of the British fleet were by then out of sight, working their way back around the bay to get back to Gibraltar and consider their next steps. The *Hannibal* was stuck just a few hundred yards away from where Archie and I watched. We debated whether Ferris should have struck his colours sooner. I thought he should have, while Archie thought that if he had done more to lighten his ship then the tide could have got him off the sandbank to escape. The tea and muffins would have to be postponed now, but we were not too downhearted. The British would have to try again, and with more favourable winds they should succeed. As we watched and chatted, boats from both the shore battery and the French ships rowed across to the *Hannibal* and took command of the ship. What followed was one of the strangest incidents I ever saw.

As the *Hannibal* had been captured by both French and Spanish guns, the joint prize crew could not decide whose flag should fly over the prize. Someone, evidently not a seaman, decided to compromise and fly the British flag over the prize but fly it upside down.

"That's odd," said Archie when he saw it.

"They will probably spend days arguing over who captured it," I replied. "With luck we will have taken the ship back before they make up their mind."

"Yes, but an upside-down flag is an internationally recognised distress signal: it means that the ship is sinking and that they need help."

"But surely people will realise that in this case it just means the ship has been captured?"

"I am not so sure. If British shipwrights help save the ship then they get a share of the prize money. If enough of them come over then they may even try to recapture the ship under the noses of the Spanish if they can get her afloat again."

208

I was doubtful the flag could clearly be seen by telescope in Gibraltar, but half an hour later Archie called me to the window again. There across the bay were around twenty launches and cutters all pulling or sailing to Algeciras. It was amazing: just two hours ago the British fleet had been undertaking a full-scale attack, but now, when an international code for help was flown, the British were sending every shipwright, artificer and seaman they could find to help keep a ship afloat in an enemy port. To this day I am not sure if this was an outstanding humanitarian act in time of war or something driven by greed and opportunism; probably a bit of both.

Whatever it was, it gave the French and Spanish a dilemma. They could hardly open fire on men responding to a distress signal, but equally they could not allow them to recapture the ship. Eventually they decided to let the boat crews board the *Hannibal* one at a time but then capture the British as soon as they were on the deck. By the end of the day virtually every skilled shipwright from Gibraltar was a prisoner in Algeciras.

Cochrane gave us the details when he returned to us that evening looking like he had been in the wars himself. His shirt was stained crimson and when we first saw him we thought he had been wounded. He explained that when the British had started their attack he had been having breakfast in the cabin of Captain Palliere on the *Dessaix*. Despite the fact that the stern windows of the cabin faced directly towards the attackers, Palliere had insisted that the attack should not spoil their breakfast and carried on with the meal. With his captor showing such *sang froid*, Cochrane was not going to show fear and so he tucked in while they watched the battle through the window. Their repast was only brought to a conclusion when a round shot crashed through the stern window and into a wine bin under one of the sofas, showering them with claret and broken glass.

~~~~~~

Chapter 19

The French and Spanish had captured a large number of prisoners, including the shipwrights, through unintended trickery and now honour demanded that they be returned. The next morning another British launch sailed into Algeciras, this time under a flag of truce, to discuss the release of prisoners. At that time there was no regulated system of exchange between warring countries but it was agreed that all the shipwrights and men of the *Hannibal* and the *Speedy* would be released. The ships officers would be released on parole, meaning that they could not resume duties against France or Spain until an officer of similar rank had been released by the British in exchange. There was, however, one significant exception to this arrangement.

The negotiation to release prisoners took the best part of a day and by lunchtime it was still not clear who would be included. As we were being brought some cold pork and bread for lunch, a young Spanish army lieutenant arrived to advise that as I had diplomatic papers I was not considered a prisoner of war and so could leave immediately. He explained that a horse and escort were waiting to take me the twenty-odd-mile journey back to Gibraltar by land. I did not want to leave by myself, but it was by no means certain then that the *Speedy*'s officers would be included in the exchange. Cochrane recommended that I went: "If they don't want to keep you as a prisoner, you would be a fool to stay. If they don't let us go, you can press the authorities in Gibraltar to push for our exchange." So, reluctantly, I said farewell and left them, leaving much of my kit behind for them to bring by boat if possible.

The young lieutenant explained that we had to leave via the commandant's office to pick up a pass that would enable the escort to cross the border. I followed him down some stairs and along two corridors until we got to there. He knocked and a hesitant voice called out ,"Enter." The commandant was a fat, nervous-looking, elderly man sitting behind an elegant desk. He beckoned for us to enter the room and I had gone about four paces when the hair at the back of my neck prickled and I whirled round. From behind the door, familiar, dark, shark-like eyes stared back at me above a self-satisfied smile.

"We meet again, Señor Flashman," said Abrantes quietly.

There are times when the human brain struggles to comprehend changes in circumstance and this was one of them. A moment ago I had been relishing the prospect of freedom, going back to Gibraltar and then on to Britain and enjoying life. A split-second later my prospects had changed to torture and death. If I was honest with myself, Abrantes was one of the reasons I had been keen to leave Spain as soon as possible. Sooner or later I thought that he might hear that the *Speedy* had been captured and come looking to see if I had still been aboard. But the ship had only been captured two days ago. It took a week for a rider to reach Madrid and another week to get back. How had he got here just two days after we had landed? I must have gaped at him as I took this in. Then I realised that if Abrantes took me away, I was a dead man. I had to somehow persuade the commandant that I was a prisoner of war and should stay in Algeciras.

I whirled back to the commandant and took a big breath as I wracked my brains for a persuasive argument. I needn't have bothered, for Abrantes had someone stop the conversation with one of his favourite methods: a musket butt slammed into my skull. There was an explosion of pain and light and then oblivion.

I came to tied to a chair opposite a large window. For a moment I thought I was back on the garrotte, but this time my arms were securely tied to the arms of the chair and there was no rope around my neck. My legs were tied to the chair legs and another rope bound my chest to the back of the chair. The back of my head throbbed from the blow, but my face hurt too. My lips were stretched and there was a nasty, salty taste in my mouth. As I came fully conscious I realised that there was a piece of cloth in my mouth held in place by another strip around my mouth: I had been gagged.

I cautiously looked around the room and saw it was an empty office. I looked out of the window and saw that I was still in Algeciras. The view was of the harbour. A British transport ship was anchored just outside in the bay. Around twenty boats were pulling between it and the shore to load it with released British prisoners. I craned my neck to look down on the beach. There were orderly lines of prisoners waiting to be embarked. I saw several of the *Speedy*'s crew in the crowd and then I saw Cochrane and Archie standing together. They were laughing and joking and I could see that Archie even had my kit bag at his feet. My possessions would make it home if I did not. They must have thought that I was well on the way to Gibraltar by land.

I had to get their attention. I struggled to get up while still tied to the chair but it was heavy and fell back hard on the stone floor. I breathed in deeply through my nose and shouted, but the noise was just an incoherent "arggh". I had to get the gag off. I was furiously trying to drag it away from my mouth by rubbing my cheek against my shoulder when I heard people enter the room behind me.

Abrantes was smiling at me as he went to sit behind the desk. Two of his men came up to me and easily lifted the chair I was tied to between them and moved me to sit in front of the desk. One of them must have made a gesture towards the gag, but Abrantes looked over my shoulder at the man and shook his head. "I am not going to have your gag removed, Flashman, as you have nothing to say that will interest me."

The black eyes suddenly bored into me. "I know all about your mission to persuade the Spanish fleet to leave Cadiz, and I am pleased to tell you that you have been successful." He smiled again, but there was triumph and not humour on his face. "I was fortunate to be in Cadiz yesterday when news of your capture and the failed British attack reached us. I could not resist coming here overnight to renew our acquaintance. The Spanish fleet is weighing anchor as we speak without the British blockade keeping it in port. It will soon join with the French warships below to make a joint

212

allied fleet that will sweep the British aside. Your government will learn to be careful what it wishes for."

He sat back, looking at me, and then continued: "We will stay here for a few days to watch the fleet combine. Hopefully the British will be foolish enough to try another attack. Then, my friend, you must answer for your crimes. There is the murder of Hernandez, the death of Guido, my specialist with the hot knife, and all those soldiers at Estepona. Did you really think I would let you sail away? You will be tried and convicted as a spy and a murderer, and then you will be hanged."

He leaned forward, resting his elbows on the desk. "I told you once that hanging is too quick a death, but I promise that it will not be so in your case. Instead of having the knot behind your ear to break your neck, the hangman will be instructed to place the knot of the rope in front of your throat so that you will be able to get rasping breaths to prolong the agony. There will be no long drop for you, but a slow haul upwards."

He had spoken calmly up to now but suddenly he let his anger show. "I promise you that it will take many minutes for you to die. You and your friends made me look a fool at Estepona, but you will pay dearly for it," he hissed.

His eyes were full of venom now and I had been staring at him, frozen like the quarry of a snake, but now the spell was broken. I tried to speak – I would have begged and pleaded and offered him anything he wanted, but I could not get a word past my gag. As I thrashed around, trying to move the gag, I felt a rising panic. I struggled to breathe and to think. I was alone and abandoned. It would take days for Cochrane to be sure that I had not been freed and start to make enquiries. Abrantes was powerful and Spanish officials were frightened of him; they would tell the British anything he wanted. With sickening certainty, I knew that this time there would be no rescue.

"Take him away," said Abrantes dismissively.

His two men lifted the chair with me still tied to it and walked out of the room. The cloth in my mouth that had been tied in with the gag was nearly at my throat after all the thrashing and was causing me to choke. For a second I wondered if it would be more merciful to die now than slowly in the noose, but my survival instinct cut in and I tried to calm myself and use my tongue to push the filthy cloth to the front of my mouth. By the time I was breathing easily we had arrived back in the room that Cochrane, Archie and I had been held in before. They left me tied up in front of the little window. Sitting, I could not see down into the harbour but I could see the tops of some of the masts. When the furthest ones started to unfurl sails, I guessed that this was the transport with the crew of the *Speedy* on board. I watched it sail slowly out of my view and wept with frustration, self-pity and fear.

~~~~~~

Chapter 20

I was held in that room for four more days, speaking to no one. They had untied me after the British transport had sailed and warned me that if I started shouting, the gag would go back on. There was no one left to shout to, and for most of that time I slumped against the window. In my time I have been in prisons and jails on nearly every continent. I have even ended up in other Spanish jails and certainly many where conditions were a lot worse. But those few days were among the most frustrating I have ever had in captivity. Your first time in prison is always hard, and in this case I was convinced that it would also probably be my last. Well, half of me was anyway. I must have been close to twenty then, and young men always have an instinctive feeling of immortality: they know death happens, but feel it will not happen to them. If you look at the groups of volunteers called 'forlorn hopes' that are brought together to storm a breach at a siege, you will invariably find that the majority are young men seeking glory. Those with the most to lose will put their faith in a gut feeling that they at least will pull through, while the hardened veterans who have seen the youthful remains of too many forlorn hopes take a more realistic view of the odds and hang back.

My heart told me that I would not die. I simply could not die this young. I would look out of the window and see Gibraltar just six miles away and convince myself that I was being missed and some sort of rescue effort would be put together. Then I would review the position with my rational brain and see little grounds for hope at all. It would take several days for people to be sure that I had not returned. The Navy would be far more concerned with defeating the French and Spanish fleets than tracking down a missing courier, and no Spaniard in his right mind would get in the way of Abrantes. That is how I spent the days, bouncing from heart to brain, optimism to pessimism, and back again, time and time again.

When I was not driving myself mad, I did have an excellent view of the French hauling their ships off the sandbanks and positioning them so that they could use their broadsides if the British attacked again. A swarm of French and Spanish shipwrights descended on the captured *Hannibal*, and as I watched it was gradually brought back to life as a fighting ship. By the fourth evening it was floated alongside the French ships and looked ready for sea. Far from capturing the French ships in their first attack, the British had just succeeded in giving them a fourth battleship for their fleet.

The Royal Navy showed no sign of making a further attack, having retired their fleet to Gibraltar. For them the situation got worse when the Spanish fleet joined the French off Algeciras on the eleventh of July. The Spanish fleet consisted of six ships of the line including two huge one-hundred-and-twelve-gun four-deckers, several frigates and a flotilla of smaller gun boats. With the French fleet now of four ships, it was a prodigious force, considerably larger than that of the British.

On the morning of the twelfth of July it was clear that the combined fleet was preparing to leave port with various provisions being rowed out to the ships. My frayed nerves were fast reaching breaking point, as once the fleet had sailed Abrantes would have little reason to stay in Algeciras and my journey to trial and execution was likely to begin. When the door to my room opened mid-morning, and instead of the usual servant with food, two guards stood in the doorway, I feared the worst. Wordlessly they beckoned for me to leave the room. One led the way and the other fell in behind. When we got outside there was a carriage and horses waiting in the courtyard, but to my surprise we turned away from them and followed the cobbled street down to the harbour. There a launch was waiting to take me out to sea.

For a brief, wildly optimistic moment I wondered if my exchange had been arranged after all, but looking around I saw no British boats waiting to collect me. The boat crew were also far too smartly dressed for such a mundane task, all wearing clean, matching shirts and trousers with a Spanish naval lieutenant in command of the boat. He looked at me with some disdain but asked, "You speak Spanish?" I confirmed that I did and so he explained what was happening. "Your colonel is to travel back to Cadiz in the *Real Carlos* and has arranged for you to accompany him as his prisoner." The lieutenant had managed to squeeze extra contempt into the words 'your colonel' and it was clear that whatever he had been doing, Abrantes had not been winning friends amongst the officers of the *Real Carlos*.

Soon it became clear that we were heading to the massive four-deckers anchored out in the bay. The *Real Carlos* and the *San Hermenegildo* were by far the biggest ships that I had ever seen and among the biggest ships afloat at that time. As we sailed between them their sides blocked out the sun; it was like rowing into a floating canyon. We approached the sides of the *Real Carlos* and I looked up at four storeys of wood and cannon muzzles, on top of which was a forest of masts and yards to power this mighty behemoth. It was truly an awe-inspiring sight and for the first time I thought that Abrantes might have had a point: keeping these beasts trapped in harbour seemed a lot more sensible than letting them loose.

Unless you were a complete land lubber and were hauled aboard in a bosun's chair, the normal way to enter a warship was to leap onto some battens on the side of the ship and climb up them onto the main deck. For such a tall ship this was impractical and so there was an entry port on the second gun deck from the bottom that we climbed through. Coming from the bright sunlight, it took my eyes a few seconds to adjust to the gloom of the gun deck, even though the gun ports were open. The place was a hive of activity. There were over eight hundred men in each of these ships; they were like floating fortified towns. I was prodded by my guards to continue and we went up two more flights of stairs through identical gun decks before we climbed again to emerge on the deck of this mighty ship.

217

Again I had to blink in the glare as my eyes adjusted back to the sunlight and then I saw a group of officers on the poop deck. I don't think I have ever seen so much gold braid in one place before or since. There were bicorn and tricorn hats, some with ostrich plumes and one with peacock feathers, old-fashioned coats of velvet with knee britches and other garments of silk. If they could fight as well as they dressed then this fleet truly would be unstoppable. The centre of their attention was an elderly officer whose uniform front was encrusted with orders and decorations and a light-blue silk sash.

"Who is that?" I asked the lieutenant from the boat who was escorting me.

"That is His Excellency Vice Admiral Moreno, the commander of the Spanish fleet."

I still was not sure why I was on the ship, although I was happy for any delay to my execution. I was now feeling very poorly dressed as I was still wearing some of my patched seagoing clothes and now had a week's growth of beard as my razor was in Gibraltar with Archie.

Suddenly, amid the group of fawning officers, I saw Abrantes. He alone was dressed in the more modern style of boots and trousers and his uniform seemed relatively plain compared to those around him, with just some gold braid around the lapels. He stood patiently, waiting for several of the other officers to be sent away on errands or with orders for their ships, and then he stepped towards the admiral and beckoned for the lieutenant.

"This is the spy I was telling you about, Excellency. As he was plotting to have your fleet sail from Cadiz, I thought it would be amusing to allow him to see the error of his ways before he suffers his punishment."

The admiral glanced at me with haughty disdain which seemed to also extend to Abrantes, and I sensed that this aristocratic-looking old man disapproved of both spies and spy catchers. This, I realised, could be my last chance. If I could appeal to the admiral I might be saved yet, but if I failed then Abrantes would make my final days a living hell.

With death my only alternative, I did not hesitate more than a heartbeat and then spoke clearly in the aristocratic Spanish accent that my mother had taught me:

"Apologies, Excellency, but I am not a spy. I am a British naval officer whom this rogue has previously tried to capture and torture. I am a prisoner of war, and I would ask for your help to be exchanged as has happened with the other British officers."

Abrantes shot me a look of annoyance, but he must have expected some outburst and was ready for it. "Excellency, I have personally witnessed this man shoot a priest. He is a dangerous criminal, as well as a spy, and I will ensure that he is hanged for his crimes." To the lieutenant he added, "Take him away."

The lieutenant pulled my arm but I wrenched it back. "The man I shot was not a priest but a spy in disguise. The priest at Estepona will still be able to vouch for me despite this villain removing his finger nails and breaking all of his fingers." I was shouting now and pointing at Abrantes. Other officers had stopped their conversations and were turning to look at this confrontation, and for the first time Abrantes looked rattled.

"Wait," said the admiral, speaking for the first time, and the lieutenant stopped hauling on my shoulder. The admiral looked at Abrantes and spoke quietly. "Did you, an officer of his most Catholic Majesty, really torture a catholic priest?"

"Sir, the man was an enemy agent who was passing on messages to his brother, who in turn was spying on your fleet for the British. I have since tracked down this brother and watched him hanged." As he said these last words he looked at me with such spite that I knew that this exchange had probably added a minute or two to my dying time. Then he continued: "I have been appointed by his most Catholic Majesty's ministers to track and capture enemy agents; it is necessarily a harsh business. But if the priest wishes to complain about my conduct, he can do so through his bishop to the minister."

The admiral was already turning away in disgust, no longer interested in this sordid matter, and Abrantes whispered furiously to the officer holding my arm, "Take him away. Put him below in chains."

That was it, my final throw of the dice. It might have damaged Abrantes's reputation with his brother officers, but it had done nothing to save me and what I had done would almost certainly result in a more painful death. The admiral was clearly a proud old aristocrat and I had taken several steps away when I realised that I still had one more card to play.

I broke free of the lieutenant and ran back several paces before shouting, "Sir, I am the grandson of the marquis of Morella. Would you see a son of that noble house thrown in chains on your ship?" I stood upright, looking as noble as I could, thinking this was how he would expect the son of a Spanish nobleman to behave. The admiral slowly turned around to look at me while Abrantes stared in astonishment.

"I knew the old marquis well," said the admiral quietly. "How are you related?" There was a note of warning in his voice as though he thought this was a trick of some kind.

"He had a daughter. She married an Englishman, my father."

He was still not convinced. "What was the name of the daughter?"

"Maria Luisa, sir."

"Ah, yes, I remember now. She was a pretty young thing and married an Englishman with a strange name. Don Pedro was furious and she was never mentioned again. What is your name, young man?"

"Thomas Flashman, sir." I held my breath; this was going better than I dared hope. I risked a glance at Abrantes. He was looking furious as the situation seemed to be slipping out of his control.

"Flashman, yes, that was it. So you are Don Pedro's grandson, are you?" The admiral's haughty demeanour relaxed slightly into a weak smile.

"With respect, sir," interrupted Abrantes, "this man is a murderer and a spy who must stand trial and suffer the consequences of his actions."

"Quite possibly," said the admiral, looking stern again. "But I will not have a grandson of Don Pedro languishing in chains aboard one of my ships without clear proof of his guilt. He is to remain at large on deck, and when we put in to Cadiz I will send word to his family and ask them to satisfy themselves as to his guilt."

"Very good, sir," said Abrantes stiffly. He walked forward and beckoned to the lieutenant holding me to follow.

Once we were out of earshot of the admiral, Abrantes turned to me. "Well, Flashman, you are full of surprises today." His voice was as cold as ice. "I give you a few days' extra life to see the folly of your actions and you try to embarrass me with the admiral. No matter, we will deal with your Spanish family."

"You can't just kill me now," I said, sounding more confident than I felt. "They will want proof. They may speak to the people at Estepona and find out what really happened there."

"You think you are safe now, do you?" Abrantes was mocking in his retort. He added in English, "All you have done is add torture to a slow death. I remember the look of horror on your face when Guido put the knives in the brazier. Well, there are lots more people with Guido's skill in Madrid. By the time they have finished with you, I promise you will be willing to sign confessions for all manner of crimes. You will confess not only to murder and spying but also to rape, buggery and piracy, plus anything else I think of along the way. Your Spanish family will be too sickened to intervene and help some heretic relative they have never met." He turned to the lieutenant. "Get him out of my sight. If he has to stay on deck, have him clean the latrines."

I struggled forward in the ship with my mind in a whirl, unsure if I had made my situation better or worse. It

221

depended on how powerful my Spanish relatives were and whether Abrantes would dare torture me if they were likely to investigate. The admiral clearly thought they would follow up on his message, but Abrantes was equally confident that they could be distracted, and he was right about one thing: I would not be able to withstand torture. I felt sick just thinking about it. But at least I felt I had a chance, whereas before there had seemed no hope at all.

The naval lieutenant obviously understood enough English to understand Abrantes's threats and, like his admiral, he clearly did not approve. He took me to the bows where the latrines, or 'heads' as they are known on ships, were situated. They were a row of box-like seats along either side of a bowsprit overhanging the sea. When the ship was moving the wind would be behind or from the side, blowing the smell away, and in rough seas the heads would be washed by the waves. Unfortunately at anchor there was a powerful smell and, with eight hundred men using them, a lot of traffic. The lieutenant had a long, whispered conversation with a bosun called Fidel, which included several glances at the admiral and Abrantes, now back on the quarterdeck. Then the lieutenant introduced me to the bosun and walked off.

Fidel gave me a long look and then gestured for me to follow him down to the heads. When we got there he gave me a bucket and a brush. "Sit there," he grunted, pointing at a corner out of the way. "If an officer comes, start scrubbing."

I sat there for most of the afternoon. You quickly got used to the smell. This was the closest thing to freedom I had experienced for nearly a fortnight. I spent my time considering my limited options and decided that if the British fleet were to attack the allied fleet, I would take my chances and jump overboard. There would be wreckage to float on and usually after a battle they sent boats for survivors. I just had to hope that the boats looking for survivors were British, which would normally mean that a British ship had been damaged or sunk. That seemed likely if

one of them was foolish enough to take on the huge
armament of the *Real Carlos*. I just had to pick the right
moment.

~~~~~~

Chapter 21

Preparations for sea took most of the afternoon. I saw the admiral go off in his barge from the *Real Carlos* to take his flag to a smaller but faster frigate. Of Abrantes I saw no sign, not that I was looking. Eventually in late afternoon the armada of ships finally got underway. The ships formed two parallel columns with the French at the front and the two mighty one-hundred-and-twelve-gun ships bringing up the rear. It was soon obvious why the two most powerful ships were at the back of the formation: ships could be seen moving on the other side of the bay. The British were setting off in pursuit. The British had eight ships in their fleet but this included a tiny armed brig and only five of them were ships of the line. In contrast, the combined allied fleet had nine ships of the line and three powerful forty-gun frigates.

The line of the allied fleet soon stretched out over two miles as the French ships seemed to be faster than the Spanish. This did not really matter, though, as the British ships seemed equally sluggish, with their bottoms fouled with weed from long blockade duty. Only one British ship seemed to be gaining on the fleet; I later discovered it was the seventy-four-gun *Superb* which had not been on blockade.

Every half hour I would move from the heads to a position where I could look astern. Each time the *Superb* looked a bit closer, but at the rate it was going, it would be nightfall before it could overhaul us. My jumping overboard plan seemed like suicide in the dark; I would never be seen. The two big one-hundred-and-twelve-gun ships were staying resolutely together and parallel, meaning that the *Superb* would have to tackle them together.

By dusk the *Superb* was well within range and I wondered if she would turn and rake the stern of one of the big ships with her broadside or if one of the Spanish monsters would turn and fire a shattering salvo at the *Superb*. The Spanish captains were clearly under orders to maintain station for they showed no sign of starting an attack. They must have been worried about getting tangled in a battle with the *Superb* that would allow the rest of the British fleet to catch them up.

I was surprised that the British ship had not tried to slow the Spanish ships down; it seemed the obvious thing to do. Instead it just kept on getting closer and closer, until I realised with astonishment that it planned to sail directly between the two huge Spanish ships. It was a desperate gamble, as the rest of the British fleet was still some two miles back and unable to offer any support. The *Superb* would be able to fire both broadsides, totalling seventy guns, at the two Spanish ships, but they would get one hundred cannons fired at them in reply. The Spanish realised the *Superb*'s intentions at roughly the same moment I did, and suddenly trumpet calls and drum beats rent the air. Soon there was a rumbling sound like thunder as over two hundred cannons were loaded and rolled out of gun ports on both sides of the two giant ships.

What happened in the next few minutes has remained a vivid memory all of my life. Slowly but surely the *Superb* began to overhaul the sterns of the two Spanish ships. Captain Keats on the *Superb* had clearly given orders to his gunners to fire as soon as their guns found a target. He was hoping that his well-trained gunners could reload quicker than the Spanish to even out the shortfall in his guns. As one of the few people on the ship with nothing to do, I watched from the foc'sle as the battle unfolded.

One by one the British guns fired, with me safely out of the way of the damage being inflicted on the stern of the ship. I saw a stern rail splinter and heard glass smash and then screams from below as one of the balls smashed through an open gun port. Smoke from the British guns blew slowly forward, obscuring their ship from my view, but despite the growing darkness you could make out the mast heads in the night sky and gauge where it was. It slowly crept further forward between the two ships, and when the Spanish judged that the whole ship was between them, a signal was given and their two massive broadsides crashed out. I have never heard such destructive power in one blast before or since.

For a moment I was deaf. The ship heeled over in the combined recoil and I lost my footing. When I got up to look again there was a massive wall of gun smoke that hid both the British ship and the Spanish one beyond. Blocks and rigging were falling down from our foremast and it seemed as though some of the *San Hermenegildo*'s shots had hit us. My hearing slowly started to come back and I heard more screams from further back in the ship. I wondered if anything could have survived that awesome firepower, but no sooner had I thought it than there was a fiery flash in the dark smoke and a boom of a cannon shot and a ball slammed into the side of the *Real Carlos*, worryingly close to me.

The first gunners to fire from the front of the *Superb* had evidently now reloaded and were firing again. The irregular spatter of shots from the invisible British ship continued to crack and create more flashes in the smoke between the two Spanish ships. Two more balls smashed into the foc'sle. I was dammed if I was going to be killed by my own side, and so I moved back into cover near the heads where I could hide behind some solid beams that supported the bowsprit. As I was moving I heard the now-familiar thunder as the Spanish guns were rolled out. They were more haphazard now, not firing in unison but as soon as they were reloaded. The *San Hermenegildo* must have been doing the same, for now there was a steady stream of flashes in the smoke and more flashes from the *Superb* so that it was impossible to judge from which ship the flash had come.

More cannon balls smashed into the *Real Carlos* and from up above me I heard the sound of splintering timber. Looking up, I saw that the top section of our foremast was coming down and that it was going to fall down the length of the ship. It seemed to move slowly at first, but then as the weight of the spars and cordage it carried snapped other lines and spars on the mainmast, it gathered speed and crashed down on the deck with terrible force. I moved to escape the snapping ropes that whipped through the air near where I was hiding and risked another look down the deck. There were screams of trapped men and the crew set to with axes to try to clear the wreckage away. In the gloom I could see frantic activity on the main deck as the gunners continued to fire while other crewmen went about chopping ropes and trying to control the huge, flapping foresails that were now spread across much of the deck.

Two more cannon balls tore through the air above my head and I ducked back down to the heads again for cover. A few moments later I heard the shout that every sailor fears: "Fire!" Curiosity battled fear for a second and then curiosity won and I decided to climb back up over the foc'sle again for another look. As I started something made me glance over my shoulder to the sea just in front of the ship, and then for a few seconds I was transfixed. The wind powering the ships was also pushing the bank of gun smoke forward. As I watched, the top of a masthead appeared through a tiny gap in the smoke, and then another. From the distance and speed it could only be the *Superb*, which had evidently continued to sail through the gap between the Spanish ships and was now pressing on to the next ships in the allied column.

I looked around. I was the only person in the heads during the battle and no one else was this far forward on the ship. Nobody else had noticed that the *Superb* was no longer between the Spanish ships. The guns of the Real Carlos were still firing, creating more gun smoke, and through it I could see the flashes from other gun muzzles in reply. Incredible as it seemed, the massive Spanish battleships were now mistakenly fighting each other.

Looking down the length of the ship, with the smoke and the darkness it was hard to see what was happening. When the guns fired the muzzle flash revealed a nightmare scene of crushed bodies, wrecked gun carriages and people scrambling about. The firing had slowed on the main top deck of the *Real Carlos*, but the three decks below were firing without interruption.

Initially the fire looked quite small, but then a fallen sail from the foremast caught light and it flared up. Flames were soon shooting up the tarred rigging ropes, and setting light to other sails. In less than a minute a small fire on the deck had turned the mainmast into a blazing beacon. Tarred ropes burn quickly and fiercely, and they were holding up aloft the massive yard arms that were bigger than the main masts of smaller ships. Cracks were heard as burning ropes snapped, and soon the mainsail yard was hanging at a crazy angle. I looked around, astonished at how fast the flames had spread. Above me they had now reached the remaining lower section of the foremast. The air around me was now hot from the flames and the heat from the burning mainmast fire was being blown straight towards me. Then there was another series of cracks from aloft and the maintop sail yard was swinging in the rigging until it was hanging directly down like a spear towards the deck, with its burning sail attached. With a final snap, the last rope burned through and it plunged straight down, smashing through the main deck and carrying the fire to the decks below.

The blazing rigging was all the *San Hermenegildo* needed to improve their gunnery. Thinking that they were destroying the *Superb*, they smashed even more balls into their sister ship and those trying to save it. Three men were working together near me to try to cut through some wreckage to get it over the side, but a cannon ball shrieked out of the darkness to turn them instantly into a bloody pulp. I was covered in a spray of their blood and gore.

The heat from the flames was getting intense around me. The pitch between the planks on the deck was melting now and sticking to my shoes; it was only a matter of time before that started to burn too. The massive ship seemed doomed, and I could not do anything to save it even if I wanted to.

I moved back down to the heads again, which was sheltered from the flames and the heat by the foc'sle, and prayed that the British fleet would soon arrive to offer a chance of rescue. I must have been down there for around five minutes, listening to the screams and shouts of those fighting the fire and continued shooting from the lower decks of the *Real Carlos*. It seemed incredible that we were still firing cannon, but the lower decks were. It must have been a scene from hell down there with flames and shattered timbers mixed with gun smoke and the crash of cannon while brave men kept the flames away from the powder. But our guns still flashed out and balls slammed into our hull in return. One ball crashed into the beam I was crouching behind, but mercifully it stood firm.

Suddenly I felt a jolt to the ship, as though we had run aground, and I stood up again to take a look. The *San Hermenegildo* had evidently tried to rake the stern of what it thought was the enemy ship. Probably at the same moment they discovered that they had been shooting at their sister ship, the crew also discovered that they had miscalculated the manoeuvre and crashed into our stern instead. The flames from our rigging illuminated the scene and showed that our stern mast, which was now also on fire, was entwined with the main mast of the *San Hermenegildo*. Even as I watched, flames spread across to the second ship.

You might imagine that I was delighted to see the two Spanish ships burn, but I wasn't, and not just because I still stood on one of them. The continual flames now illuminated a scene from Dante's *Inferno*. I saw an officer shoot one man trapped across the thighs under a yardarm who was screaming as flames licked around his legs. Powder charges for the guns exploded, killing anyone standing near them. Two men ran around the deck with their clothes ablaze, one eventually sinking to the deck but the other managing to get over the rail and drop into the sea. That was the first time I smelt burning human flesh, but sadly not the last.

The guns had stopped firing now and more men appeared on deck to try to fight the flames, but it was already far too late. Even the heads were no longer offering the refuge that they had. The wind had been blowing sparks and burning cinders and now the big foresails were ablaze above and in front of me. Smoke was pouring out of the foc'sle hatch behind me and the pitch between the planks on the deck underneath me was now burning in a couple of places. I was surrounded by flames. Several other Spanish sailors had now sought shelter in the heads too. One had even managed to climb out to the tip of the bowsprit, underneath the burning sails. I had burning cinders on my coat and the smoke and heat was making it hard to breathe. I reasoned that the British fleet must be closing in on this inferno, which would be lighting the darkness for miles around. It was time to leave the ship.

I am not a strong swimmer and so I took off my coat and boots first and then climbed on the edge, ready to jump. I hesitated as I stood on the rail. Jumping into the sea from four storeys up is no easy thing. If a gout of flame had not burst out of the forward hatch, startling me and causing me to lose my balance, I might not have made it. Suddenly I was falling and spinning in the air, remembering just in time to take a deep breath and hold my nose before I hit the water with a hell of a jolt. I hit the water head and shoulders first, which literally knocked some of the wind out of me, and went in deep.

The only time I had dived before it had been from a few feet in daylight so the surface was easy to see. When I opened my eyes this time all I could see was black. I had no idea which way was up. I started to panic, and then something incredible happened. Simultaneously I felt several impacts which vibrated through the water and hit my chest and the blackness to my right turned gold. A huge sheet of flame rolled over the surface of the ocean, illuminating me and two startled fish. I knew now which way was up, and swam towards it with my last gasping breath burning in my lungs.

Still a yard or two from the surface, the light was already diminishing, but I saw something splash above me and fall quickly to the deep. Glancing across, I saw that it was a cannon barrel that had been blown off its gun carriage. More splashes appeared; some things stayed on the surface, others went down past me. I realised that there must have been an explosion on one of the ships, but nothing prepared me for the view when I was finally able to gasp for air.

The surface of the sea was covered in wreckage – some of it still burning, which provided light to show that the two mighty ships had simply disappeared. The fire on one of them must have found the magazine, which had then blown both of them to smithereens. I was surrounded by floating spars and pieces of planking, and bodies, and bits of bodies. I heard the odd groan from other survivors, but did not see any in the dark.

I swam forward and bumped into two badly burned corpses, one still smoking, but pushed them away. Then I found four big timbers that were still attached together. They formed a kind of raft, and after a bit of a struggle when I got tangled in a rope, I managed to climb on. I looked around for a sign of rescue; surely the British fleet had to be nearby. But apart from some smouldering wreckage, all I could see was blackness.

It was a summer night and not too cold, but suddenly I found I was shivering from shock. I tried to convince myself that after all I had been through I would be safe now. They couldn't leave me to die on some floating planks. Someone would come looking for survivors. I was floating in the straits of Gibraltar, one of the busiest sea lanes; a ship would see me in daylight.

After a few minutes of trying to convince myself of my own survival, I saw more flashes in the darkness and then a moment later heard the dull rumble of more gunfire. Whether it came from the British fleet that had been behind us or the Allied fleet in front I was not sure. I just hoped that whoever came looking for survivors in the morning was British. Exhausted, I lay back on my planks and waited for the dawn.

The gunfire, it turned out, was the *Superb* attacking, and this time capturing, another allied ship. As dawn lit the eastern sky I woke up from a fretful doze and almost wept with relief to see the *Superb* and her prize sailing back towards me with boats already in the water to look for

231

survivors. A cutter pulled towards me on my raft and a sailor in the bows, seeing me waving, called back, "It's all right, Pedro, we've seen you."

"I'm British," I called back.

"Well, what the bleedin' 'ell are you doin' 'ere then?"

"I was held as a prisoner on the *Real Carlos*."

By now the cutter was just a few yards away and the sailor in the bows surveyed the scene revealed by the dawn. Hundreds of corpses were floating in the water with bits of planking, cordage and other flotsam and just a handful of other survivors waving pitifully for rescue.

"Well," said the sailor as he looked around, "you are one lucky bugger then, aren't you."

~~~~~~~

Chapter 22

Less than twenty people survived from the two ships to be rescued that morning. Most had died in the explosion or from wounds afterwards. I am very happy to report that Abrantes was not one of those pulled onto the boats. It had been an incredibly one-sided battle: the allied French and Spanish fleet had lost three ships and over seventeen hundred men; the British dead numbered just seventeen. The battle is known to history as the Battle of the Gut of Gibraltar, although to this day I am not sure what the 'gut' bit is all about; must be one of those naval terms

Captain Keats of the *Superb* welcomed me aboard and I offered him my heartfelt thanks. He had been amazed that the Spanish had continued firing after his ship had sailed past and so I explained to him what I had seen from the deck of the *Real Carlos* and how the Spanish had thought his ship was still between them. The officers and crew were delighted that they had effectively destroyed two of the biggest warships afloat and captured a third ship with so few casualties. It was double rum rations all round, and then once the boats had collected the last of the survivors we set course for Gibraltar, which was still visible on the horizon.

Word of the victory had reached the port before us and as we docked bands were playing and crowds gathered and Captain Keats was rightly hailed a hero. Admiral Saumarez was one of the first up the gangplank to congratulate him. For getting me out of Abrantes's clutches and killing the bastard to boot, he should have got a knighthood at the very least in my book. Other naval officers from the fleet were flooding aboard to congratulate Keats while I was trying to get off the ship. I looked up and there was Cochrane, looking astonished at finding me.

"Flashman, what the devil are you doing here? I have been looking for you everywhere."

"That bastard Abrantes got me in Algeciras and was going to have me tortured and hanged. We were travelling back to Cadiz on the *Real Carlos* and I only just managed to jump off the thing before it blew up."

"Good God," said Cochrane, and then there was nothing for it but for me to tell him the details of what had happened. Then others wanted to hear the story, and even Admiral Saumarez showed an interest, especially when he heard that the *Real Carlos* had been planning to put in at Cadiz. He wondered if, without their big ships, the Spanish may return their fleet to port.

I was exhausted when a hand clapped my shoulder and I looked up to see the twinkling eyes of Governor O'Hara. "Well, young Flashman, I have been hearing lots about you and your adventures. When we last met you promised to come back and tell me all about them, and I have a strong feeling that this will be a tale worth hearing."

He smiled genially and continued: "I have already had a letter of thanks from a French diplomat whom you and Cochrane apparently rescued from under the nose of the dey of Algiers. Come and stay with me at Government House. The only rent I will charge is your story over a good dinner that I will provide. We will invite Cochrane to that dinner too. But not tonight, for I am arranging a celebration dinner for Keats and you are both invited."

Despite the short notice, the celebration dinner was a grand affair, organised in the society rooms of Mrs Harris. Every Army and naval officer in Gibraltar seemed to be there with piles of food and limitless wine. There were loads of congratulatory speeches to Keats that night and virtually everyone proposed a toast to him and his crew. I got a toast from all present simply for surviving. Reunited with Cochrane, Archie and Guthrie, I drank every toast with enthusiasm and when eventually I collapsed, exhausted, they got me sent me back to my rooms at Government House where I slept until noon the next day.

The following evening Cochrane and I joined Governor O'Hara for dinner. It was a very relaxed affair, but I quickly realised that O'Hara was a very shrewd gatherer of information and passed frequent despatches back to London, which explained why Wickham knew him so well. Together, Cochrane and I told the story of the last eight months since I first arrived in Gibraltar. O'Hara had already heard of the defence of the tower at Estepona but was interested to learn of Abrantes and the fear he spread amongst local officials. He expressed amazement at the ingenuity shown in evading the two frigates. Cochrane and I had told the tale for our mutual credit and Cochrane had implied that 'Flashman's broadside' was my idea.

While he had read the official report, O'Hara wanted to know about the capture of the *Gamo* and probed about the level of morale amongst the Spanish forces. He asked why Cochrane had not been promoted as a result of the action. When we explained the circumstances surrounding our trip to Algiers, he was appalled. He told us that Auclair had sent messages through him for both the Admiralty and the Foreign Office expressing thanks for his rescue. While we were at war with France, rescuing a diplomat from a pirate kingdom that threatened all nations would be seen as a worthy humanitarian gesture.

At the end of the tale he turned to us both and said that we had earned considerable credit. Cochrane was facing an automatic court martial for the loss of the *Speedy*, but O'Hara was sure he would be acquitted. I was not so certain, for Cochrane had not told O'Hara of the letter he had sent to St Vincent effectively accusing him of cowardice. I had been mentioned in despatches to the Foreign Office with Wickham extolling my virtues as a resourceful and courageous agent. This was the start of a reputation that, like a millstone, would drag me into countless dangerous situations in the future. O'Hara also gave me some post that had been sent care of Gibraltar and this included a letter from my father. He evidently still did not trust me with money and as I was under twenty-one he had persuaded the bank to hand over to him all the prize money I had earned to date. I would have been furious but for the fact that he was using it to build a row of apartments on some land in London that he already owned. He wrote to say that he was transferring the land into my name and the apartments, known as Flashman's Row, would provide me with a rental income of two hundred and fifty guineas per annum, which he hoped would give me financial security.

I was more than ready to go home now, but I had one final duty to perform, as a witness for Cochrane at his court martial for the loss of the *Speedy*. Everyone said that, as Cochrane had done all that could be expected from him when confronted by three battleships, he was bound to be acquitted. But you could never take things like that for certain with the Navy, especially when they involved Cochrane. What made it interesting was that Manley Dixon and the merchant were very anxious that their use of *Speedy* to carry the mail did not come to light. Cochrane was offered fifty guineas to keep this fact to himself, but insisted that prize money for all his crew was confirmed before he gave evidence. Whether O'Hara pulled any strings behind the scenes or not I don't know, but in addition to the prize money I had already received, I had an Admiralty bank draft for three hundred guineas in my pocket when I was waiting for the trial to start.

The court martial took place on the ship *Pompeii*. We all went aboard and waited in an anteroom as Cochrane submitted his evidence to the panel of captains who served as judges. They sat with Cochrane's sword lying on the table in front of them, and when they gave their verdict the sword would be pointed blade-first at him if he was found guilty or hilt-first if he was innocent. In the event, our evidence was not required as Cochrane was immediately acquitted with full honour and his sword was returned. . Cochrane was to benefit directly from the recent battle too as he was to be formally exchanged for the captain of the ship whom the *Superb* had captured.

The very next day Cochrane, Archie and I set sail for home on the brig *Louisa*. We sailed for protection with Saumarez's fleet, which was returning to blockade the Spanish fleet back in Cadiz. Once the Spanish were confirmed back in port, the *Louisa* continued on home with news of the recent engagements.

As the Spanish coast fell away over the horizon, Cochrane and I stood on the quarterdeck looking back over the stern rail. Cochrane said, "You know, we made a good team. We should sail again together some time."

We did too, nearly twenty years later, on the other side of the world. We helped liberate a nation, and we nearly liberated an emperor and changed a continent, but that is another story.

~~~~~~~

Historical Notes

For those interested in learning more about Cochrane then the excellent biography of Cochrane by Donald Thomas, called *Britannia's Sea Wolf*, is recommended. Cochrane's own description of his life is now back in print and called *The Autobiography of a Seaman*. It is an illuminating read and is now available through at least one leading online book retailer. Both of these books have been invaluable in helping check the historical facts detailed in Flashman's memoirs.

All of the events involving Cochrane are confirmed in the above-mentioned reference books with the exception of the defence of the tower at Estepona; although this does bear a striking similarity, including the use of the bug trap pit, to his defence of a fort in the town of Rosas a few years later. The visit to the dey of Algiers is not mentioned in Donald Thomas's work, but is mentioned in Cochrane's own autobiography. In that work Cochrane questions why the *Speedy*, the smallest ship on the station and least likely to intimidate anyone, was sent to threaten the dey. He also confirms that the *Gamo* was sold to the dey for a pittance, but he stops short of suggesting that these facts were linked to get rid of him. This is probably because by the time he wrote his memoirs he was back in the Navy as a senior admiral and he would not have wanted to embarrass the service.

Incredible as it may seem, the loss of the *Real Carlos* and her sister ship also took place as described.

While Cochrane had made an extraordinary start to his naval career, it was nothing to what was to come. From the point where this book ends he was finally promoted to post captain, but initially not given a command. After a prolonged campaign by his supporters, he was finally given a ship, a near-wrecked collier called the *Arab*, which was even less suited to warfare than the *Speedy*. He was then given a series of mundane naval tasks, such as guarding a non-existent fishing fleet in the Orkneys, as Lord St Vincent took his revenge after Cochrane's slur against his courage. But St Vincent had made too many enemies with his reforms and was replaced in 1805, which enabled Cochrane to get the command he had always dreamed of: a fast frigate.

In the *Pallas* on just his first cruise he captured numerous prizes and evaded three French battleships. When he returned to port he had captured so much treasure that he had five-foot solid-gold candlesticks tied to each mast head and his personal share of the prize money was seventy-five thousand pounds.

He subsequently entered Parliament, winning the seat of Honiton, as described in this book, and combined the career of an MP with that of a naval captain. He took a radical stance in politics and made enemies in Parliament, but at sea in a new frigate called the *Imperieuse* he had more success, particularly raiding the French and Spanish coast. He was made a Knight of the Order of the Bath.

But in 1809 he was involved in an attack on Rochfort in France, an engagement called the Battle of the Basque Roads. Cochrane had been instrumental in planning the attack, which involved the use of fire ships. While everything did not go according to plan, some fire ships got through and as a result the French ships cut their cables and many were beached and defenceless at the next low tide. Cochrane wanted the fleet to go in and destroy them, but the commanding officer, Admiral Gambier, declined to attack. Cochrane launched an attack alone in the *Imperieuse* and then sent a false distress signal to force the admiral to send some ships in to support. Due to time wasted and the lack of a full attack, the French were able to refloat unharmed many of their ships. Cochrane was furious and openly critical of his commanding officer. When a vote of thanks to Gambier was proposed in Parliament, he declared he would not support it. As a result, Admiral Gambier asked for a court martial to clear his name. After a heated hearing before a panel of admirals, Gambier was cleared. But the reputations of both Gambier and Cochrane had been damaged by the affair and neither was to have a command for the remainder of the war.

Cochrane concentrated on his political career, but his radical views just resulted in more enemies. In 1814 these opponents struck when Cochrane was implicated in a Stock Exchange fraud. Despite some dubious evidence Cochrane was found guilty, and sentenced to twelve months in prison and a one thousand pound fine. His disgrace also resulted in him being expelled from the Navy and Parliament, and he had his knighthood revoked. A month later he was re-elected, unopposed, to his old parliamentary seat after an outcry over the court case, but he was not able to appear in Parliament until after he had finished his prison sentence. He remained an MP until 1818 when, still in disgrace, he was offered command of the Chilean navy in its war of independence against Spain. He had a series of spectacular victories before he achieved the capture of Valdivia, the last significant port held by the Spanish, in an audacious raid with just three hundred men.

Following this success, he was offered command of the Brazilian navy in 1823, and after another series of creative deceptions and victories, he helped secure the independence of that nation from Portugal. This appointment was followed by one to command the Greek navy in their war against Turkey. There were few ships to command and Cochrane was often disgusted at the savagery shown by both sides. In the event, a combined French and British fleet destroyed the Turkish fleet at Navarino.

In 1832 Cochrane was granted a pardon for the Stock Exchange conviction and restored to the Navy list. He was an early proponent of steam warships, having had one built for the Chilean navy, which arrived too late to take part in the war. In 1847, after the personal intervention of Queen Victoria, he was restored as a Knight of the Order of the Bath.

In 1854, when Cochrane was seventy-nine years old, he was considered by the Cabinet for command of the Baltic fleet during the Crimean War with Russia. With most of the action taking place in the Black Sea, the ministers were looking for an admiral to fight a holding action in the Baltic.

Despite his age, they felt that this near octogenarian was too 'adventurous', and so declined to offer him the command. Some months later, with the British Army suffering heavy casualties at the siege of Sebastopol in the Crimea, Cochrane approached the Admiralty again, this time with a proposal for 'stink vessels'. These were fire ships with a mixture of chemicals in their holds that would create great amounts of noxious fumes, forcing a defending army downwind of their approach to abandon their position. An attacking army could then move quickly in when these vessels sank and the fumes then stopped. In the event, the siege was over before a decision could be made on their use and the details were covered by the Official Secrets Act until poison gas was used in the First World War.

Cochrane died a few weeks before his eighty-fifth birthday. His grave is in the central part of the knave of Westminster Abbey, and even now, on a day every May, the Chilean navy holds a wreath-laying ceremony at his gravestone.

Other Characters:
Pitt, Castlereagh, Canning and **Wickham** all existed as described in this book and details on their lives can be found in various books and online sources.

Charles Stewart was Castlereagh's half-brother and he held various posts and positions, often supporting his brother. His character seems to have been accurately described by Flashman, as the book *Rites of Peace: The Fall of Napoleon and the Congress of Vienna* by Adam Zamoyski describes how he made a spectacle of himself at the Congress of Vienna with his loutish behaviour, being apparently rather often inebriated, frequenting prostitutes quite openly, touching up young women in public, and once even starting a fist fight in the middle of the street with a Viennese coach driver.

O'Hara was the governor of Gibraltar at the time and did have the singular distinction of having surrendered to both Washington and Bonaparte. He was a lively soul, as described, and built a lookout post at the very top of the rock of Gibraltar in the hope that it would enable the British to see the port of Cadiz on a clear day. This was not possible, but the gun battery subsequently sited on the spot is to this day known as O'Hara's Battery.

James Leander Cathcart is another extraordinary character from history and his biography, written by his daughter from his recollections, can be read for free on various websites. The details in this confirm the situation that Flashman and Cochrane found in Algiers when they visited, including the description of the galley slave prison and its adjoining menagerie, the means of punishment for prisoners and the political intrigues at the time in Algiers.

The existence and actions of various other characters, including **Archie, Guthrie** and **Manley Dixon**, have also been confirmed in historical research. I have not been able to find Mansfield in any reference work, but he may have got work later in the Admiralty itself as clearly someone with a vindictive streak did, as the following note confirms.

The final footnote must be spared for poor **Lieutenant William Parker** who, readers will recall, was severely wounded in the attack on the *Gamo*. This note also serves to demonstrate the power of clerks to admirals and the Admiralty. Cochrane's autobiography describes how repeated requests by him for Parker's advancement were turned down, doubtless due to his association with Cochrane himself. In the end Parker retired on half-pay to a farm near Kinsale with his wife and four daughters. Some malevolent official in the Admiralty then sent him orders to command the sloop *Rainbow* in the West Indies. Thinking he was at last getting the recognition he was due, the man sold his farm and furniture and used the money to travel with his family to Barbados to take his commission. However, when he arrived there, after a lengthy search of the region, he found that the ship did not exist. Returning to England, he complained to the first lord of the Admiralty, who promised that he would be amply compensated for the loss and expense of this fruitless voyage and that he would be given another command at the first opportunity. Sadly the malevolent force intervened again and he received neither. With his prospects still in ruin, domestic arrangements destroyed and pride wounded, his spirit gave way and he sank into an early grave, leaving his wife and four daughters with little support. Cochrane, writing his autobiography in his eighties, advises that despite then being a senior admiral again in the Navy, he was never able to identify who had so cruelly deprived his former comrade.

~~~~~

Thank you for reading this book, and I hope you enjoyed it. I aim to write about more of Thomas Flashman's adventures in the future, so look out for further instalments.